Bet on It

Bet on It

JODIE SLAUGHTER

ST. MARTIN'S GRIFFIN
NEW YORK

First published in the United States by St. Martin's Griffin, an imprint of St. Martin's Publishing Group

BET ON IT. Copyright © 2022 by Jodie Slaughter. All rights reserved. Printed in the United States of America. For information, address St. Martin's Publishing Group, 120 Broadway, New York, NY 10271.

www.stmartins.com

Designed by Gabriel Guma

Library of Congress Cataloging-in-Publication Data

Names: Slaughter, Jodie, author.
Title: Bet on it / Jodie Slaughter.
Description: First edition. | New York : St. Martin's Griffin, 2022.
Identifiers: LCCN 2022002671 | ISBN 9781250821829 (trade paperback) |
    ISBN 9781250821836 (ebook)
Subjects: LCGFT: Romance fiction. | Novels.
Classification: LCC PS3619.L3776 B48 2022 | DDC 813/.6—dc2/
    eng/20220225
LC record available at https://lccn.loc.gov/2022002671

Our books may be purchased in bulk for promotional, educational, or business use. Please contact your local bookseller or the Macmillan Corporate and Premium Sales Department at 1-800-221-7945, extension 5442, or by email at MacmillanSpecialMarkets@macmillan.com.

First Edition: 2022

10 9 8 7 6 5 4 3 2 1

To me because, bitch, we did it!

Some of the thematic material in *Bet on It* discusses mental illness, panic attacks, drug abuse, and child endangerment. For a more detailed description of sensitive content, please visit jodieslaughter.com.

Chapter 1

All things considered, the frozen dinner section of the Piggly Wiggly was one of the better public places to have a panic attack. It was late, only a half hour before closing in a small town where being outside after 9 P.M. on a weeknight automatically branded you a degenerate. That meant the other poor souls wandering the aisles were too glassy-eyed to pay Aja Owens any notice.

Forehead pressed against the cold, wet glass of a freezer door and bright, fluorescent lights heating the back of her neck, she gripped her handheld basket tight. Less than two minutes ago she'd been anxious but steady. Then she'd pulled the freezer door open, and a box of Hot Pockets had come barreling off the shelf and into her chest before clattering to the floor. The life had nearly been startled out of her, sending what was left of "composed Aja" out of her body to levitate above like a spirit, watching with shrewd eyes as her corporeal form descended into outright panic. The sudden fear made her body tense, her throat tightening immediately. Every second that passed saw her heart rate speed up until she could hear the pounding in her ears, drowning everything else out.

She tried to push past her light-headedness enough to calm herself. *One, two, three, four, five. Hold. Keep holding. Now, release.*

Even after three full minutes of reciting her silent mantra, the technique was barely working. Her breaths came fast, burning her chest as air was pushed and pulled through her overexerted lungs to no relief. She knew exactly where her anxiety meds were; the transparent orange bottle was tucked safely in a pocket on the interior of her purse. Only, her purse was currently locked in the trunk of her car. It didn't matter how much relief the Ativan could give if her pills were hundreds of more steps away than she could take.

Aja's teeth ground together as a tinny voice came through the store speakers announcing that it was 9:15—fifteen minutes until closing. She needed to pull away from the glass. Yank her heart out of her throat, pay for her items, and go home where she could feel some semblance of safety and security. But she couldn't make her feet move, and the frustration of that made her eyes burn.

Another minute had passed, her forehead freezing against the clammy glass, when she heard a pair of shoes beating against the floor towards her. She figured it was an employee. It would be absolutely mortifying if some frazzled sixteen-year-old grocery clerk approached, begging her to *please get the fuck out of the store* so they could close up. It might not be all bad though. Her regular, everyday anxiety about being a public nuisance would probably override the attack she was having and send her scrambling. Without her Pepperoni Pizza Hot Pockets, sure, but the end result would be worth it. A groan slipped through her panting lips when the feet stopped behind her. The person said nothing, made no move to get her attention or usher her out. So, it wasn't an employee. Probably a customer, then. Fan-fucking-tastic. The embarrassment welled up further, making her belly twist into a hard knot. The clench was familiar but that only served to make it worse.

"I saw you when I was walkin' past the aisle earlier," the deep voice said, nearly making her jump in surprise. "I saw you still standin' here when I came back around ten minutes later. I figured I'd . . . see if you were all right."

She clenched her eyes tight, half hoping to disappear into thin air, half hoping the guy would get tired of waiting and walk off.

"But I can clearly see that you aren't . . ."

Aja kept silent, and when he still made no move to leave, she gritted her teeth and managed a few hoarse, ragged words. "I'm fine."

He grunted. "Well, we've got seven minutes until they lock down the store. You mind if I stay right here with you until then?"

She didn't know what to say. Yes, she minded a stranger seeing her like this. But no, she didn't want him to walk away. She felt overwhelmed by his presence and desperately lonely at the same time. The back and forth would have made her head hurt if her temples hadn't already been throbbing.

"I . . . I just need . . ." She swallowed.

"A minute," he chimed in, his accent making the words run over her like thick, smooth honey over a warm biscuit. Her fist tightened so hard around the basket handle that it dug into her skin, no doubt leaving a lasting mark. "I get it," he said.

Whether or not he really "got it," she wasn't sure, but his tone was colored with empathy. They didn't say anything else, but he didn't move from his spot across the aisle, and she felt him the same as she did the chill from the freezer against her face.

One, two, three, four, five. Hold. Keep holding. Now, release.
One, two, three, four, five. Hold. Keep holding. Now, release.
One, two, three, four, five. Hold. Keep holding. Now, release.

When her heart finally slowed, some of the tension in her shoulders fell away. She flexed her toes in her tennis shoes and ran a dry tongue over drier lips. She didn't pull away from the door until she could breathe through her nose, and she didn't turn around until the heat in her cheeks was a steady burn rather than a scorch.

Aja could hardly look at him, her eyes still trying to focus as they flitted across his face and body. She caught nothing concrete other than the red birthmark that splayed out on the right side of his lightly tanned neck.

"Thank you for . . ." She paused, not exactly sure why she was thanking him. Maybe for helping her feel a little less alone, or for not trying to get her to calm down the way other people did—with tons of unnecessary touching and useless suggestions to *find your center.*

"For standing here with me."

His chuckle was deep and throaty, and her fingers flexed in response. "Don't worry about it. Like I said, I get it. Plus . . . those Hot Pockets are the only reason I even came in, and I'm not leavin' until I get them."

On another night, she might have laughed. But while the worst of her panic attack was over, her body was still eaten up with anxiety, and she desperately craved the comfort of her bed. So she just kept her eyes on his shirt and flashed him a shaky smile before turning and dragging her heavy feet back down the aisle—cringing at how she was about to force a cashier to check her out only minutes before closing.

Chapter 2

There were few places in the world more superstitious than the Greenbelt City Bingo Hall. It was a place where Friday the thirteenth and knocking on wood meant next to nothing. Instead, something as small as a chihuahua bobblehead or an old string of Mardi Gras beads was thought powerful enough to turn the tides of a game when called upon.

Aja hadn't known how seriously people took bingo until she'd first attended and was nearly coldcocked by a little old lady for daring to sit in the seat she had claimed three years before Aja had even been born. That first warning had been the only one she'd ever needed. After that, she picked a seat in the middle row on the right side of the room, right near a thick pole that kept one side of her closed off. The pole was there to keep the building's structural integrity sound, but for her it meant she didn't have to spend bingo being stressed out about sitting between two strangers.

Every Wednesday evening, she spent twenty dollars on a pack of bingo sheets, blue and yellow daubers, and a large order of crinkle-cut fries. And for three full hours she felt good. Calm. Involved. All the things that seemed so far out of reach when she stepped outside of those walls.

The inside of the hall reminded her of the poorly lit church basement she'd spent so much of her childhood in. Even with their often-snappish behavior, Aja had built an easy camaraderie with her fellow players. She kept mostly to herself, but they provided plenty of entertainment from her place on the sidelines. They were so uninterested in pretense that she was confident no one was paying nearly as much attention to her as she tended to think people were.

Her favorite was Ms. May Abbott—who'd made sure to put an emphasis on the "miz" when introducing herself. A white woman in her mid-sixties, with dyed red hair, thin lips, and wrinkles around her mouth, she spoke entirely in a conspiratorial un-whisper-like whisper. Her normal seat was right next to Aja's, and she spent the majority of her Wednesday nights giving her a running commentary of other people's bingo faux pas. They didn't know each other outside of the hall, but inside, they were damn near best friends. After they had formed a kinship over the house-made chicken wings and their mutual love of Tina Turner, Aja looked forward to their visits.

The older woman hadn't shown up in three weeks though, and Aja regretted every time she'd been too nervous to exchange numbers with her. Four days after the Piggly Wiggly Incident, she planned to walk into bingo and finally work up the courage to ask one of the gossipy little church ladies in the front row if they'd heard anything. But before she could bring herself to, Ms. May came strolling in through the double doors, hair slightly askew, leopard-print leggings tight as ever, and both of her arms in bright-pink casts. The first thing Aja felt was relief that she wouldn't have to melt under the scrutinous eyes of the church ladies. The second was pure shock.

It must have shown, because when Ms. May locked eyes with her from across the room, her lips curled into a rueful smile, and she shook her head.

"Oh my God . . ." Aja breathed when the other woman was finally in front of her.

Ms. May waved a dismissive hand as best she could with her arm obstructed. "It's nothin'."

"Nothing?" Her voice was damn-near hysterical. She knew she must have been overreacting, but she suddenly couldn't get the distressing images of Ms. May out of her head. Bloody, bruised, battered, and worse. She'd been hurt, and that reminded Aja that the people she cared about *could* be hurt—something she spent an inordinate amount of time trying, and failing, to keep her mind off of.

"I fell down those damned steps of mine." Ms. May rolled her eyes. "You should have heard me callin' out the screen door for my no-good neighbors to come help. It would have been hilarious if I hadn't wound up like this."

Aja wasn't sure how she could find any humor in that. She could have been there for hours without anyone noticing, she could have been hurt even worse. Aja inhaled shakily and pressed a hand against her sternum underneath the V-neck of her shirt. She needed to calm the hell down. Ms. May was fine. She was standing right there, heart beating and pink in her cheeks. It was hard to remember that, but very important. Every bad thing tended to feel like a tragedy in Aja's mind, and it was never easy to convince herself it wasn't.

"Well, do you need anything?" She pulled out Ms. May's chair and motioned for her to sit. "You need me to get your bingo packs and daubers?"

Ms. May twisted so her back was to Aja, her head looking towards the entrance. Aja had no idea what she was searching for.

"No, honey, Wally's bringin' them. He's here takin' care of me for a little while so he's goin' to play my packs for me until I get these things off."

Aja was glad Ms. May was facing away so the surprised look on her face went unnoticed. Wally was her grandson, the one who made her expression turn slightly crestfallen on the odd times she brought him up. Aja didn't know much about Wally. Only that he lived in Charleston, wrote for a newspaper, loved baseball, and never, ever visited. She had never met a "Wally" her age before, and she had a hard time picturing him because of it. Had his name been Chase or Tyler or Jaden, she would have had a clear image. Even if that image was completely wrong. In her head, Wally was the spitting image of his grandmother. Even down to the dyed red hair. Just younger, and maybe a little taller.

"Oh!" Ms. May turned and gasped like she was surprised to see him even though she knew he was there. "That's him comin' over now."

Wally was the exact opposite of the blurry outline of a man she'd pictured in her head. Instead of red hair, his was dirty blond and a little wavy, falling somewhere below his ears but above his jawline. He was tall and broad shouldered and had a plump bottom lip that was close to making his clean-shaven face appear pouty.

For a few seconds, the only thing that ran through her head was how unexpectedly *fine* Wally was.

Then she noticed his neck. The collar of his long-sleeved raglan shirt left the expanse of it exposed and there, right against his peachy skin, was a large, red birthmark. Had she never seen him before, it would have been barely a blip on her radar. Now, it was nothing less than a glaring reminder. Physical proof she hadn't imagined the person who'd seen her in a dark, panicked state at the Piggly Wiggly. Verification that she'd been so out of it she hadn't even managed to move the image of his face into her long-term memory.

He seemed to float over to them like something straight out of a movie. There was nothing on his face that looked remotely like recognition when his eyes grazed over Aja, but she wished she could disappear into thin air anyway. As a general rule, she preferred to know someone a little longer before she had a panic attack in front of them. That way there was already an established repartee when it inevitably came time for her to downplay the moment and pretend it was no big deal.

"You want these right here, Gram?" His voice was the same— deep and measured—as he gestured to the table in front of Ms. May's seat with an eight-pack of bingo sheets and a pink dauber in hand.

Ms. May nodded. "I'll show you how I want the sheets set up in a minute. But first"—she made a show of turning her entire body in her seat until she was facing Aja with a giant, wolfish grin— "Wally, this is Aja. She's my bingo buddy. Aja, this is Wally, my grandbaby who never comes to see me."

Aja looked up to see Wally redden and grit his teeth before he schooled his features into a kind, if insincere, smile. "It's Walker, actually. Walker Abbott."

She mulled the name over in her head.

Walker.

Walker Abbott.

It was a nice name. It fit him. And the way he said it—so succinctly and with a sharpness that acted in direct contrast to the slow stickiness of his drawl—piqued her interest. There was something almost defiant in the words, like he was daring her to say something slick.

He thrust his hand out and she resisted the urge to grimace. She hated handshakes. It wasn't the touching that bothered her so much as the fear that her grip wasn't sure enough. That a seconds-long clasping of hands would be so inadequate that the other person would sense how weak she was.

"I'm Aja." She cleared her throat, trying to make her voice sound less broken. "Owens."

Walker had blue eyes. She'd never been much interested in blue eyes. Any eye color was fine, of course. But she maintained that there was something extra special about brown eyes. She found them rich and beautiful and romantic. Easier to fall into than a heated pool. It was possible her feelings towards the color were an internalization of being fed the idea her entire life that brown eyes were somehow less beautiful, but she stood by her views nonetheless. Walker's eyes weren't clear and bright; they were a murky blue, a little cloudy and hard to fully put a name to. As they raked over her, she bit the inside of her bottom lip to keep it from dropping open. It wasn't until his gaze met hers again that she finally saw recognition hit him.

Her tongue grew heavy in her mouth and the heels of her feet dug into the linoleum floor. Her breath caught as she waited for him to acknowledge what they'd shared. To embarrass her so thoroughly that this innocuous Wednesday became seared into her memory for years to come. But it didn't happen. As quickly as the recognition appeared, it was gone. In its place was another small smile, this one a little more honest.

"Nice to meet you," he murmured. "You here by yourself, or . . . ?"

He looked behind her like he was searching for the grandparent she was supposed to be accompanying. Her mouth popped open slightly in surprise.

"Aja is the youngest bingo player here by almost twenty years," Ms. May butted in, looking oddly proud.

Aja's face heated, and suddenly she would have traded the possibility of ever winning a bingo game just to be swallowed whole by one of the cracks in the fabric of her weathered chair.

"How old are you, Aja?" Walker saying her name made her eyes close briefly. Between her embarrassment and the way his voice made her feel, she was in the beginning stages of being totally overwhelmed. She was used to intense emotions and racing thoughts and flip-floppy feelings, but that didn't mean she enjoyed it when they happened all at once.

"Twenty-eight . . . twenty-nine in six months." She looked at Ms. May. "Then I'll only be the youngest by nineteen years. If we're right about Patty Kinnaird's age, that is."

Aja forced herself to joke like she hadn't been thrown out of her comfort zone. She'd never really talked to Ms. May about her anxiety, and the woman wasn't afraid to ask well-meaning but invasive questions. If she let it show that Walker's presence had thrown her for a loop, it might cause a whole chain of ridiculous events that led to her admitting how a dented box of Hot Pockets had been the catalyst for her spending the last three days in a lump under her bed covers.

That was the last thing she wanted. She didn't come to bingo to talk about her anxiety—her virtual therapy sessions on Friday afternoons were for that. She came to feel normal. It was a crappy thing to think, she knew. Problematic and self-hating. She understood logically that normal was subjective. She even hated herself for thinking how much she wanted it sometimes, but that didn't make the desire any less real.

"Well, now that I'm here, you're only the youngest by a little over a year." Walker winked.

Her face heated again. The action shouldn't have flustered her. It should have been so corny that it made her cringe. But she'd be damned if it wasn't charming as hell.

She didn't get a chance to respond, thanks to three chimes sounding over the speaker system, signaling the start of the first game. She took her seat, noticing that Ms. May had pushed her chair farther away from Aja's and used her legs to scoot another one in between them for Walker.

While Walker was busy stacking the bingo papers the way his grandmother had instructed, Aja caught her friend's look. Ms. May's smile was full of false innocence and Aja narrowed her eyes in response before she started setting up her own pack.

The bingo caller had barely gotten five balls out of the roller before Ms. May started fussing at Walker for not being fast enough locating the numbers.

"Look, it's right there," she said in that loud whisper of hers. "You've got to be quicker than that, Wally. Keep up!"

Aja caught a glimpse of his exasperated expression before he turned it on his grandmother. She had to smother a laugh.

"I'm tryin' to find the numbers on eight different cards, Gram. It's impossible to be that quick." His whisper was much quieter than his grandmother's but more frustrated.

"Well, Aja seems to be doin' just fine."

Aja tried to convey sympathy on her face when he swiveled his head to look at her cards. She definitely hadn't had any issues. Jim Collins was the caller tonight and he was a slow talker, much to the dismay of her fellow players.

"And look, little miss Anita is movin' right along. Arthritis and all."

Walker grumbled, "Little miss Anita is movin' so fast it's almost like she already knows what numbers are comin' up next."

Ms. May flicked his earlobe and he gave an exaggerated wince. "You watch it, Walker Abbott. People have been kicked out of this bingo hall for far less than accusin' one of its most esteemed members of cheatin'."

Most of the players were well over fifty and had very little patience for inefficiency or what they considered to be tomfoolery. Bingo callers who walked too slowly down the aisles to confirm winners were met with ornery yells to "move it the hell along." She'd even seen two elderly women nearly come to scraps over a bingo ball that had gotten stuck in the spinning cage. Aja lived in fear of causing a holdup in the game and bearing the brunt of that fury. Luckily, it hadn't been an issue. In the eight months that she'd been coming to Wednesday night bingo she hadn't won a single game. If the thrill of gambling had been her sole reason for being there, she would have turned in her daubers and headed to the state's only casino a long time ago.

Walker turned to Aja, a curious eyebrow raised and a gossipy look in his eyes.

"It's true," she confirmed quietly, one ear still glued to the caller. "They got Stanley Jones out of here because he told the concession stand lady that she needed to change the grease for her fries."

Walker's eyes widened.

"The second anyone steps out of line," Aja continued conspiratorially, "they come together like a swarm of wasps to push them out."

"Exactly." Ms. May nodded. "And I'm not tryin' to drive all the way to damned Port Royal for my Wednesday night bingo games, so you'd better stay in line, little boy."

Aja couldn't help but snicker. She'd been on the uncomfortable receiving end of his grandmother's scolding and seeing it from the outside was hilarious. Walker grumbled under his breath but focused his attention on the bingo sheets, his face moving closer like it would help him see better.

Aja didn't get a number from one of her sheets called until the eighth ball was pulled.

"B90—the end of the line."

Aja loved the quirky, sometimes totally bizarre sayings that accompanied the numbers in bingo. When the number 90 was called, it was accompanied by the phrase "top of the shop" or the "end of the line." Not because the game was over, but because 90 was the last number used in a bingo roll call. There was "legs 11" for the number 11 simply because two ones next to each other looked like a pair of legs. There was also "buckle my shoe," which came after the number 32, because it rhymed.

There was technically a phrase for every number in the roll, but the callers themselves decided which ones to use and when. Aja had heard them hundreds of times by now and she still got a kick out of them. She didn't think they'd ever get old.

She took a peek at Walker's stack and immediately spotted the same number, right there on top. He was running his eyes over the cards frantically, completely missing it. Moving her pinkie finger across the table, she slid it towards the little square on the upper far left of the top card. The second she touched the square she heard his intake of breath.

"Thank you," he mouthed, and the gratitude in his eyes was so palpable it made her throat tighten.

She had no idea what came over her. The pluckiness that welled up inside was something she hadn't felt in . . . forever. It didn't sit with her for long though, spending only enough time in her chest for her to shoot Walker a wink of her own. Then, it was gone. Leaving her with a racing heart and a look from the man next to her that made her light-headed.

Chapter 3

Outside of his grandmother, there were exactly three things that Walker had missed about Greenbelt, South Carolina. The first was the lack of traffic. In Charleston, he had to leave home nearly twenty minutes early to get to work on time even though he lived a five-minute drive from the office. In Greenbelt, it wasn't uncommon to get clear across town without catching a single red light.

The second was the quiet. He'd known what he was getting himself into when he'd decided to move to the largest city in the state, but he'd underestimated the noise. He lived downtown, in an older building near the city's center, and something was always happening. Always. Here, things were quiet more often than not. He never had to worry about being woken up by a music festival two miles away or a news helicopter flying overhead. There was only sweet country silence in the woods next to Gram's place.

And last, there was the peach cobbler at Minnie's Diner.

Normally he hated cooked fruit. It was too soft and too mushy and no matter what it was put in, way too damn sweet. But Minnie's cobbler had a special place in his heart.

He'd been six the first time he'd had it. The night before, he and his father, Benny, had been pulled over by the cops while driving home. The entire memory was blurry for Walker—whether because of his age or the trauma, he didn't know. One second, he was buckled into the front seat of whatever hooptie his dad had gotten his hands on, and the next, he was standing on the curb watching Benny get ushered into a police car for possession of a controlled substance. They hadn't taken Walker down to the station, and since his mother had split town years before, there was only one person to call.

Gram had picked him up right at the scene. The next day, she'd forced him out of bed early, cleaned him up, and taken him to Minnie's, where she'd let him pick whatever he wanted for breakfast, nutrition and propriety be damned. He'd chosen cobbler. It wasn't the first time Walker had eaten dessert for breakfast, but it was the first time it hadn't made him feel all wrong inside.

Crisp, buttery crust; warm peaches covered in syrupy goodness; and ice cream to top it all off. It may have sounded ridiculous, but that cobbler had healed him. Not of his shaky childhood or the trauma it left him with, but the place in him that had never known true satisfaction before.

That feeling had never really gone away, even if he had. He'd been chasing it in peach cobblers around the state for over a decade and hadn't been able to recreate it in a single one. Which was why he found himself standing in front of the Minnie's dessert counter on an early Friday afternoon a week after arriving in town.

He'd shown up at the perfect time; heat was rising off the freshly made cobbler and steaming up the glass display case. He was sure the other treats were incredible too, but Walker's eyes were on the only prize that mattered.

"Got your eye on somethin' special, Sugar?"

He recognized the voice immediately. There was a singularly unique cadence, high and nasally, with an accent that was clearly exaggerated. At one point he'd been used to hearing it. Now it sent a shock through his system that made him jerk his head up.

Louise Smith hadn't changed much in the twelve years he'd been gone. She'd kept the same dark, wispy bangs across her forehead, still used foundation a couple shades too dark for her pale skin and hadn't bothered to switch up the dark purple lipstick she'd always worn. She would have been in her mid-fifties by now, and he could see lines and wear in her face that hadn't been there before. Otherwise she was exactly the same. Almost as if she'd been preserved in time the moment his Greyhound bus had left the city limits. She looked him over but didn't seem to recognize him.

As a teenager, Walker had been tall and gangly. He'd had no idea what to do with his long limbs, so he had simply carried them around with a begrudging sort of acceptance. He'd spent most of his adolescence trying to remain invisible—folding into himself, keeping his head down and his eyes ahead. It hadn't worked—not after he'd become so prone to public panic attacks that he got pitying, but judgmental, looks everywhere he went.

He was thirty now—broader, bulkier, and less attached to his own shadow. Therapy and Zoloft had reduced his number of panic attacks by a whole hell of a lot. But he wasn't perfect. He wasn't free from his issues and never would be, not completely. But he was much more secure than he'd been. At least, that was what he'd thought until he'd gotten back to Greenbelt and found himself accosted by reminders of a past he'd done his level best to avoid.

But he wanted that fucking cobbler. And the only thing that stood between him and those warm summer peaches was Louise Smith. A woman who was decades older but had spread rumors about his life like they'd been in the same graduating class.

"I heard Wally Abbott's no-good daddy got him strung out on meth young. That's why he can barely go a month without freakin' out like somebody's about to kill him."

"Somebody said when that granny of his finally took him from Benny, Wally tried to fight her. You know, like, physically."

"That boy ain't right in the head. Both of 'em fucked him up so bad, he never stood a chance. Poor thing."

Louise, like his Gram, had a whisper a few decibels short of quiet. Unlike his Gram, she used hers to shit talk anybody she came across—even innocent, struggling kids. Walker had never liked her. He'd outright hated her at one point. Now all he wanted was to get away from her.

Just . . . not without having his cobbler in hand first.

"Yeah," he answered, flashing her a smile so as not to display his disgust. "I'll take two slices of that peach cobbler. To go."

She nodded, already opening the glass case. "You want ice cream with that?"

"No thank you." He and Gram had just bought a pint of Blue Bell French Vanilla, and house-made scoops would melt on the way back.

She was efficient as she spooned two slices of cobbler into a couple of small plastic containers and walked them the few steps to the

register. Walker was pleasantly surprised that the price of his favorite dessert hadn't even gone up a whole dollar. Their exchange
halted when she narrowed her eyes at him. He narrowed his right
back, his mouth pinching at the corners.

"Well, I'll be good godd—" she stopped herself, putting a hand
on her chest and giggling. "Wally Abbott, is that you?"

There were a thousand things he wanted to say, not a single one
nice. *Go fuck yourself* was at the top of the list. It sat right there
on the tip of his tongue, itching for him to spit it out, but he held
back. His Gram had raised him better than that, and she would
have been mortified to hear that he'd said something like that to
Louise. And like any Southern boy worth his salt, he made it his
business to offend his grandmother as little as possible. He was already on thin ice with her as it was. So he choked the words down
but made a point not to appear too friendly.

"Yep," he grunted. "I go by Walker now."

"I had no idea you were back in town, Wally," she said smiling,
and he grit his teeth hard. "I know your poor granny had that bad
fall. You here takin' care of her?"

"Yep," he answered.

A silence stretched between them, and Walker reveled in the
awkwardness that settled on her face.

Louise cleared her throat. "Well, how's she doin'?"

"She's healin' up well."

She released an exasperated breath that briefly lifted her bangs
away from her face. "How long are you in town for again?"

She was fishing for information. He didn't know if it was for
gossip or her own curiosity, but he didn't plan on giving her shit.

"Until I decide to leave." He slid exact change across the counter and picked up the containers. "You have a nice day, ma'am."

He kept his head held high as he walked out, but he couldn't keep the satisfied smirk off his face. He hadn't given her the dressing down he'd wanted to, but he sure as hell hadn't given her what she wanted either. That was enough for now.

The plan was to take both pieces of cobbler to Gram's place and eat one in front of the TV. He'd save the other for later—for when he really needed some peace. With the level of simmering tension that he'd been feeling since he'd been back, that time was coming sooner than later.

The early June sun had moved higher in the ten minutes he'd been in Minnie's and beat down on his arms, making the short hairs stand on end. He took a pause right there in the middle of the parking lot, closing his eyes and tilting his face up towards the sky to feel the heat more intimately. Once he was sufficiently warmed, he opened his eyes. And he saw her.

He'd parked his black pickup near the back of the parking lot where there were very few cars. There was still an open spot on either side, but in one space over to the left was a little lime-green sedan. And leaning against the closed trunk was Aja Owens.

Walker had never been good at remembering names. He often had the same trouble with dates and appointments. They all took a little extra work to lock down. Normally that meant he had to catalog things in his phone the second they became set in stone. Names were a different matter. He had to employ a specific amount of brain power to keep them in his head. He usually tried to turn them into a song or make them rhyme with something. It was a lot of work—work that he didn't have the energy to do with most people he met.

The second he met Aja he'd made an effort to remember her name. He'd repeated it in his head six different times. He would have written it down, but he had no idea how she spelled it. So he turned it into a little tune instead.

Aja. Aja. Aja Ow-ens.

Aja. Aja. Aja Ow-ens.

It was catchy. So much so, it had gotten stuck in his head. He'd found himself singing it while showering and while eating his late-night apples and peanut butter. The tune had run its course when he'd gotten up the next morning, but the name had remained. Seared so deeply into his memory that he wasn't sure it was even possible to forget.

Her face was there too, sweet and round. All dark hooded eyes and lips so full he could have shed a tear over them. Her eyes were glued to her phone, and as far as he knew, she hadn't noticed him, so he took the opportunity to stare a little longer.

He hadn't been paying much attention to her looks during their first not-quite-meeting at the Piggly Wiggly. He'd heard her breathing an aisle away, and while he hadn't been able to see her face, he'd felt pretty certain that she was having a panic attack. They could be like snowflakes, each one different and more complex than the last, but he'd had enough to recognize the signs. And then he had been too focused on preparing himself to help her if things escalated to gauge whether he found her attractive. But when Gram had introduced them at bingo, he knew immediately he definitely did.

Now she wore a black maxi dress that was a bit tight around

her upper body and had spaghetti straps. He could see the fullness of her upper arms and the lush way her breasts pressed out of the top. Her skin was a dark golden brown that caught the sun just right, making his breath hitch.

As discreet as he tried to be, Aja must have felt his eyes on her. After a few sweeps of his gaze, she looked up from her phone and stared ahead—right at him. He saw her eyes widen from across the parking lot and a stricken look flash across her face. She looked like she wanted to run. When she didn't, Walker approached.

"Hey," he drawled, flashing her a slow, easy smile.

"Uhm, hi." It was clear that she was unsure what to say. The last thing Walker wanted was to make her uncomfortable. He contemplated walking away with only a greeting, but her mouth was faster than his feet.

"Got some pie?" she asked, gesturing to his takeout containers.

"Cobbler actually. Were you headin' into Minnie's too?"

Aja shook her head. "No, I have a hair appointment. I'm getting braids for the summer." She pointed to the salon two doors over from Minnie's in the strip mall. "But I'm here early so . . ."

Her hair looked thick, full of tightly coiled curls that fell a little above her shoulders. He wondered briefly what she was getting done. They were quiet for a few seconds, a slight awkwardness building in the space between them. Walker could end it by bidding her good-bye and leaving, but he didn't want to. He knew next to nothing about the woman, but he was intrigued by her.

Gram had started mentioning her new bingo buddy on their weekly phone calls months ago. Bingo talk always made him zone out, but from what he'd picked up, Gram considered her sweet but quiet. Meeting Aja in person hadn't disproven those things, but he'd caught wind of something more. She'd joked with him and Gram on Wednesday night, even giving him a wink after being generous enough to help him as he fumbled through his first game. Plus, there was something a little mischievous behind her eyes.

He'd always been drawn to women who were less than forthcoming with their entire personalities. He liked to be the one to draw hidden shit out of people, loved it when they trusted him enough to open up and let him see everything they kept shut away. His therapist said it probably had something to do with elevated empathy in response to his childhood trauma. Part of him thought it was just him being fake deep in an effort to connect with people, another thing that was rarely easy for him. Either way, it was there, and it refused to let him walk away from Aja.

"You ever had Minnie's cobbler before?" he asked.

"Nope." She shook her head, tucking her hair behind her ear. "I've actually never eaten there before."

Walker's eyes widened almost comically. "Seriously?"

Her lips twitched into a smile. "Seriously."

"Minnie's is an institution. I can't believe no one's brought you here."

"I haven't even been in town a year yet . . . and I don't know that many people."

"That's a damned shame." He smiled, but he was only half joking.

He wanted to ask about her friends, but when he'd lived in Greenbelt, he hadn't had many either. Looking down at the containers in his hand, he felt a brief flash of regret for the late-night piece of cobbler he was giving up. But he figured being able to spend a few more minutes in Aja's company would make his aching sweet tooth worth it.

"Here." He held one of the containers out to her. "Everybody needs to try Minnie's cobbler at least once. It has healin' powers, you know."

She raised an eyebrow but accepted the cobbler once he wiggled it around in the air a little.

"Healing powers?" He could hear the skepticism in her voice, and that simply wouldn't do.

"Yup. This cobbler has kept families together, it's turned around a high school football team's losin' streaks—hell, it even made me come back here after twelve years of refusin' to get within a twenty-mile radius of Greenbelt."

Aja thought on his words for a bit, her face turned upwards, letting him see the soft line of her jaw and her full cheeks clearly. "How long was the losing streak?" she asked.

"Twenty-two games." He grinned.

She grimaced in fake sympathy. "Well, if the cobbler's that good, I guess I have no choice but to try it . . . you didn't happen to grab any forks, did you?"

"Nah, I was goin' to eat these at home on the couch like the hermit I am. But I can go back in and get some."

He dreaded the idea of having to encounter Louise again so soon, but for Aja, he was willing.

"It's all right, I have a ton of disposable ones in my glove compartment." Aja placed her cobbler on the roof of her car before she opened her driver's side door, put her knees on the seat, and leaned in.

Had he been a better man, he would have looked away. Kept his eyes trained on the worn signs of the shops in front of him and

not stared at her ass. But her dress stretched over her oh so perfectly, tightening so that he could make out the shape of the most
perfect behind he'd ever had the pleasure of seeing. Full and round
and so grabbable that his fingers ached. Walker's teeth dug into
his bottom lip as his mouth watered for something other than cobbler for the first time in days. He jerked out of his trance once she
straightened, shutting his eyes briefly so he could keep the picture
of her bent over in front of him at the forefront of his brain.

"Here you go," she said, handing him a white spoon wrapped
in cellophane.

The only sound between them was the rustling of their utensils being unwrapped. Once she'd gotten her first spoonful, she
paused, waiting.

"You go first," he prompted, his mouth watering as the scent
of cobbler became stronger. "You deserve to experience this all on
your own for the first time."

"Are you always this dramatic?" she asked.

"Only about cobbler. Now . . ." His gesture told her to speed
things up. He could only be patient for so long when faced with
something so tempting.

With a roll of her eyes, she took her first bite. Walker could
see the exact moment she fell in love with it. Her eyes widened
some, then closed. She chewed slowly, working her jaw carefully
as if she was trying to savor every taste. Once she'd swallowed it
down, she ran her tongue over her lips twice, no doubt searching
for more. It was a look he recognized well. Had there been a photo
of him taking his first bite, he probably would have looked the
same.

"Whoa . . ." She breathed the word.

Seeing her so pleased made it impossible to hold off on his piece any longer. The groan he let out would have been embarrassing had he cared enough to feel that way. The flavor hit every one of his taste buds, pure satisfaction worming its way into his heart the longer it sat on his tongue. He let himself take one more bite before speaking.

"Incredible, right?"

"I'll be honest, I thought you were just being goofy but . . . that might be the best peach cobbler I've ever had." She shook her head in disbelief. "And I have an auntie who's won first place in the cobbler contest at the Prince George's County Fair seven times. She'd kill me for saying that too. Either that or force me to peel peaches until my fingers fall off."

She took two more small bites in quick succession, and he followed suit.

"This cobbler transcends familial ties, Aja. I'm pretty sure Minnie sold her soul to some kind of demon for this recipe." He forewent all manners, speaking with his mouth full.

"I guess that would explain the, uh, 'healing properties' then."

"No finger quotes needed," he argued. "I never said it wasn't demon magic that did the healing, just that it existed."

Aja shook her head, grinning at him for the first time. It was brighter than the sun behind her, and prettier too. She popped her spoon into her mouth and closed the container, leaving her cobbler half eaten.

"I've got to head inside." She sounded almost sad about it. "I've got four very long hours in one of those chairs ahead of me so I'm going to save the rest for later."

"Smart girl," he chuckled.

"Thank you, Walker. It really is incredible."

"No problem. Like I said, everybody needs to try this at least once."

"I have a feeling I'm not going to be satisfied with just one piece."

"You won't," he assured her. "Now that you've tried it, you won't be able to help yourself from comin' back to get some more."

She smiled again, then waved good-bye. "I'll see you Wednesday?"

"Gram would kill me if I disrupted her bingo night, so yes, definitely."

Walker kept an eye on her as she started walking away, and he moved two spots over to his truck. But instead of getting inside and driving back to Gram's, he leaned against the closed truck bed. He'd idle a while, finish his dessert, feel the sun on his skin a little longer. It was beautiful out, and he was suddenly feeling good. Aja didn't seem to want to rush inside either, keeping her strides short enough to make her ass bounce with each step. Walker watched her, ankles crossed as he stood, digging into his cobbler. When she was halfway there, she looked over her shoulder at him, and he smiled, lazy and satisfied.

He couldn't be sure, it wouldn't have been the first time his imagination had run away with him, but he could have sworn he saw her smile right back.

Chapter 4

Aja tried not to spend too much time overthinking how her best friend, her only true friend in the world, really, was ten years older than her and her sister-in-law. Upon further contemplation, maybe it was less weird and more just sad as hell. But it was what she had. Most of the time she was grateful—until Reniece got into one of her moods and decided to treat Aja like the younger sibling she often forgot she was.

"You need to make sure you're greasing that scalp regularly. And don't forget to moisturize them with some leave-in either." Reniece's hazel eyes were scrutinous even through the slightly fuzzy FaceTime feed.

"Believe it or not, this isn't the first time I've had braids, Niecy, I know what to do."

Aja had her phone propped up against a bag of rice in the kitchen while she snapped fresh green beans into thirds. She had no idea what was going on in Reniece's house, but her nephew's high-pitched voice was in the background, joyful as you please. It put a smile on her face.

"Uh-uh," her sister-in-law snorted. "The last time you got some they lasted for all of a week before you were in my kitchen begging me to take them out for you."

"They were too tight," Aja argued. "The lady I went to had my edges in a death grip. If I hadn't gotten them out when I did, who knows where I'd be right now. Probably involuntarily bald. Which is why I don't need you holding that situation over my head."

Reniece hummed, pursing her lips like she had something shady to say but was trying to keep it in.

"Anyway," Aja continued. "Is there something you wanted to talk about? I need to get this food prepped before bingo tonight."

The other woman paused, and Aja looked up from her green beans to see Reniece's mouth screwed up in a different way. Whatever she wanted to say next wasn't shady, it was concerned. Aja's stomach knotted. She preferred, by far, good-natured jabs to delicately asked questions about her shaky well-being.

"I was just wondering if you made it out to that mixer you were thinking about going to."

The First Church of Zion in downtown Greenbelt had been advertising their Black Women Rising mixer for months. She'd seen posters around town and had heard people speak about it in passing. She had even been approached in the Piggly Wiggly by a church leader who had given her a welcoming smile and a flyer. Aja didn't consider herself to be religious by any means, but she'd really wanted to go.

The only people she knew in town were either from the few businesses she frequented or some of the older ladies at bingo. She was well versed in how rewarding friendships with older women could be, sure. But there were disparities that made most of the decades older and much, much whiter crowd less than desirable for the kind of companionship she was looking for. She wanted to make friends—real friends. It seemed like such a simple thing on paper but had proved to be almost maddening in its difficulty.

After running into Walker on Friday, having a great experience at the new salon, and trying Minnie's cobbler, she'd been determined to carry her good mood to the event on Sunday evening. But when the actual day had rolled around, she'd been a tight ball of nervous energy.

She worried about the possibility of wearing the wrong type of clothes and standing out. She worried about whether she had anything worthwhile to say to the other women. She even worried about the minute possibility of being asked to lead a prayer circle. Aja wondered how she could attend an event like that when most of the time she didn't feel like she was a Black Woman Rising. She felt like she was falling into an ocean of fear and doubt, the water unyielding as it surrounded her up to her ears.

So she hadn't gone. She'd made a pizza instead. Spent hours distracting herself with a homemade dough and topped it with the things she loved most. Then, after she was full, she did a little work. Her job as a remote social media manager for a medium-sized millennial-focused clothing company meant there was practically always something to be done, even when she was off the clock. Once she couldn't spend any more time drafting corporate tweets, she fell asleep on her couch with some awful action movie playing. When she woke up on Monday, her anxiety had dampened down, but in its place was shame. A shame that hadn't subsided enough to not make her want to throw up when Reniece broached the subject.

"No, I didn't end up making it."

There was silence, and Aja was too afraid of what she'd see on the screen if she looked up, so she kept her eyes on the green beans.

"Well, that's all right. You know Black churches love to throw an event, so there'll be plenty more," Reniece joked. "In the mean-time, you've got me."

"Don't remind me." Aja tried to blink back the tears in her eyes.

"Keep playin' with me, little girl. I'm about to send your dar-ling little nephew out there for the summer and see how apprecia-tive you are of me once I pick his little bad ass up."

"Justin is not bad! Leave that baby alone!"

Reniece growled. "He's six, and he's a menace. Yesterday he damn near threw a fit when we didn't let him ride his bike off the roof of my car onto the driveway. He's still got training wheels, Aja!"

"Oh, he gets that from his daddy," Aja laughed. "Tyson was obsessed with *Jackass* when he was younger. It got to the point where Mama banned him from ever watching those 'goofy-ass white boys' in her house."

"You see what I'm dealing with all alone here without you?" The other woman sighed deep from her core. "You picked a hell of a time to leave me."

"I haven't left you, Niecy. I just needed to live somewhere that wasn't so . . . *on* all the time. Especially while I try to get myself together. It's not like I'll never be back in DC."

Her decision to move to Greenbelt had been rather abrupt. She'd known for a long time that she needed a change, a chance to get out of the city and someplace quieter. Some late-night internet browsing had brought her to an article where Greenbelt had been named one of the quietest small towns in the country. All it had taken was a few pictures on Google Images and a little research before she'd decided to make it home. The distance it put between her and her family had been about the only downside, one she'd realized she could live with.

"Yeah, I know . . . I'm just saying, you're missing out on a lot down there. Especially all the new brunch spots. We went to one last week where the bottomless mimosas were basically just champagne with the nearly dissipated spirit of orange juice."

Aja snorted. "The next time I'm there you can drag me to all the brunch spots you want, Sis. But I have to go. I have a lot to get done before I leave, and you're distracting me."

"Yeah, yeah." Reniece waved a dismissive hand at her. "You have fun at your little elderly gambling den or whatever."

• • •

The energy at bingo was always kind of strange during the weeks in the middle of the month. She wasn't sure what caused it, but something in the air made people behave differently. Worse somehow. Accidentally claiming a false bingo was enough to get you booted out. Players were especially finicky about the speed of the game. Even the cooks at the food counter were on edge lest someone try to jump over the counter at them for serving chicken wings without enough lemon pepper seasoning.

Aja hadn't been the only one to notice the mid-month mayhem. The bingo hall always made sure to assign Mr. Rodney Zane as the caller during these weeks. A no-nonsense Black man with a barrel chest and a stark white beard, he reminded her of her middle school principal. Stern and unflinching.

She was surprised to see that Walker and Ms. May were already seated when she got there. Ms. May normally showed up fifteen minutes into the first game, shout-whispering her apologies as she skirted the dirty looks to squeeze past other, more dedicated players. Aja didn't think Ms. May had ever shown up before her.

"Hey," she said to them both with a smile before turning to her friend. "You're here early."

Ms. May rolled her eyes as she adjusted her pink casts on the table. "This one rushed me out the door." She jerked her head towards Walker, who was sitting in the seat closest to Aja's again. "Couldn't get here fast enough."

Walker groaned low in his throat, which Aja found hilarious.

"Well, maybe he fell in love with the game. You know how easy it is to get hooked on that bingo adrenaline rush." Aja kept her eyes on him while she spoke, unable to keep the smirk off her face.

"Uh-uh," Ms. May commented blandly. "I'm sure his enthusiasm had nothin' to do with the fact that he gets to sit next to some hot young thing after spendin' all day with my old behind."

Aja raised an eyebrow at Walker. "You're about to go sit next to little miss Anita, huh?"

He looked back and forth between them, the tips of his ears reddening. "Now y'all are just tryin' to embarrass me."

"Just havin' a little fun, baby." Ms. May patted his cheek.

It was Wednesday, and Aja felt good. All the shame and anxiety inside her wasn't gone, but it was sleeping. Like always, it decided when she got relief, not the other way around. And it would only last so long, so she decided to go with it.

"You shared your cobbler with me, Walker." She gripped the back of her chair, swallowing when his eyes caught the movement and his gaze narrowed in on it, "I figured we were friends now."

He pointed his long index finger in her direction. "You're mean." Then he turned to his grandmother. "And you're meaner."

Ms. May shrugged. "It's tradition to haze the newbies. Ain't that right, Aja?"

"My second time here, the man at the front desk pretended to refuse to sell me bingo cards for, like, five minutes. I almost cried."

She tried to keep her tone light. She recognized that the joke had been in good fun. And the last thing she wanted was to come across as someone who couldn't have fun. But the whole thing had mortified her. She'd been hot and humiliated and forced to try and remain calm under all those staring eyes. She almost hadn't come back. The only thing that had gotten her to step foot back in the hall again was her incredible need to be around other people. Even if those people were elderly folks who thought shitty pranks were funny.

Walker frowned at her, his eyes stormy. "I see folks in Greenbelt still love messin' with people for no reason."

The air between them became thicker as his tone changed into something much less playful.

"It's all in good fun, Wally," Ms. May said.

He grunted, turning his head away from his grandmother as he rolled his eyes.

When Aja sat down, he leaned closer. Her nostrils flared as they met his cologne. It was incredible, a light scent she couldn't describe but was eager to breathe in. His warm breath caressed her cheek and neck as he whispered in her ear, and it made her shiver.

"If you want me to beat up the dude at the front desk, let me know." His tone was playful again. "I don't have any qualms about knockin' out an elder."

"He already apologized," she said. "He gave me a free pack of bingo cards the next time I came in."

"Well, good, but still . . . If you're anything like me, it's not easy to brush that kind of shit off. I'm sorry more people don't care to understand that not everybody can brush it off easily."

She found herself at a loss for words. Her brain loved to overthink things. Find hidden meanings in moments without any. She was always digging through simple conversations for unspoken things that she'd already convinced herself were real, even against all logic. She'd been with her new therapist for six months and they'd been working on that. Progress with mental health was slow, but Aja had been doing that digging less and less.

Walker's words made her pause. They were obviously supportive but also vague. She could have sworn he was referencing a part of her he only knew because of their moment in the grocery store. He'd been so understanding in those few minutes. Quiet and sure and as far from frantic as possible. He'd been the exact opposite of her. But if she thought hard about it now, it was almost like he'd been coming from a place of experience.

If you're anything like me, he'd said.

If you're anything like me.

She drew in a breath, willing herself to calm down. It wouldn't do her any favors to jump to conclusions, especially not off something as simple as a few kind words. Was she so desperate to connect with someone who understood her on *that* level that she was willing to read so deeply into some random man's actions? All

Walker had done was share his cobbler with her for fuck's sake. He wasn't trying to send her coded messages about shared mental illnesses over bingo games.

"Thank you." The words left her in a croak. "But I'm over it. Promise."

He nodded his head at her with a soft expression and turned to his sheets as Mr. Rodney prepared to call the first number. They were mostly silent for the rest of the game, Ms. May fussing at Walker while Aja hyperfocused on her own sheets to keep herself from overanalyzing everything he did.

Neither of them won any games, but Aja got the feeling Walker and Ms. May cared about that as much as she did—which was not at all. She was gathering up her used cards and daubers when she heard Walker clear his throat. She'd been deep in her own mind and had been slightly startled by the abrasive sound but didn't even think enough of it to look up from her actions. When he did it a second time, louder, she finally turned to face him.

His smile was wide, and strong arms dusted with light golden hairs folded across his chest, flexing in a way that was so sexy it sent annoyance running through her.

"So, Gram and I are pretty hungry . . ." he said.

"Yeah, me too. I made dinner earlier so I could eat as soon as I got home." Her mouth watered thinking about the pulled chicken and sautéed green beans she had tucked away in her fridge.

Walker's face fell, but Ms. May kept her pleasant smile.

"We were goin' to go on over to Kenny Mack's, but I think I'm goin' to go to the bar with the girls instead." She turned and awkwardly waggled her fingers at a couple of ladies standing near the door. Aja had never seen her talk to any of them before, and certainly not with enough familiarity to refer to them as "the girls." "But I remember you tellin' me last month that you'd been dying to try one of those big ol' burgers they have there. Isn't that right?" she asked, completely putting Aja on front street.

"Well . . . yeah, but—"

"Well, Wally was tellin' me the same thing when we drove by the other day," Ms. May said. "Why don't you two go together . . . he's payin', if that sweetens the deal any."

Aja looked between them, trying to figure out her next move.

"Hey." She looked up at Walker and his eyes were soft. "It's just an invitation. If you don't want to, that's fine."

It wasn't that she didn't want to. When she thought about it, she found that she did. She wasn't ready to go home yet, wasn't ready to be lonely again. There was some anxiety about being with someone she didn't know, a man she didn't fully trust yet, but it wasn't overwhelming. She wanted to make friends in town and maybe this was a start. Maybe Walker Abbott could be her friend. Even if that title didn't settle very well in her stomach.

"I want to," she blurted out, trying to move past that troubling thought. "But I want to drive my own car."

Both Walker and his grandmother grinned big enough to make her eyes hurt. She got the distinct feeling that she'd been set up, and she didn't know whether to laugh or run. She grabbed her purse instead, putting the long strap across her body.

"I guess you can follow me then," she told Walker.

"Lead the way," he licked his bottom lip until it was shiny. "I'll be right behind you."

Chapter 5

On the spectrum of things that were sexy and things that were patently not sexy, Walker had always seen food as being much closer to the latter than the former. He'd never gotten the appeal of licking whipped cream off of warm skin or dipping strawberries into secret, very delicately balanced places. Just the thought of trying to swallow down hot fudge while trying to get his rocks off made him kind of queasy.

That said, watching Aja Owens devour one of Kenny Mack's giant cheese-covered burgers made him strangely, shockingly hot. The restaurant was a sports bar—loud and a little rowdy, with TVs covering almost every square inch of wall space. Since it was Wednesday and not a game night, it was a bit quieter than it probably was usually, but it wasn't what he would have called cozy. The hostess had sequestered them in a small booth off to the side where he got to sit close enough to smell Aja's honeyed perfume and see the brightness of her eyes. He didn't care that they were surrounded by half-drunk fools stinking of bloomin' onions; he was having a great fucking time.

"You're not hungry anymore?" Aja asked after a swallow of her peach sweet tea.

He had managed to take a knife to his burger, cutting it down the middle so it was easier to eat, but he hadn't gotten more than a couple of fries down. How was he supposed to focus on beef and lettuce and onion when the woman across from him looked more appetizing than anything on his plate? For however good his meal proved to be, he was willing to bet she tasted better.

"I just got a little distracted is all," he replied before taking his first real bite of food.

Aja kept her expectant gaze on him as he chewed. He made a show of it, working his teeth a little slower than normal, savoring the flavor of the food as well as the feeling of her eyes on him.

"Good, huh?" she asked once he'd finally swallowed.

"It's a damned good burger," he said. "Not the best I've ever had, but very good."

She seemed to mull this over a little bit before conceding with an agreeing nod.

"I agree actually." She paused to eat one of the tater tots she'd gotten on the side. "When I was little, my brother and I would beg my mama to get us McDonald's when we were out. Sometimes she did, but more often than not she'd be like 'I can make a burger better than that at home.' And then she'd whip up these fat patties in the cast-iron skillet, all filled with fat chunks of onions and green peppers and stuff. Back then, you couldn't have paid me to say those burgers were better than McDonald's but thinking back . . .

I'm not sure I've ever had a burger that's lived up to the ones she made."

"Gram used to do that with chicken nuggets," he chuckled. "She wouldn't even let me have the little frozen dinosaur ones from the grocery store. If she even got a whiff that I wanted some, she'd go tearin' into some poor chicken breasts and bread and fry them up like she did on Sundays with the legs and wings. They were definitely better than anythin' she could have bought me."

Aja's expression was fond, her eyes looking towards him but still far away.

"It's so weird to think about what we took for granted when we were kids," she said. "Me and my brother used to bitch and moan about those burgers she made us eat all the time, and now I wish I could go back and flick seven-year-old me on the ear for being ungrateful."

"I guess that's the nature of kids," Walker commented. "Self-centered as hell until somebody teaches them not to be. Seems like it worked for you though."

"I guess . . ."

She went quiet but looked like she wanted to say something else. He kept his mouth shut, patient.

"I think I'd rather eat paint chips than be a kid again, but there are things about it that I miss . . . the freedom, the unabashed happiness, the lack of . . . worry," she pinched her lips together. "I mean, I know not everyone had that type of childhood, but mine was . . . really good. And I miss it, you know?"

Walker didn't say anything. He couldn't relate. When he thought about himself as a kid, he didn't see someone running free, entrenched in innocence. He saw a little boy who was quiet and buzzing with anxious energy. One who felt more comfortable huddled in the back of a closet than he did anywhere else.

The first ten years of his childhood had been tumultuous and damaging. What adolescence he'd maintained after he'd gone to live with Gram had been mostly eaten up by the aftereffects of what came before. The past few years had been good to him. He felt stable and happy. Work was good, his personal life was . . . fine. He wasn't perfect, and his PTSD sure as hell wasn't gone, but he was managing it for the first time in his life. It didn't matter how content he felt, how well he was doing, he had never been able to look back on his childhood with much fondness.

This was something he'd been working on in therapy, developing a more rounded view of his life. The process was slow and agonizing, and even he didn't know how his therapist had been able to sit through the hours of him lamenting. About seven months before he'd gotten Gram's call for help, Dr. Guthrie had informed him that he was going to stop seeing patients to spend more time with his husband and children. Walker had seen nearly a dozen therapists since, and none had fit. Too cold, too familiar, too invested in trying to get him to incorporate Christianity into his treatment plan when he'd explicitly said he wasn't interested. It got to a point where the search for a counselor just became another anxiety trigger. He'd been adjusting . . . fine. But he knew he couldn't go on forever without some help.

One thing at a time, he figured. He'd continue the search when he got home. He could already tell he was going to have a lot of shit to unpack.

He nodded at Aja, trying his best to convey empathy for desires that he didn't actually possess.

They finished the rest of their food in silence. The quiet between them wasn't exactly tense, but it made his knee shake under the table anyway. Walker ate slower than he normally would have. The conversation between them hadn't really gone the way he'd expected. It was much less flirty and much, much more intense. But he still wasn't ready to leave. He found that sitting in silence with her, leg shaking and belly full of grease, was more appealing than spending the evening with his eyes glued to his phone in his old bedroom. As long as she was willing to sit there with him, he was willing to keep his ass parked in that booth. He was even considering ordering an outrageously large milkshake as an excuse to sit there longer.

"Are we ever going to talk about it?" Aja's voice shocked him out of his dessert menu perusing, and he looked up to see her leaning across the table with that round jaw clenched. He tried not to glance at the soft-looking cleavage that glowed golden brown even under the harsh light above. He failed. Spectacularly.

"Uhh . . . what 'it' are we supposed to be talkin' about?"

She sighed, leaning back and narrowing her eyes at him. "That night in the grocery store, Walker. It's weird that you haven't brought it up yet."

Walker cursed under his breath. "I didn't think you'd want me to bring it up, to be honest."

"Well, I didn't, but you not bringing it up feels even weirder than if you had."

He couldn't make heads nor tails of her reasoning. All he knew was that he had plenty of experience with having panic attacks in public places. And he'd always hated it when the people who witnessed the attacks treated them and him like some kind of fucking sideshow after. He didn't know Aja, not then and not really now either. He didn't know whether she would want him to acknowledge it, so he hadn't. It definitely hadn't seemed like a new experience for her, so he figured the last thing she needed was to rehash a traumatizing moment with a stranger.

"So . . . did you want to talk about it?"

She floundered, her mouth opening and closing a couple of times.

"No," she said finally. "Not particularly. I just needed to acknowledge that it happened because I can't stop thinking about it. And I wanted to thank you for . . . for just being there. It helped me a lot."

"No need for thanks." He swallowed. "Like I said then—I get it. I spent my entire childhood with undiagnosed and untreated complex PTSD. I'm very familiar with freakin' the fuck out."

"Complex PTSD?" Her voice was soft.

Walker nodded but didn't clarify any further.

"Generalized anxiety disorder." She said the words matter-of-factly, like she was introducing herself to him for the first time.

He smiled.

"Is it awful that it makes me feel better that you understand firsthand that way?" she asked. "I feel like that's an awful thing to feel comforted by."

His mouth tilted downwards in thought. "I don't think it's a bad thing to want somebody to understand you in that way. I mean, I know we live in a time where some people feel more comfortable talkin' about mental health than they have in the past, but it's still easy to feel alone when you're in the thick of it. Plus, it's not like society as a whole makes it safe for people to be as open as they might want to be about this kind of thing."

"Yeah." The nod of her head was emphatic. "When I was first diagnosed, I remember feeling a ton of . . . shame. Some of it is gone, but not all of it, and what's left definitely keeps me from opening up to people about my anxiety. Even if it would make life easier for me in the moment."

"I was twenty before I saw a psychiatrist and got diagnosed, and I didn't tell anybody about it for a long time after that. Not even Gram." The unexpected intimacy of the conversation had his throat dry, so he took a sip of his sweet tea. "Shit's hard. It's important to be open and honest when you're ready and willin'. But I don't think we owe it to anybody to tell them shit we aren't comfortable tellin' them either."

Aja bit down on her bottom lip, seeming to mull his words over. He hoped he didn't sound like some know-it-all pushing his opinions down her throat. But if he'd only learned one thing in life, it was that not everyone deserved to know all of him. His soft spots were his to expose, and he had the right to be very fucking discerning. He must have felt some kind of kinship with Aja, seen parts of himself in her that made it easy to be so open and honest.

"This is a hell of a conversation for a . . ." She paused, then cleared her throat with a wince.

Walker couldn't have stopped the smirk from overtaking his face if he tried.

"A . . ." he prompted.

"Nothing, just a"—she waved a hand around in the air—"an outing."

"An outing otherwise known as a date?"

Her eye roll was drenched in exasperation, but he could tell she was a little flustered. She did this thing where she widened her eyes and pinched her chin between the knuckles of her middle and pointer fingers whenever she was unnerved. She'd done it when Gram had introduced them at bingo, and she was doing it now. The very last thing Walker wanted was to make her uncomfortable, so he watched her closely, hoping that his teasing hadn't toed over the line.

"Please," she smirked, and it was so wildly sexy that it made his fingers twitch, "if this were a date, I definitely wouldn't have worn leggings and a grungy sweatshirt."

He didn't give a damn what she had on. When he'd gotten a look at her at bingo earlier, he'd had a hell of a time taking his eyes off her for the sake of decency. Even in her unassuming clothes he could see how spectacular she was. Dark material stretched over the wide expanse of her thighs, her stomach pressed against her sweatshirt, refusing to be hidden. He'd had to stop himself from thinking about what she looked like naked in order to keep his head on straight. All he knew was that the woman was damn gorgeous. She could have been wearing a burlap sack covered in sawdust and his opinion on the matter wouldn't have changed.

"It's all right," he drawled, trying to see how far he could take the flirting. "I wouldn't bring you here on a first date anyway. You seem like the type of woman who likes a little winin' and dinin'. You'd have me takin' you to someplace with eighty-dollar steaks, where they make sure you're wearin' a tie before they let you in."

Aja tilted her head to the side, her lips pursed. "I don't know why, but I have a hard time picturing you in a tie."

It was probably because he could count on two hands the number of times in his life he'd worn one. When he was on his own time, he was a jeans and T-shirt type of guy. *The Charleston Journal* didn't have a very strict dress code for beat reporters; most days he wore a dryer-ironed button up and slacks to work. On days when his boss wasn't around he wore jeans and a sweatshirt. Walker didn't consider himself to be some kind of rough-and-tumble country boy, but he couldn't deny that the whole suit-and-tie getup made him feel stuffy and claustrophobic. That didn't mean he wouldn't be willing to get choked to death by the stiff collar of a button-up shirt for the chance to see Aja all dressed up in her Sunday best.

But odds were his wish would never come true. He was in Greenbelt for one reason only: Gram needed him. Her doctor had said that it would take about eight weeks for her fractures to heal. He'd gotten the go-ahead from his boss to work from home in the meantime, but he had every intention of leaving as soon as Gram was self-sufficient. As beautiful as Aja was, and as intriguing as he found her, none of those things could hold up to the bitter taste this town left in his mouth.

If they'd been in Charleston, he would have taken her words as an opening to ask her to go out with him. And he wanted to. He wanted to sit across from her in some place with low lighting and listen to her talk about whatever the fuck she wanted while he admired her. But to what end? In two months, he'd probably never see her again.

He wasn't the type of guy who could thrive in a long-distance relationship. He craved affection and physical closeness as much as he valued emotional connection. It wasn't that he was afraid he'd cheat—he liked to believe he had more integrity than that. But he knew that type of arrangement wouldn't work for him. He could deal with it for a while, but in time the physical distance would cause him to become emotionally distant. He'd pull away slowly, inching towards the end until all he could manage was a terse once-a-week phone call until the inevitable breakup.

He was confident that this would be the outcome for him. Largely because it was almost an exact mirror of how his relationship with Gram had deteriorated once he'd left town and couldn't feel her hugs or love so keenly.

So no, he couldn't ask her out on a date. Not if he was trying to be responsible with both of their feelings. That didn't mean they couldn't be friends though. Eight weeks wasn't a very long time, but it was too long for him to exist with only his grandmother for company. And he sure as fuck wasn't about to hang out with anybody else in town. They already had a few things in common, and if her presence was any indication, she didn't hate his company. He could keep his desire for her in check long enough to maintain a casual friendship with her . . . if she wanted one.

"That's probably because I only own two of them," he laughed. "And both are balled up in a drawer in my apartment back in Charleston."

"I thought you were some fancy journalist," she said. "The way your grandmother talks, you work for some sophisticated paper and practically wear a three-piece suit to work every day."

The pride Gram felt for him and his career should have made him feel pleased, but it only served to make guilt bite at the back of his neck. "Not at all. I love my job. I write about sports—mostly baseball. It definitely ain't fancy though. The last time I wore a tie to work was during my interview."

"Maybe don't tell her that, then. Because she's definitely told everyone at bingo that you're some kind of Don Draper type."

He shuddered at the thought. He didn't know if he'd have it in him to bust up Gram's vision like that, but he didn't like the thought of people thinking of him as that particular brand of asshole.

"I'm definitely not that," he said. "I like to think of myself as more of a Michael O'Neal in *My Best Friend's Wedding* kind of guy."

"You're missing the sexy scar though."

He snorted. "Anyway, speaking of friends . . . I was thinkin' that we should spend more time together."

Aja's eyes went comically wide, and she rolled her left wrist. "What . . . brings you to that conclusion?"

"Greenbelt is borin'. And aside from Gram, you're about the only person in town I can stand to be around for more than two minutes. If I have to sit in that house with only my grandmother for company for the next two months, I will absolutely lose my mind. And it's already far gone enough as it is."

"I can definitely understand that," she murmured. "But I'm not exactly sure what you think we should do. Like you said, Greenbelt isn't the most poppin' place on the planet. And I don't invite people I don't know well into my house. Most activities around here are either thrown by churches, are for kids, or are some combination of both. That doesn't leave us with a whole lot of outing options."

Walker shrugged. "It doesn't have to be anythin' super exciting, I'm sure we could make our own fun wherever we go."

She bit down on her bottom lip, eyes narrowed in thought. "How would you feel about doing another night of bingo every week?"

He mulled it over. Gram had practically dragged him into the bingo hall by his ear, but he hadn't hated it nearly as much as he expected. He knew that it likely would have been much more boring without Aja's presence, but luckily he didn't have to experience that. He would gladly sit through a hundred games, struggling to identify the numbers on his cards before the caller moved on, so long as he could fail while sitting next to her.

"I wouldn't hate that. If my last couple games are any indication, I could use some practice. Maybe you could even teach me a few things. Hell, all of your supreme expertise might even help me win a game or two."

Her answering laugh was clearly mocking him, but the sound was so sweet he couldn't find it in himself to mind. "I don't know about that," she said. "You can barely keep up with the calls; I might not have enough 'expertise' to carry you *that* far, dude."

Walker's jaw dropped open, and he put a hand on his chest in mock offense. "It hurts that you don't think I have what it takes to win, Aja. Like I can actually feel the pain, right here in my chest."

She shrugged.

He pursed his lips for a second, eyes squinting. "How about we make a little wager? Since you're so confident in my inability to win."

"Let me get this straight." She put her forearms on the table and leaned in. He mimicked her movement until their faces were inches apart. "I know you're horrible at bingo, you know you're horrible at bingo, your granny knows you're horrible at bingo. And even with your chances of winning being as dismal as they are, you still want to make a bet with me?"

"Absolutely. If you're not too scared to take me on. . . ."

"You're ridiculous. Do you know that? Has anyone ever told you how ridiculous you are?"

"A few times," he remarked. "But that's still not goin' to make me back down."

Aja was quiet for a couple beats before she was shaking her head at him. When her eyes rolled, he knew he had her. "All right, I'll take you on. But I'm going to need the promise of some kind of prize if I'm going to keep entertaining your mess while you keep losing right along with me."

"I feel like we should be discussin' what I get when I inevitably prove you wrong, actually."

"And what do you feel like your grand prize should be, Walker?"

He screwed his face up, going all out in his exaggeration. "Think you could get your hands on a signed Hank Aaron Topps baseball card? I'd prefer 1962; he was with the Braves then."

"*Who?*"

He made a disgusted scoffing sound in the back of his throat. "You don't know who Hank Aaron is?"

She shook her head again. "I have neither the energy nor the brain space to get into sports."

"You're breakin' my heart."

"I might break more than that soon if the next thing out of your mouth involves any form of the word 'ball'."

A grin spread across his lips slowly. He was enjoying the hell out of riling her up. She was gorgeous, even when she was threatening him. He couldn't help but keep it going just a little longer.

"How about you find a way to hook me up with that actress from the movie you were talking to Gram about earlier." He snapped his fingers, searching for her name. "Gemma Chan."

Her face went blank. "If I had her number, I'd tell her to avoid you at all costs."

His bark of laughter made the people in the booth behind Aja turn around to glance at them.

She sighed and shook her head. "Next thing I know you're going to request claim to my virtue as your prize."

He raised an eyebrow. "Virtue?"

"It was the first, most ridiculous word that came to mind." She waved a hand dismissively in the air. "You know what I mean."

"I'm not quite sure I do actually."

"I'm just saying, your little demands are getting progressively more . . . demanding is all."

Walker placed a hand over his heart again. "I can assure you, I have no interest in stealin' anything from you, least of all your virtue. But if you're thinkin' about givin' me some type of winner's prize for all my hard work, I sure as hell won't be turnin' you down."

He was being bold. So bold that it made his heart race. All it had taken was a couple of slightly provocative words to bring out the lecher in him. He probably would have been ashamed of himself if he hadn't wanted so badly—against all reason—to see where the conversation would lead. He watched as Aja's eyes narrowed. The expression on her face wasn't necessarily suspicious, but he couldn't really discern its meaning. He stared back, trying not to break under her gaze.

"It's not a completely awful idea, I guess." When she finally spoke, he breathed audibly. First from relief that she'd broken the tension, then out of surprise at her words. "Hypothetically speaking, of course. I don't know if anyone's ever gotten horny over a game of bingo before, but it's definitely not the worst idea I've ever heard."

His mouth went dry. "I don't know . . . those daubers *are* very phallic. I guess bingo is as good a place as any to get turned on." Hell, sitting next to Aja for three hours, smelling her skin, the anticipation of waiting for her to say something, *anything*, to him had made not getting turned on a job in and of itself.

Aja looked at him silently, then shook her head, a small smile stretching across her mouth. "Not that I'm happy about admitting it, but you're not wrong, I guess. The energy in there can get pretty intense sometimes. And I imagine the adrenaline rush that comes with winning is pretty heady too."

"Imagine? You've never won a game before?"

She shook her head.

Walker relaxed into the booth some more, splaying his arms out along the back. He picked at the hard, cracking vinyl fabric, channeling his nervousness about the turn of their conversation into desecrating the worn furniture. "So, what you're sayin' is that you've actually been projectin' your desire to steal *my* virtue as your winner's prize this entire time?"

"Yes," she deadpanned. "I honestly didn't think you'd find me out."

"How could I not? It's written all over your face."

"This face?" She pointed a finger at herself, her expression blank again.

He grinned. "It's all behind the eyes, Aja."

"Mmmhmm." She rolled her eyes. "I think your virtue is going to be safe with me, but lucky for you I wouldn't mind getting out of the house more, so I'll take you up on your request. Monday nights are usually pretty bare, if you want to go then. All the little old ladies have choir practice that night."

"Let's do that. We can have a little more privacy."

"And they let Mrs. Schofield call the bingo balls on Monday nights . . . she talks really, *really* slowly, so maybe you'll have a chance of keeping up."

Unable to stop himself, he caught her gaze. Her eyes were bright and open, and he found himself saving the image of her looking at him that way in his head.

"I don't know about that." Walker crossed his arms over his chest. "Somethin' tells me I might have a hard time maintainin' my focus with you there to distract me."

Chapter 6

It was nothing short of a privilege that she was able to work from home. Her shiny bachelor's degree had left her with a mountain of student loans, but it had also gotten her a job at a new-age company that made up for lackluster salaries with "radical flexibility." Whatever the hell that meant, it had allowed her to move across the country when living in busy-ass DC had become too detrimental to her mental health. Critiques and all, Aja was endlessly grateful for her job, and she loved that she was allowed as much solitude as she desired. But she also knew something absolutely had to give.

She'd rehashed the conversation with Reniece in her weekly virtual therapy with Dr. Sharp. Her therapist was a Black woman in her mid-forties who had an incredibly kind face but also had a sternness to her that always made Aja sit up straight. She had half expected Dr. Sharp to say she didn't need to rush to make new friends. Instead, the woman had told her that fostering new relationships would be beneficial to her. The professional opinion startled Aja. She knew it was the truth, just like she knew it was what she genuinely wanted. It was just that she was . . . stuck.

As a child, before an insurmountable level of anxiety had descended upon her as a teenager, it had been easy for her to make friends. She'd been quiet enough not to hog the spotlight but had enough personality to make her fun and interesting. By the time she was sixteen, she was quietly drowning in anxiety more often than not, but she already had a strong group of friends. She hadn't sought out counseling until her sophomore year of college, and with therapy and meds, she was more outgoing than she'd ever been. That didn't last forever though. Life happened, friendships ended for reasons other than her disorder, and the older she got, the more difficult it became to cultivate new ones. Admittedly, after a while she'd stopped trying. She self-isolated, putting strain on what connections she had left, until her closest friend was someone she was related to. It sucked. A lot. She wanted to meet people she could go out with, have fun with, *talk to*, but she wasn't sure she knew how to do that anymore.

Walker and his grandmother were the first new connections she'd made in a long time. And she didn't really feel like Ms. May counted since they only ever spoke in a very specific setting. She didn't think Walker counted either. Mostly because she knew that whatever friendship they might build was temporary and because the way she felt couldn't be contained to pure friendliness. She needed friends who weren't white ladies twice her age and white dudes she kind of, maybe, sort of, possibly wanted to rub herself up against like an overly affectionate cat.

She spent hours racking her brain for ways to make friends as a grown woman who worked from home and had a hard time opening up to people. She'd sat down at her desk with an actual pen and paper, relying on memories and anecdotes of how outgoing women like her mother and Reniece made friends to try and form her plan:

1. *New mom clubs*
2. *Facebook groups*
3. *Friendly neighbors*
4. *Water aerobics classes*
5. *Black sorority gatherings*
6. *Target checkout-line conversations*
7. *Cultivating sparkling personalities*

She'd felt no better when she finished the list. In fact, she'd felt even crappier about her options. None of them felt particularly doable for her, and that only served to increase the hopelessness in her spirit.

Had she been in DC, she probably could have bitten the bullet and gone to a few day parties and professional-development brunches before wiggling her way into the life of the first person who showed her kindness. Greenbelt didn't have much in the way of those things. Unless you counted the Saturday afternoon rush at Minnie's to be a popping brunch spot. Now all she could do was wait for another church event and hopefully force herself out of her own head long enough to meet some people.

The reality of it was defeating and filled her with the need to do something to make herself feel better. When neither cake baking nor staring at pictures of Trevante Rhodes was sufficient, she settled on something she hadn't done in a very long time—a manicure.

Fresh Coat was located in a strip mall downtown, tucked between a dentist's office and the only Pizza Hut in Greenbelt. Aja had done a quick online search for nail salons in town and quickly realized there were only two. They had the same number of reviews and star ratings, so she went with the one closest to her apartment. She hadn't planned on getting anything extravagant, so she figured if the place was clean and the nail tech could polish sufficiently well, she didn't need to be picky.

It was midmorning on a Monday, and she hadn't expected the place to be busy, but when she walked in, she was shocked to find no other customers. None in the tiny little waiting area, none in the pedicure chairs that lined the right side of the shop, and definitely none at the nail stations. It was eerily quiet too—not even the small flat-screen TV mounted above the front desk was on. Aja took a few steps back until she was outside the door, making sure the little neon sign out front said "open" like she'd originally thought, before sliding back into the shop. Her feet had only just barely made it inside when someone finally appeared out of a back room.

It was a tall Black woman with dark-umber skin and a perfectly laid light-brown bob wig. The look of pure shock on her face was startling.

"Uh . . . hi." Aja waved awkwardly and regretted it immediately. It seemed she was determined to act like a dork at any given moment.

"Oh my God." The woman put the top back on the bottle of soda she'd been drinking and set it down on a nearby table before making her way towards her. "Hi," she said with a grin. "You're not lost, are you?"

Aja frowned. "I don't think so. . . . I wanted to get my nails done. . . . Are you guys closed?"

"Hell no!" The woman winced the second the words were out of her mouth, and Aja couldn't help but chuckle. "I mean, no ma'am, we are definitely open. What services were you interested in today?"

"Well, I need a manicure and . . . I don't know. I wasn't planning on getting anything fancy, but . . . maybe if I see something I really like . . ."

"Lucky for you you're currently looking at the best nail tech in Greenbelt." The woman reached into the back pocket of her dark jeans and pulled out her phone, tapping on her screen before handing it to Aja. "This is my Instagram."

Aside from a few photos of the woman herself, the entire page was full of nail art. Each set was more gorgeous than the last. Nails of all shapes and lengths outfitted with designs so perfectly done they made Aja excited about the possibility of wearing the art on her own body. She peeked at the woman's hands, noting the long coffin shape of them painted with a milky white coat of polish and a sporadic gold leaf design. Aja wondered if she'd done them herself. Based on the quality of her online portfolio, she probably had.

"These are amazing," she breathed, handing the phone back. "Yeah . . . I'm definitely interested in getting some art."

The woman grinned, her cheeks scrunching up, making her gorgeous face turn absolutely adorable. The smile was infectious, and Aja couldn't help but return it.

"That's great to hear. I'm goin' to set you up at the second table over there." She walked ahead, leading Aja forward, but turned her head to talk. "I'm Miriam, by the way, but everybody calls me Miri, since I apparently forgot all the home trainin' my mama gave me and didn't introduce myself earlier."

"I'm Aja."

"Nice to meet you, Aja," Miri said as she pulled out the chair for Aja. "And thank you for choosing Fresh Coat."

A moment later, Aja was sitting across from Miri, who inspected her hands.

"You have beautiful nails," Miri told her. "They're real strong . . . healthy."

"Thank you. I started taking care of them myself last year after I decided to finally try to stop biting them. Spending so much time and energy making them look nice made it harder to want to tear them apart." Aja chuckled softly. "It's kind of a soothing thing for me now."

"Well, you do a good job. I mean, your cuticles need some love, and your nail shape could be a little more refined, but I can tell you've been takin' care of them; I can see the love you put in."

Aja took pride in the validation. After spending years with haggard nails from both anxiety-induced biting and just a habit she had a hard time breaking, she loved that they were in good shape. It was even better that their health had come by her hand, by a concentrated effort to take care of herself. It was a small thing. She was sure there were plenty of other personal growth endeavors to undertake with such fervor that probably would have benefited her life. But she should be grateful she had even this because she didn't always, wouldn't always.

Miri had connected her phone to a little speaker on the manicure station next to them. Her playlist seemed to be mostly modern R&B. Some songs Aja recognized and others she didn't, but they were all nice, vibey in a way that relaxed her with every thump of bass. The longer they sat there, the more comfortable she became. Miri's hands were soft and strong and incredibly steady as she went to work shaping Aja's nails with a little file.

Their silence wasn't necessarily uncomfortable, but it was. Aja had never made a habit of going to the nail salon regularly, and from the few times she had, she knew conversation wasn't required. But Aja found herself itching to speak. It wasn't an unfamiliar feeling, but she surprised herself when she actually followed through with the desire.

"Is this your place?" she asked.

For some reason she couldn't see Miri owning the spot. Guessing ages was a slippery slope that she'd never found steady footing on, but had she been made to guess, she would have said Miri was somewhere around her age. Aja sure as hell didn't know many millennials who owned their own brick-and-mortar businesses, especially not Black ones.

There was also the vibe of the place. Fresh Coat was nice, clean, and well maintained, but the decor was definitely what she would consider . . . auntie-ish. The entire color scheme was various shades of brown. Rich chocolate-colored chairs, tan walls, even the artwork was tinged in the color, along with burnt oranges and reds. Aja obviously didn't know the woman, but she had a hard time imagining Miri picking those things. She wore a thigh-length dress with a muted green-and-pink geometric pattern that showed off her arms and the bold, black heart tattoo in the center of her cleavage. She wore a couple of black chokers with gold star and moon pendants dangling from the front. Even her shoes, thick-soled platform sandals, were stylish.

In short, Miri looked cool as fuck. So cool that Aja couldn't picture her decorating a place she owned in this particular fashion.

"Uh-uh," Miri said as she worked her rough file against Aja's nails, slowly turning them into more pronounced oval shapes. "My auntie owns it, but she's only workin' a couple days a week while she gets ready to retire, so I'm holdin' the fort down."

"Oh, right." That made a lot more sense. "Well, I'm glad I made it in here before the rush."

Miri snorted, gripping her file a little tighter. "Girl, you're probably one of maybe three customers I'll have all day. And that's if I'm lucky . . . and I might actually be the unluckiest person this side of the Atlantic."

"What do you mean?"

"You didn't see how surprised I looked when I saw you in here?"

"I mean, yeah," Aja said, nodding, "but I figured that was because I'm here kind of early in the day . . . and it's a Monday."

"Nope. It's because you're the first brand-new customer we've gotten in, like, three months. Everyone else who comes in has had a standing appointment for damn near as long as I've been alive."

Aja was silent in her shock, and Miri looked up at her, chuckling at the expression on her face.

"We were the only nail salon in town for years. If you weren't comin' to Fresh Coat, you'd have to go to Beaufort or Yemassee for the chance at getting a decent shellac." Miri put her file away and pulled cuticle cream from a drawer attached to the table. "But a couple of years ago the mayor's wife's sister opened up this fancy new shop in the part of town where all the rich folks live. They've got massage chairs at every station and free bottomless mimosas and all kinds of other shit we can't afford to do and well"—she gestured to the empty space around them—"everybody who wasn't already deathly loyal to my auntie started flockin' there."

There was more than a hint of bitterness in her tone, and Aja couldn't fault her for it. Greenbelt was a small town, so their customer base would have already been limited. To have it poached so blatantly would have made her feel bitter too. Her money wasn't going to make their situation any better, but she felt even happier about choosing Fresh Coat over the other place.

Miri huffed. "Anyway, you didn't come here to hear our boring sob story. You came to get these pretty nails done. Do you have an idea of the kind of art you want?"

Aja wanted to reassure Miri that she didn't view anything as a sob story, nor did she mind hearing her talk about something weighing heavy on her heart. This was the first conversation she'd had in person in days. It was also the first time she'd been touched since Walker had rested his hand on her lower back on the way out of Kenny Mack's. She didn't know if other people viewed getting their nails done as an act of intimacy, but it was beginning to feel like one.

She also recognized how much she hated being pushed when she obviously didn't want to talk about something though. Trying her hardest to extend Miri the same courtesy, she bit down on her words.

"I saw some on your page that were kind of like . . . marbled?" She thought back to Miri's Instagram. Out of all the gorgeous designs, those had stood out.

"Oh yeah, I did those for my friend Jade. I was inspired by a picture of this tacky-ass bathroom that was floor-to-ceiling marble," she snorted. "I wanted to take that idea and make it . . . not shitty, I guess. They'd be real pretty on you. What are you thinkin' in terms of color? We could do a white base or . . . maybe red, but I think I like pink for you. We could put some gold and gray in there, glam it up a bit."

Aja wouldn't have described herself as glamorous, but Miri sounded so excited at the prospect that Aja probably would have agreed to mini portraits of Big Bird if it looked like it would make the other woman happy.

"Let's do it," she said.

Miri grinned, big and white, and Aja's stomach flipped. Was there a word for something that felt an awful lot like a crush but wasn't? Something that didn't connotate romance but felt similar in so many ways? Whatever this feeling was, Aja hadn't felt it in a long time. Not since she'd been young and found herself on one side of a budding new friendship. It was exciting and scary, and she was probably going to spend an inordinate amount of time later making sure her brain understood that Miri was only being nice because she had to. She wasn't trying to be Aja's friend. Aja had come for a service, and Mira was providing it—and doing an excellent job, no less.

Miri was diligent. She prepared the tools she needed for the designs as Aja soaked her hands. During the hand massage portion they decided that instead of acrylic tips, they would just strengthen Aja's natural nails and do the art on top, using gel polish.

Aja watched in awe as Miri worked, constantly surprised that the other woman was able to carry on a conversation as she created spectacular artwork on such a small scale. Aja sat as still as possible, her eyes glued to the marbled nails slowly coming together in front of her. They spoke some about Aja's work—Miri seemed incredibly tickled that she was working as the manager of an account she'd *definitely* seen on Twitter. They also talked about how Miri had gotten into her career. Aja admired the story of the little girl who'd started cleaning up in her aunt's salon to make extra money to take home to her mother and became enamored with the beauty of nails. Her own career was born out of necessity rather than passion. And while that was perfectly fine with her, she enjoyed seeing people who did something they felt called to do.

For all the problems Fresh Coat may have had, Miri obviously loved it. She was warm and funny and her passion for her work was infectious. Even before they'd finished, Aja had decided that making regular trips there would be a regular part of her schedule. She might not make friends, but she could have this. It was a connection, even if it was temporary and transactional.

When she was finished, Miri took time to inspect her work. Her eyes were sharp as she looked over each of Aja's nails. Aja wasn't sure what she was searching for, nor did she see anything she would change. Still, Miri would go back with more polish in some spots or gold dusting in others. The result was more stunning than Aja had imagined.

Each nail had a pale pink base. The faux marble design was darker pink and gray in some spots, and white and gold in others. The designs were incredibly cohesive, but clearly done by hand rather than a stencil. Each nail had slight differences, little cracks or shades, making each one unique. Aja wasn't sure how she was going to tear her eyes away from them long enough to get anything done.

When Miri was finally satisfied, she made sure Aja was happy before guiding her hands underneath a UV light to dry. They were quiet as Miri went about sanitizing the station.

"You got any plans tonight?" Miri asked almost absent-mindedly. "A hot date?"

Aja snorted. She was excited but nervous as hell about her plans with Walker for the night, and she sure as hell wouldn't have called them "hot." "I'm uh . . . I'm going to bingo actually."

"Bingo?" Miri made no effort to hide the mirth on her face. "Like, real bingo, or are you talking about some new club I don't know about?"

"Yeah, actual bingo." Aja cleared her throat. "I go every week. It helps me get out of the house."

Miri's full lips turned down, along with her eyebrows. "Baby girl, if you need to get out the house there are tons of things you can do besides sitting around with them mean old ladies that go to the Greenbelt City Bingo Hall. You know . . . they ran my granny out after accusing her of cheating by screwing one of the bingo callers. As if my granny would mess around with one of them boring old duds," she scoffed.

They shared a laugh. Aja understood where she was coming from. There was a reason she was the youngest person there, but bingo had saved her sanity more than once, and she wasn't ashamed of it.

"I'm . . . not really outgoing." That wasn't the whole story, but it was the only explanation she was willing to give. "I get anxious around new people, and I don't know that many people in town, so . . . bingo is what helps me socialize right now."

Miri eyed her for a few silent moments before her gaze went soft.

"Well, I'm definitely not goin' to judge you for that. It ain't like I'm out here doing hip shit everyday either. *But* on the off chance that you're interested, me and some friends get together at my house sometimes to watch movies and drink way too much wine. You can come through if you want."

Aja's heart jumped into her throat. Had she just received an actual invitation to hang out from a real-life person or was she completely tripping? She ran over Miri's words twice in her head before she realized that, yes, it had happened. Even still, it was a bombshell.

Miri seemed to take her silence as something other than surprise though, because she fidgeted with the gold bangles on her wrist and frowned. "It's not even a party," she insisted. "Just me and two other girls. My friend Jade, who I was telling you about earlier, and my other friend Olivia. You don't need to dress up or put on makeup or anything. It's very chill, I promise. But . . . you can say no, of course. No hard feelin's or anything."

Aja didn't want to say no. With the way her heart was pounding in excitement, she was surprised she hadn't jumped into the woman's arms out of pure glee. She didn't care what they were doing. She probably would have been just as happy if Miri had invited her over to do yard work. She'd gotten a genuine invitation from a woman who was cooler than Aja could ever even hope to be. It was like her brain was moving so fast her mouth couldn't keep up enough to get any words out. When they finally came, she didn't even bother trying to mask her joy.

"I'd love that," she said with a grin. "Actually, I'd love that a lot."

Chapter 7

Walker tried hard to make himself look as un-creepy as possible. But as a grown man of considerable height standing in a sparse parking lot under a half-darkened sky wearing a baseball cap, he knew that it was unlikely he had succeeded. He and Aja had confirmed their plans via a couple of very straightforward text messages, and he'd been so anxious to see her ever since, he'd shown up to the bingo hall almost twenty minutes early.

It was a gorgeous night, dusk settling over the horizon, and surprisingly cool and not humid. Instead of sitting in the cabin of his truck, he got out and hopped up on the bed, his legs dangling over the edge. It was pretty quiet; the main street that led to the bingo hall was sparsely traveled. Every once in a while a car would drive up and pull into a parking spot, but other than that, the only other sounds were chirping crickets and Walker's fingers drumming against his jeans.

He saw her bright green car coming from what seemed like a mile away, and the sight immediately widened his smile. He noted, not for the first time, how interesting it was that such a reserved person drove such a loud vehicle. Like when she made a snappy joke or lost herself in a flirty turn of phrase, it showed him that her timidity was backed by something else. Something vibrant.

He stayed seated as she pulled into the spot next to him, greeting her with a grin when she finally approached.

"Good evenin', Miss Aja." He was almost embarrassed by how much he sounded like the worst kind of Southern-boy cliché. But she smiled, and her pretty eyes blinked up at him so slow and tantalizing that the shame refused to show its face.

"You sure look like you're having a good time." She gathered her long, dark braids and let them fall over her right shoulder.

"It's a nice night."

She tilted her head back, giving Walker an unobstructed view of her neck. Long and elegant, in contrast with her soft, round face. His hands and mouth ached with want. In an instant, he became aware of how close she was. How easy it would be to widen his legs and pull her between his thighs until they were brushed up against one another so intimately that he could feel nothing but her, smell nothing but her.

Feeling himself harden beneath his jeans, he dug his thumbnails into his palms. Not enough to hurt, but enough to send him plummeting back to reality. These were not the thoughts he was supposed to be having about a woman he was trying to cultivate a friendship with. He shouldn't have been wondering what kind of panties she had on underneath those little cutoff shorts she wore. And he sure as fuck didn't need to be thinking about laying her out across one of those long bingo-hall tables and working those panties off with his teeth. Aja was doing him a favor by hanging out. She was keeping him from being lonelier than he already was in Greenbelt. That was all. He just . . . had to make sure his dick understood that.

"You ready?" she asked, jutting a thumb towards the hall's entrance. "Monday nights are never as packed as Wednesdays, but I still want to get a good seat."

He was hopping off the truck bed before she could finish talking. His heart stilled as his body accidentally brushed hers, and he moved away quickly, playing it off with false nonchalance. The hair on his arms stood to attention as he pushed the tailgate back up into place. He took a second to catch his breath, trying to forget what the brief second of being so close to her felt like before he turned towards her with another grin. This time his jaw ached from the force of it.

"I'm right behind you."

When they entered the hall, it became clear to him that Monday night bingo was an entirely different scene from Wednesday nights. Aja was right. On Wednesdays, the largest bingo room in the building was packed full, with barely any free seats left for the taking. Now Walker counted only a couple of handfuls of people, and they were spread out pretty far, leaving most of the highly desired spots open. It was also quiet—not somber, just calm. The people there didn't seem nearly as intimidating either. His shoulders loosened, tension leaving his body as the chill atmosphere soaked into his skin.

The room was warm—even hotter than it was outside. It was almost like they didn't want to bother wasting money blasting the air conditioner for so few people. He was sure that by the time they left his clothes would be sticking to his body.

Even though plenty of seats were open, Aja insisted they sit towards the back. "We'll probably be talking some," she said.

Walker followed behind her, obedient as a puppy and without a single objection. Sure, his eyes had been so glued to her wide hips and full ass that he hadn't even considered arguing, but still . . .

The area they chose was completely empty, but he still sat in the chair directly to her left. He rationalized that choosing that particular seat would allow them to keep their voices down. But he knew full well he mostly wanted to be close, to live in the possibility of the brush of their arms or thighs. It was pathetic, sure enough, but Walker's sense of shame was wearing thinner the more time he spent in the presence of Aja Owens.

Once she'd set her purse and water bottle on the table in front of her, she cleared her throat.

"I feel like Ms. May threw you to the wolves with this, so I'm going to give you a rundown of my own."

"Sounds good."

"We always start with the blue sheets first." She isolated the blue sheets from the stack of six they'd each gotten. "I don't know why, but they always do."

Instead of keeping the sheets in a stack like he'd seen most other people do, she laid them all out on the table in front of her.

"You're not a pro at this," she said. "You can't just stack your sheets and expect to flip through them fast enough to find the numbers."

"That's how everybody else does it though," he argued. "It's how Gram told me to do it."

"Everybody else has been playing this game since 1976,

Walker. They all have some kind of superpower that allows them to memorize the sheets at a glance or something." She paused to lick her lips and his eyes glued themselves to the shine her tongue left behind. "You and I don't have that power, so I suggest you do what I do and make it easier on yourself."

"People will look at me funny though," he said, pouting.

Aja's answering eye roll was more adorable than it had a right to be. "You're a tall, handsome young man who spends multiple weeknights in a bingo hall surrounded by senior citizens. People are going to look at you funny either way."

If his ears had been able to perk up like a dog's, they would have. "Handsome?"

"No." She snapped, then pointed a stern finger at him. "Focus."

He pouted again, and she ignored him.

"You can't memorize the sheets, but it doesn't hurt to give them a good, long look to get familiar."

As she began arranging her sheets, he did as she said. His eyes scanned over the numbers. Spread across six sheets with six different bingo cards on each one, there were hundreds of them. He started feeling overwhelmed all over again.

"You have any tricks you'd recommend?" he asked.

"It's important to remember that you're not just searching for random numbers across the sheets. If the number they call is BI5, focus only on the B columns. Don't let all the numbers make you feel like you're going on a wild goose chase."

That made sense. Perfect sense actually. He knew the rules of the game. Understood that the only way to get a bingo was to match both numbers and letters with the ones called. But in the previous games he'd played, he'd been disconnected from the point she'd made. His eyes had flitted across the pages with each call, searching for matches in places they couldn't be. Aja's words reminded him what he already knew but had failed to fully grasp in practice.

They both straightened up, eyes to the front as the bingo caller announced from the podium that they were about to begin.

Walker followed Aja's lead as he unscrewed the top on his green dauber. The game started with little fanfare. He couldn't remember the name of the woman calling the numbers, but she moved much slower than the other two callers he'd encountered. He wasn't mad at it though; he got through the first three numbers easily. He didn't have any matches, but he didn't feel flustered the way he usually did.

"Maybe I don't need as much practice as I thought," he commented to Aja.

"Don't get too cocky," she laughed. "I told you, Mrs. Schofield likes to go at a snail's pace—but this is how she always sounds, even in regular conversations. She talks so slow that sometimes people bring their kids on Monday nights because it's the only time the little ones have a chance of keeping up."

"And, just like that, my confidence is shot."

"No!" Her hand shot out to touch his forearm, sparking lightning behind his skin. "I didn't mean it like that. I was playing with you."

"I know, Aja." His voice was rough, his eyes on her hand resting against him. She'd gotten new nails. Pretty and pink and marbled, and he immediately thought about what they would look like clutching at his back or wrapped around his . . . "I'm just fuckin' around. Don't worry."

"Right . . ."

He could tell she was embarrassed. Her eyes dropped to the table and her face morphed into a light grimace. "What kind of friends would we be if we couldn't fuck with each other every now and then?"

She was quiet for a few seconds, studying him. He wasn't sure what she was looking for, or if she found it, but the tension around her eyes faded. He groaned internally when she moved her hand off his arm, immediately missing her touch.

"So, we're friends now?" she asked, her eyes back on her sheets. "I didn't know that."

It took everything in him to take his eyes off her. "Do you make a habit of hanging out with random men and helping them get better at bingo so they can find a way to not be bored to death in this awful town?"

"Only if you call four or five guys a habit." The words came out in an exaggerated whisper, and he had to bite back a bark of laughter.

"So this was all some ploy to make me think this was my idea before you turn around and play me." His confidence was bolstered as he easily found another called number on one of his sheets. "You lure me in with those irresistible eyes and get my defenses down long enough to what? Rob me? Convince me to join some multilevel marketing scheme where you make me hawk shitty leggings to sad moms?"

Those eyes turned to him, just as irresistible as he'd claimed them to be. "All of this may or may not just be a long con to get you to move my furniture around my apartment."

"I'd say it's working pretty well. I can start doing my stretches to get my back ready to move a couch all by my lonesome if that's what you want from me, Aja."

"You'd offer your services up that easily? I barely had to do any work to get you to commit to that."

The air between them sparked with something new. Walker's brain told him that this conversation was far too charged for one between friends. Some part of him—his heart or his dick or something else, he didn't know—was feeding off it. He felt excited and electrified and horny as hell. Those were dangerous things to feel for a woman he was trying not to bed. But that knowledge didn't stop him from pushing past the limit he'd set for himself just a little bit more.

"How else am I supposed to show you how eager I am to please?" His words were low and brazen.

Aja's eyelids got even lower as she blinked at him slowly. He could see her chest rise and fall a little faster. Her skin was too dark to show any kind of natural blush, but he was willing to guess that her cheeks were as warm as his. They stared at each other, that crackling air settling into something so charged he wasn't sure how it didn't suffocate them both. When her plush lips parted again, he held his breath, waiting impatiently for her next words.

"I think you're trying to get me into some trouble, Walker Abbott," she said softly. "Either that or you're purposely trying to distract me so I don't win before you do."

"Too bad, I'll never tell," he whispered conspiratorially, using every bit of his strength to turn his attention to his sheets, suddenly much less interested in the game when faced with the reality of Aja fucking Owens.

●●●

He took the long way home, driving just at the speed limit on side streets and through neighborhoods he knew would make his drive time longer. He'd had an amazing time with Aja. Neither of them had won or even come close, but it was the most fun he'd had all week. Even if he'd had to spend the majority of that time holding himself back from flirting with her.

Gram was a night owl, and he knew she'd be awake when he got home. Their conversation would likely be awkward and strained in the way it often was these days. Sure enough, she was sitting on the couch when he came in. The television was on but muted, and the low light from one of the side-table lamps gave the old room a soft glow.

She looked up from the *People* magazine she had propped up on a reading table in front of her. The glasses she never wore outside the house sat low on her pointed nose. If the sight of her struggling to get comfortable with her bright pink casts weren't so dismal, it might have been funny.

"You have a good time?"

"Yep." He moved to sit on the other side of the couch, knowing it would make her sad if he shuffled off to his room immediately. "Aja says hey."

Gram's lips twitched into a smirk, and he had to fight the urge to roll his eyes. Injured or no, that foolishness wouldn't be tolerated.

"Gram, please . . ."

"What?" Her eyes widened. "I didn't say anything."

"Yeah, but I know what you're thinkin', and it ain't like that," he lied through his teeth. "We're just hangin' out. She's helpin' me get more bingo practice in because I'm tired of you pinchin' my ears every time I move too slow for your likin'. That's *it*."

The words sounded unconvincing, even to him. She didn't seem to buy them either.

"Does that mean you aren't goin' to ask her out?"

He threw his head back on the couch with a groan way too juvenile for a thirty-year-old man.

Gram kept going. "Because you could do far, far worse, you know. Aja is beautiful, and kind, and she has her own job. Some kind of internet nonsense, but still, it makes her good money I think."

"And she lives in Greenbelt."

"What's wrong with that?" Gram sniffed.

"In a little over a month, when I go home, how am I supposed to date somebody who lives in a place I hate? How are we supposed to go on dates when I refuse to step foot in this place after I'm gone?"

"When you left twelve years ago, you told me you'd never come back, and here you are."

"The only reason I'm here is because you need me and I love you," he argued. "And because you refused to come down to Charleston while you recovered."

She completely ignored the second portion of his statement. "Well, what if you—"

"*Please* don't say it," he cut her off.

She was obstinate. "What if you fell in love with her? Would that be enough to make you stay?"

"I'm not goin' to fall in love with Aja, Gram, because we are *not* dating. I'm goin' to bingo with her, not courtin' her."

"You never know," she insisted. "It's not like love is something you can plan. Maybe you and Aja will fall in love, and she'll convince you to stay right here where you belong."

His last nerve had officially been worked. He sighed, standing up from the couch, schooling his face as much as possible so that he didn't show every bit of the fury he was feeling.

"I don't belong here, Gram. I spent my entire childhood not being sure of anything other than that I did not belong here. I don't care if Aja Owens turns out to be my one true love or the best woman to ever walk the face of the Earth. Nothing can convince me to stay in a place I hate as much as Greenbelt."

Ignoring the sheer devastation on his grandmother's face as he walked away was hard, but he managed. He'd done it before, after all.

He had FaceTime up on his phone before he even had the door to his old room shut. His first call went unanswered, making his jaw tighten in stress. His second call was picked up within seconds.

"What's going on?" Adya's light brown face was pressed close to the camera. There was music playing in the background and dishes clinking together.

"I called Corey and he didn't pick up. . . ."

Adya rolled her eyes, her chin-length brown hair swishing back and forth. "Corey," she yelled. "Our very tall white son is nervous because he can't get ahold of you."

"I'm not—" He stopped himself at the lie. He had been nervous when Corey hadn't answered. There had been no logical reason for that nervousness. Corey was a grown man who obviously had his own life and shit to do. But Walker's other emotions—namely anxiety—always got harder to control when he was agitated.

"What's wrong, man?" Corey's face appeared in the camera next to his longtime girlfriend's. His shirt was off, he had on his favorite purple du-rag, and he was drying a plate with a printed cloth.

Walker knew that cloth. He'd used it countless times when the duo had forced him to clean up the kitchen on the heels of a dinner they'd invited him over for.

"I just . . ." he grumbled incoherently, squeezing himself into the hard wooden chair at the desk in front of the only window in the room. "I just miss bein' home is all. I miss bein' there with y'all."

Adya's bottom lip poked out. "Aww, we miss you too, buddy."

"We had Jamie and Nate over earlier. I made sliders and we played Clue." Corey's back was to the camera, but his voice was clear.

The sound Walker released was downright pathetic.

"It was fun, but it wasn't the same without you there playing as Professor Plum," Adya said.

"You didn't let Nate play him in my place, did you?"

Corey turned and the looks on his and his girlfriend's faces were nearly identical and completely offended. "Of course not. We would never betray you like that."

Walker rolled his eyes, but his body relaxed more into the chair. "I just want to make sure y'all aren't chomping at the bit to replace me."

His best friend screwed his face up. Corey's first instinct would be to call him ridiculous, but Walker knew he would find a way to crush that impulse before it made an impact.

"I've been your best friend for over a decade, Walker," Corey said. "There's no replacing that shit."

The words were a balm, instantly cooling the fast-burning irritation overtaking Walker's body. There was security in Corey's words that settled over him like a weighted blanket, letting something solid and calm settle into his bones.

"I'm fuckin' countin' down the days, man." Walker closed his eyes. "In less than two months I'll be back in my own bed and back to my real life."

"Walker . . ." Adya's voice made him open his eyes. "Fuck that town. This is a blip on your radar. A couple months out of your entire life. You'll be back here with us soon, and none of them will matter."

"I know it's not easy, man, and being there sucks and makes it harder for you to stay on track, but I don't care if you have to walk around telling everybody to go fuck themselves. You're there to take care of your granny, but that doesn't mean you can't put your needs first too," Corey added.

"Right. You're right. You both are. I just need to remind myself that this is temporary, and I'll be there to watch the Saints get their asses beat to hell and back by September."

Corey's face screwed up, arms folding across his bare chest as he stared Walker down. "A'ight, it's time to go. For a second there you almost made me forget how much I can't fucking stand you a good ninety percent of the time."

Walker's laugh was a loud bark that he had to shush for fear of Gram hearing him and coming to investigate. Corey walked away from the camera, grumbling how shitty it was to have a best friend who refused to respect the sanctity of football teams.

Adya shook her head. "Now I have to go calm him down so . . . thank you for that."

"Right. I'll just stay here and think about what I've done."

"You do that. And remember, we can't stand you . . . but we love you."

Even after they hung up, their words continued to wrap him up tight, squeezing his insides until he finally decided to take his ass to bed.

Chapter 8

"You want to grab a bite?" Walker whispered the words in her ear, and she had to clench her teeth to dampen her shiver.

The game was nearly over—only three more balls needed to be pulled from the cage—but Aja and Walker were so far from winning they'd already given up hope.

"Did you want to go back to Kenny Mack's?" she asked, keeping her eyes on her sheets.

Walker sighed. "Gram wants to go to Minnie's. . . ."

"She's not going to fake other plans and ditch us this time?"

He rolled his eyes. "Apparently she has a very real hankerin' for some meat loaf tonight. But if I'm goin' to eat in a room full of people I can't stand, I'd at least like to have a friendly face with me."

"And your grandmother isn't a friendly face?"

"Not when she's shoveling ground beef into her mouth she's not."

If she went, this would be the second time Walker had convinced her to forgo a home-prepped dinner for restaurant food. Her dinner routine was normally very precious to her. The older she'd gotten, the more she'd come around to her mother's "I can make it better than them" way of thinking. But here she was considering it anyway because that was what Walker did to her. He was constantly driving her to consider things she hadn't before.

The man overwhelmed her. The way he smelled, the slight slouch of his shoulders, the way he looked at her so fucking intensely anytime he was within eye range. It was all so much. Her head told her to deny him. To go home and eat the shredded chicken and sweet potatoes she had tucked away in her fridge. But the rest of her, the parts that thumped and beat and pulsed and wetted whenever he was near, screamed at her to do the opposite. To go to that old strip mall diner with him and his grandmother for the chance to be near him a little longer.

It was utterly ridiculous. And she was ashamed of her own weakness as she nodded her head.

"All right, I'll go," she whispered. "But only because I want some more cobbler."

He put a hand to his chest. "I knew you were a woman after my own heart."

Fuuuuuuuck.

Even nearing 10 P.M. on a Wednesday, Minnie's Diner was packed. Still, their makeshift host, an obviously disgruntled cashier, managed to secure them a booth against one of the parking lot–facing windows. Aja was surprised when Walker slid into the booth next to her rather than his grandmother. They were even closer than usual. The booth wasn't large, and with the way her thighs spread, even with her legs closed, it was impossible for him not to brush against her. Neither of them acknowledged their closeness, but somehow that made it even more thrilling.

She picked up her laminated menu with a shaky breath, suddenly reexamining her decision to come out. Aja had grossly overestimated her ability to be near Walker so much without losing her mind. She was *so* not strong enough to push her lusty feelings down until they turned to dust. She didn't have that kind of power. She was more the type to yearn so much for something to no end that it just became a part of her personality. Which was exactly why she should have been keeping her distance.

Guilt inched its way up her esophagus. Walker and Ms. May were nice people, good people, people who had befriended her. She shouldn't be feeling so wary about being with them when they'd been nothing but kind. She feared for her emotional well-being though. Or, at least, she feared that she might explode from the amount of lust filling her body.

"Well, I already know what I'm gettin'." Ms. May placed her menu on the table and crossed her hands on top of it. "Minnie makes the best meat loaf I've ever had, Aja. You should give it a try."

Aja tried not to let the disgust show on her face. Meat loaf was one of the only dishes her mother had never quite perfected but still refused to stop making. Her childhood had been filled with nights trying to choke down enough to satisfy her mother and be excused from the table. She didn't care if Minnie had gotten her meat loaf recipe from some kind of Lowcountry-dwelling food deity, she wasn't going to be eating it.

A miniscule look of revulsion must have slipped through because Walker chuckled. She felt his breath against the curve of her ear and another rubber band holding her sanity together snapped.

"Gram, I think you're the only person in Greenbelt who has

ever ordered the meat loaf," he said, laughing. "I'm pretty sure they keep it on the menu for you alone."

"Not true!" Ms. May pointed a finger at him. "I know plenty of people who eat Minnie's meat loaf."

"Do any of them happen to be younger than sixty?" Walker asked, eyebrows raised.

"Don't be ageist, Wally," his grandmother snapped playfully. "Good food does not have an age limit."

"Mmhm, if you say so." He raised his menu in front of his face long enough to shoot a wink at Aja. "I think I'm goin' to stick with a good old-fashioned smothered pork chop."

Aja flashed Ms. May an apologetic smile. "And I'm really craving a club sandwich, so . . ."

Ms. May released a long, deep sigh.

"Maybe next time," Aja lied, knowing full well that she'd rather spend the rest of her life avoiding Minnie's Diner altogether than eat that meat loaf.

Their waitress appeared a few moments later, the bright smile on her face dimming some as she took in the people sitting around the table.

"Hey, y'all." Aja didn't know her, but the woman spoke with an air of familiarity. She had a name tag attached to her polyester uniform that identified her as "Louise."

"Hey there, girlie." Ms. May grinned. "Since when do you work evenings?"

"I'm just fillin' in for Donna." Louise tapped her pen against her wrist. "I'm tryin' to save up for a vacation to LA."

Ms. May perked up even more. "Have you ever been?"

Aja kept one ear on their conversation, trying to stay alert but barely listening as she turned her attention to Walker.

His expression had turned sour. It may have been subtle to most people, but it was glaringly obvious to her. His mouth was tight, lips pressed together and turned down slightly. Those dark eyes were softly narrowed as they focused on Louise. He looked like he was trying to either hold himself back from saying something unpleasant or from getting up and walking out of the restaurant completely. Aja had never seen him look like this before. So uncomfortable, angry. It had happened so fast too. Seemingly out of nowhere. Had their waitress done something offensive?

Her anxiety tended to make her hypervigilant, especially when it came to other people's actions. It was rare that she missed the little tics or micro expressions they tried to hide. Misinterpreted them? Yes, often. But she rarely ever missed them. She was sure that if Louise had done or said something shady, she would have caught it. But she hadn't. So why the hell did Walker look so disgusted about being in her presence?

"Are you OK?" She moved her face closer to his so she could keep her voice down low.

"Huh?" He startled. "Why wouldn't I be?"

His words were as tight as his jaw, and she looked down to see his fist clenched against his thigh.

"You look"—Aja tried to be delicate in her wording—"upset."

The muscles in his face flexed as his jaw ground even harder. "I'm all right."

It was clear he wasn't, but it was also obvious he wasn't interested in talking about it. That, she understood. So she let it go, but the overwhelming need to comfort him still sat on her heart. There was very little she could do with so many people around, in such a tight space, with the limitations they already had thanks to the nature of their relationship. Had things been different, she might have kissed him or stroked her hand softly along his jaw to show him that she was there for him. Two things that were wholly inappropriate in their current reality. She did the only thing she could think to do. She put her hand on his, right over the fist he had balled up on his leg.

She ran her thumb over his knuckles, feeling the skin stretched tightly over the bones. She folded her fingers around his hand for a few seconds. Then, when her fingers unflexed, his started to as well. The movements were slow, but piece by piece his fist fell away until his hand was palm down on his leg with hers on top.

He caught her gaze; his eyes were still dark and clouded, but his appreciation was as clear as a summer sky. When his shoulders loosened, she smiled. There was an awkward moment where she realized that she didn't know how long it would be appropriate to keep her hand on his. Now that he seemed less troubled, should she move it? She liked the feeling of his skin on hers, but she didn't want to make him uncomfortable or for him to think she was trying to take advantage of his compromised state in some way.

The second she went to pull her hand away Walker turned his over. His palm was warm and dry as it met hers, and she barely had time to register the action before he was linking their fingers together. Her heart sputtered in her chest. She felt like she was floating in the middle of the ocean, her body weightless and lazy, being carried along by something more powerful than herself.

It was then that she became sure Walker Abbott was going to kill her.

It would be accidental, but she was positive that her heart would give out completely if he kept making it thump and soar like it was. She didn't think he was doing it on purpose, which made him even more deadly.

She didn't get a chance to say anything to him—not that she knew what to say—before Louise and Ms. May finished their conversation and the waitress left with their orders.

Dinner was relatively quiet. No one else in the restaurant made an effort to keep their conversations hushed, but their table was content with stilted pleasantries and small talk as they enjoyed their respective meals. Underneath the table, Walker's hand stayed clasped in hers. This made it difficult to eat and drink, but she pulled through, as unwilling to lose the comfort of his touch as he seemed to be of hers.

Every time Louise came by to check in, Walker spoke very little and kept his gaze turned towards Aja. When the check came and questions about dessert were asked, he requested three pieces of peach cobbler to go. Louise informed him that there would be a fifteen-minute wait, since the latest batch was still in the oven. Ms. May, finally noticing her grandson's discomfort, insisted that she would stay and wait while he went outside and got some air. Aja could barely blink before Walker was throwing his credit card on the table and pulling her out of the booth along with him.

The second the door to the diner swung shut behind him, he let out a long, shaky breath. He clutched her hand a little tighter, remaining silent as he led them through the parking lot towards where their cars were parked. When he finally let go, she had to wipe her clammy palm on her jeans. Once her hand was dry again, she was overcome with missing the weight of his.

Walker pulled the tailgate of his truck down and motioned her over. His hands stretched out near her lower body, then paused.

"Can I help you up?" he asked, his voice rough. "I don't want to just put my hands all over you without—"

"Yes," she interrupted him. "Go ahead."

His hands were only on her waist for a few seconds, but she was sure she'd never get over how delicious his grip was. She pressed her thighs together as she sat, watching him hoist himself up on the truck. Heat rushed to her center. No matter how the rest of the night turned out, she knew exactly how her next fantasy of him was going to go.

"I fucking *hate* her." His voice in the quiet night shocked her out of her lust.

"Who?" He couldn't possibly have been talking about his grandmother, could he?

"Louise fuckin' Smith," he growled. "And I fuckin' hate that Gram talks to her like that. Like she's not an awful fuckin' person."

"What did she do?" Her heart started thudding, this time for all the worst reasons. "Did she hurt you?"

He didn't answer. He just clenched his jaw so tightly that she was sure she could hear his teeth grinding into a chalky powder. He crossed his arms over his chest and tilted his face up towards the sky. She knew exactly what he was doing: closing himself off, refusing, for whatever reason, to give her the information she was seeking.

A pang of hurt ran through her. She had no real right to feel it though. She and Walker hadn't known each other long. What had she done to make him feel comfortable enough to share things that were obviously painful for him?

Whatever it was, it had him mad enough to spit. He kept his eyes clenched shut and the expression on his face was more thunderous than any summer storm she'd ever experienced. It didn't matter how badly Aja wanted to know exactly what was bothering him and why. He wasn't interested in sharing. Her mind reeled with possibilities, each situation more awful than the last. Every single one made her ache for him, and the pain written across his face made her want to wrap him up in her arms and give him what little comfort she could provide.

She didn't know if he'd be open to that though, and there was no way in hell she was about to ask. Not when she could practically feel the sparks flying off his skin. So she pushed down her need to know and reminded herself that she and Walker weren't as different as she liked to think. If you replaced his anger with anxiety, their reactions to situations like this were strikingly similar. She tended to close off too, retreating into a place where it felt like no one could see or touch or hurt her. She knew full well that she wouldn't be open to baring her shit to a near stranger either. So she gave him the same grace she hoped he would have given her and kept quiet.

She stayed sitting beside him, not touching him, not speaking to him. Just there, waiting for the moment he finally wanted to talk or leave.

The latter happened when Ms. May appeared in the doorway of Minnie's, to-go boxes in a plastic bag hanging off one of her casts and a grim look on her face. The former never came.

Chapter 9

Walker spent the rest of Wednesday night and most of Thursday trying to muster the self-consciousness he was supposed to be feeling about behaving the way he did with Aja. When it didn't come, he decided to move on. Push it to the part of his brain where he kept the things that he didn't feel like dealing with. It would come back sooner or later, he was sure. Sooner, when Aja asked him about it, or later, when he vomited out the story to one of his Charleston friends. Either way, he wasn't about to unpack those feelings now.

In the aftermath of his emotional breakdown, his mouth had been uncharacteristically quiet. Giving Gram the silent treatment wasn't something he was particularly proud of, but it was what it was. He couldn't get over how she'd had a whole entire conversation with Louise like she was completely unaware of their history. Asked about her fucking vacation plans like she hadn't been the one to comfort him every time that woman started some new bullshit rumor about them. He didn't understand what the hell Gram was thinking—but then, he never really did. When he was younger, the rift made him sad. Now it pissed him off.

That anger kept him in bed for most of Friday morning. It hadn't stopped him from getting up early to make Gram breakfast and put it in the microwave, but it had kept him from speaking to her directly. He'd taken his work stuff from the dining room table up to his room and gotten some work done from his bed. Around noon, he was still tucked under his covers, dressed in nothing but his boxers, scrolling mindlessly through Twitter on his phone when his best friend texted.

Corey: You missed Jamie make a total fucking fool out of himself at karaoke last night. Shit was amazing.

Walker: I know, I saw the Instagram Live. I can't believe y'all let him take all those tequila shots. You know how he gets. You're lucky he didn't set something on fire.

Corey: We weren't thinking. That's why we need you around to keep us in line.

Walker rolled his eyes. Corey Whittaker was one of the first friends he'd made after leaving Greenbelt. They had met during freshman orientation at the College of Charleston. Walker had been like he always was in those days: quiet, reserved, desperately sticking to the back of the crowd. Corey had been none of those things, but he'd zeroed in on Walker's Atlanta Braves shirt and latched on. Twelve years later and Corey still hadn't gotten the urge to untangle himself.

When he was home in Charleston, Walker lived a good, if calm, life. He woke up every morning, went on a forty-minute run, then went to work. There he spent roughly forty percent of his day doing what he got paid for and the rest trying to look busy so he didn't piss his editor off. He worked a sports beat, but most of his coverage was focused on baseball. Some MLB, but more recently college and high school, which meant that he was at games at least three nights a week on average. When he wasn't working or enjoying his own company at home, he was with his friends. They were a small group, just him, Corey, Adya, Jamie, Andre, and Nate.

Walker's social circle wasn't exactly what he would call full. He'd come a long way from his friendless days in Greenbelt, but his past meant that he rarely felt comfortable letting new people in. Not when he knew that he couldn't trust his trauma with just anybody. And there was no way for him to live his life without acknowledging it. Even if he could, he wouldn't have wanted to. His friends had all come into his life in different ways at different times. But he trusted them with his life. Instead of feeling bad that his birthday celebrations were normally composed of fewer than ten people, he found himself in awe that he'd come so far.

As a kid, it had only been him and Gram and sometimes his father, Benny, during the short times when Benny was sober. Back then, he never would have imagined he'd have so many people not related to him giving a fuck about his well-being. He often had to shake himself out of the awe he felt whenever he dwelled on it for too long. That awe was exactly why he continued to put up with the boys' antics whenever they insisted on going out and acting like ridiculous-ass frat boys.

Walker: Only a few more weeks, man

I was seconds away from calling in the rescue team the other night

Corey: Again? What happened?

Walker: Just Greenbelt being Greenbelt we went out to dinner and our waitress was this shitty woman who said all this shitty stuff to and about me, and Gram straight up didn't give a fuck

She went full on little nice old Southern lady and I was mad enough to spit

Corey: Damn . . .

Corey: I'm sorry, man, that must have been fucking infuriating

Have you talked to Ms. May about it?

Walker: Nope not sure what to say tbh

Corey: Well . . . you could just tell her that it makes you feel like shit when she gets all buddy-buddy with folks who were cruel to you

Walker: Honestly, I don't even know if it's worth the time it would take to get the words out

I don't think she sees it like that

Corey: Dude, you won't know for sure until you talk to her

Walker: Jesus what are you, my new therapist?

Corey: Best friend, therapist, same fucking thing.

Corey: Just talk to your granny before I come up there and knock you upside your head

Walker: Yeah

Corey: What else is going on down there? Hook up with any of the girls you couldn't bag in high school?

Walker: Those girls have either booked it to someplace less awful than Greenbelt or they're married with kids

I did make a new friend though

Corey: Well that's boring as fuc.

Walker: She's actually very fun, you asshole

Corey: . . .

Corey: And this fun you're having with your new friend, it wouldn't be of the fucking variety, would it?

Walker: Absolutely not

Just a good, perfectly wholesome time. We go to bingo together.

Corey: And I'm supposed to think bingo isn't a euphemism for eating pussy???

Walker: Hate to disappoint but it's literally just regular old-fashioned bingo with the daubers and numbers and old people and everything

Corey: That's a fucking bummer

Walker: You're telling me. . . .

Corey: Wait, what? So you DO want to get it with your new friend then?

Walker: Sorry man, I need to go

About to have that talk with Gram like you suggested.

Corey: You squirrelly little motherfucker

Corey: Fine, go experience some emotional growth or what the fuck ever

He barked a laugh into the quiet of his room. Leave it to Corey to curse him out and make him feel better over the course of one short conversation. He paused when he heard the TV downstairs, knowing immediately that Gram had finally left her bed for the comfort of the couch.

The house they lived in was old. Gram and his grandfather, Mitchell, had bought it before his dad had even been born. Walker's grandfather had died when Benny was thirteen, and instead of selling and moving on, Gram had decided to hunker down and stay put. The old house had been well maintained and stood strong, but its age meant it was damn near impossible to not hear everything that happened inside of it. The precautions he'd had to take to jerk off in peace were damn near CIA levels of covert ops. He had plenty of experience keeping an ear out for which part of the house Gram was moving around in. This came in handy when he was trying to do something private or sneaky—and when he was trying to avoid her.

Now the noise helped guide him towards her and the conversation they needed to have. He heaved a long sigh, getting out of bed to pull on a pair of jogging pants and a T-shirt before he slipped out of the room. When he got downstairs, she was sitting in the right corner of the couch, one of her casts resting on the couch's arm, using the remote to flip through the TV channels. Her dark satin robe was a little wrinkled and her hair was all over the place, but she seemed relaxed. She looked up when she saw him, the lines around her mouth pinching tighter as her lips pursed and pressed together.

"Hey, Gram," he said, taking a seat on the other side of the couch.

"Oh, we're speakin' to each other now?" Her eyes burned.

He sunk in on himself then, a wave crashing over him, leaving him weak and soaked in shame. "Gram . . . I'm sorry. . . ."

"Don't worry. It's not like I'm not used to it. You spent years lockin' me out."

"I didn't lock you out." Walker struggled to keep indignation out of his tone. "I was just—" He stopped and shook his head. Now wasn't the time for that. "I was angry."

Gram's exasperated sigh made his temples ache. "You've been here three weeks, Wally. What could you possibly have to be angry about already?"

There were all kinds of infuriating things he wanted to reveal. The way he hated the looks he got in town anytime someone recognized him. The fact that he couldn't even get himself off at a time when he needed the relief most because his grandmother refused to knock before entering a room. The way she still refused to acknowledge his PTSD by name. So many grievances rushed to the front of his mind at once that his head spun.

"The other night, when we were at the diner and you were talkin' to Louise Smith—that bothered me. It made me angry," was what he said instead.

Her face screwed up and he could see that she truly didn't understand. That only made the knots in his stomach pull tighter.

"Why would that have made you mad?" she asked. "We were just talkin' about her vacation."

Tendons tight, he stretched his neck, grimacing as he moved his head from side to side. Tension rose in his body right along with frustration. For him, that combination had always been dangerous. He was trying not to get too worked up, but he wasn't doing a great job of it. The backs of his neck and knees slicked wet with sweat as anxiety invaded his body.

This was it. This was the reason he hadn't been back to Greenbelt in over a decade, the reason he avoided even thinking about the place unless he was in a safe space—like a therapist's office.

Whenever he delved in too deep, he started feeling sick. His heart raced and his skin got clammy. Irritability inched its way up his spine, mingling with the anxiety already digging into the base. It wasn't a panic attack that he felt coming, but anger. Not just the frustrated sighs and slightly irritated tone that his grandmother perceived as him being angry. Real anger—the kind that made his head hurt with the force of it. The kind that made him want to find the nearest small space and fold his body into it for so long that his muscles started to groan. The kind that would only go away when some other part of him started to hurt, whether from sheer sadness or physical strain.

In the past he would have flicked himself between the eyes or jammed his elbow against something sharp. Whatever it took to distract him from the chaos in his head. He couldn't do those things anymore though. Hurting himself wasn't healthy and it didn't serve him. That's what he'd been told time and time again.

Hurting myself isn't healthy and it doesn't serve me.

Hurting myself isn't healthy and it doesn't serve me.

It doesn't serve me.

It doesn't serve me.

Repetition had always been his self-soothing technique of choice. It had worked when he was a kid, and it worked now—to an extent. Not enough to make the anger go away, but enough to clear the fog.

"So you don't remember when I was little, and she started all those rumors about us? Telling people that dad had tried to trade me in for a fix and that you used to lock me in a closet at night and that's why I had panic attacks? You don't remember that?"

She grunted. "Wally, there's nothin' to do in Greenbelt but

gossip. You think we're the first family in a small town to get talked about like dogs?"

"No, Gram, I don't think that. I know other people got it too, but I don't see them goin' out of their way to be friendly with the people who treated them like crap."

"If I avoided everybody in this town who ever whispered about my failings in raising you and your daddy, I'd never have anybody to talk to," she snapped. "You left and you made a home somewhere else and found a family somewhere else. Greenbelt is my home, and these people are my family."

"I'm your family!" He strained to keep his voice level.

"You haven't much acted like it for the past twelve years." She turned her head towards the window and sniffed. Walker couldn't see her face, but he could picture the tears welling up in her eyes, and it made his ribs ache. "A short call once a week, makin' me drive all the way to Charleston a couple times a year just to see you. I barely know anything about your life, Wally. I barely know you."

Her words felt like a punch to the sternum. She hadn't done a perfect job of raising him, they could both acknowledge that. But he hadn't done a perfect job of being there for her either. She was right. For as little family as he had, Gram had about the same amount. Her husband was long dead, her only son may have been sober, finally, but he was as distant as distant could get, and the grandson she'd raised had all but cut her out of his life. Walker knew his feelings were valid. He had a right to be angry about the help he'd gone so long without. But he loved her.

For all she hadn't done to help him, there were a million things she had. She never flinched when she found him sleeping on the floor of his closet. Whenever things got too rough that he couldn't deal, she pulled him out of school for a few days without a word. In the end, she'd always been there for him. Even when she complained about not seeing him enough or him not visiting, it was always with a certain lightness. Like she was telling him subliminally that asking for her forgiveness wasn't necessary because he'd never need it. He'd never been forced to hear the pure devastation in her voice when she brought up the state of their relationship. Whatever real grief she felt, she did a good job of hiding it. All so he didn't have to acknowledge that he was hurting her too. It fucking sucked. It made self-loathing color every part of his vision.

His original plan had been to leave Greenbelt behind, not his Gram. At first, he hadn't. His first year at school, they'd spoken on the phone damn near every day. But the more distance he put between him and his hometown, the longer he had to come into himself without the constant outside stressors weighing him down, the harder it got to keep up with her. When he started therapy and learned that his issues with Greenbelt were intertwined with his family issues, he'd found himself stumped. Torn between feeling eternally grateful to her for taking him in and raising him and feeling the brunt of the damage caused when she allowed him to flounder in his trauma without any real help, he had pulled away.

That struggle became his proof that counseling wasn't a cure-all for his issues. He also had to be willing to tackle them, and this was one that he hadn't been open to taking on in the past. He didn't even know if he was willing now. All he knew was that something had to give. For both of them.

"I want you to know me," he admitted, laying his body down across the couch, his head in her lap. Even impaired, one of her hands immediately moved to stroke his hair. It was familiar, comforting. Back when she'd seen him suffering from something she couldn't put a name to, this had been the only way she knew how to calm him. But they'd lost this too somewhere along the way. "I just wanted you to know that it . . . it *hurts* me that you're friends with someone who hurt me."

Gram's hand stilled, her eyes free of tears but no less distraught. She stared down at him, taking in every inch of his face like it was the first time she was seeing him—or maybe the last.

"I never want to hurt you, baby," she said quietly. "I've only ever wanted to protect you, to make up for those times I couldn't."

He went to speak, and she put a finger against his lips and kept talking.

"I know I didn't do a perfect job. I should have done more for you. I knew it then, and I know it now. You needed help, and I thought my love was enough to make you better, and it wasn't. It just wasn't. I can understand why you . . . why you hate bein' around me."

Walker's hand was cupping her cheek before he could even fathom his own actions. "I don't hate bein' around you, Gram. I love you more than anythin'. It's just hard when we have all this . . . stuff between us. This stuff we never talk about. I never know if it's safe to tell you how I feel or to talk about my problems. I don't want to make you feel bad and I don't want to make you think that I'm not grateful, that you're not the most important person in my life. I just . . . I don't know how to connect with you anymore."

She nodded, understanding written across her face. The relief made his cheeks flush. He felt like a child again. Safe and warm and comforted in her arms. Tucked away from everything bad and wrong and scary he had ever felt. He hadn't realized how much he'd missed this.

"Well, we're not dead yet, Wally. We have time to get it right. *I* have time to get it right."

His throat was thick, and his eyes were full. When the tears started to escape at the corners, she wiped them away.

"We can get it right," he choked out. "We have to."

Chapter 10

Dr. Sharp's face was pixelated through the screen of Aja's computer. The older woman sat at her desk, shelves of books stacked high behind her. With her salt-and-pepper locks gathered in a ponytail at the nape of her neck and her glasses on the bridge of her nose, she looked like she always did but pixelated. Kind and open but ready to throw down.

After their initial greeting, they sat in silence. Aja knew she was the only one who found that silence awkward. Dr. Sharp was patient as always. But if Aja didn't speak up soon and say what was weighing on her mind, the other woman would have no choice but to use her counselor magic to get her to open up.

"So . . ." Aja cleared her throat, tucking a braid behind her ear. "I had a pretty good week actually."

Dr. Sharp smiled. "I'm glad to hear that. Did anything special happen?"

Aja started to shake her head, then stopped abruptly. "Well, kind of. I went to get my nails done, and the nail tech was really nice. She, uh, she invited me over to her place to hang with her and her friends tonight."

A slow smile spread across Dr. Sharp's plum-painted lips. "You've been trying for a while to make some new friends down there. Are you happy about the invitation?"

"Absolutely." Aja swallowed. "I almost cried after she asked me. But I'm not sure I'm going. . . ."

"Why not?"

Aja didn't answer right away, taking time to gather her thoughts. She'd been in therapy for years and had seen no fewer than six different counselors. There was still a part of her that felt a little intimidated by them. Logically she knew they couldn't read her mind, but sometimes it felt like they could. It was counter-productive to keep things from your therapist, but everyone did at some point. Dr. Sharp had a talent for dragging things out of Aja that she didn't want to bring up with *anyone*. Sometimes it just took time for her to choke the words out.

"I don't want to get there, meet her friends, and have them all realize that they don't like me."

"What makes you think they wouldn't like you, Aja?"

Aja rubbed a hand across her forehead and shook her head, silently indicating that she didn't want to speak.

"Do you have any evidence that you're unlikeable? Has anyone ever told you that before?"

They hadn't, but that didn't keep her from thinking it. She tried her level best to maintain as much confidence in herself as she could. But her anxiety made it next to impossible sometimes. Trying to fight off the insistent whispers in her head telling her that she wasn't worth knowing was exhausting. And at times like this, when she was already distracted by a ton of other things, she didn't have the energy to raise her fists.

"No," she whispered, the mic on her laptop surely struggling to pick it up. "But you know me. I've never needed evidence to harp on something."

"I know you're a smart woman." Dr. Sharp adjusted her glasses. "I also know that you're resilient and clever and hungry for connection. Personally, I have a hard time seeing why anyone wouldn't want to know you."

"How many young people out there are up for dealing with a friend who can barely sit in a half-crowded movie theater without panicking?"

Dr. Sharp pursed her lips. "You'd be surprised how many people don't feel that accommodating the needs of the people they care about can be boiled down to just 'dealing' with it."

Therein lay the biggest issue. Aja didn't believe anyone aside from her family could ever care about her enough to view her as anything other than a burden. She wanted to believe it. So badly it hurt inside. She just . . . didn't know how.

"How do I make myself believe that?" she asked, voice full of desperation. "What do I have to do to convince myself that people can care about me?"

Dr. Sharp shook her head, a small, sympathetic smile on her face. "I don't think there's a single thing I can tell you that would make you believe, Aja. You have to do that work yourself. And you can start by going to that gathering tonight. Pay attention to how they treat you, how they respond to you. And if you don't find any evidence that they think you're unlikable, try letting them in. They might surprise you."

●●●

Miri's house was a cute, compact white structure in a neighborhood full of homes that were similarly cute and compact. All the houses were older and clearly weathered but with well-manicured lawns that made the level of care obvious. It was warm outside, and the sun hadn't started to set yet, and from inside her car she could hear sprinkler systems going off and children playing—a neighborhood alive in the summer. The entire scene was so sweet and wholesome that it looked like something out of a movie from the 1960s.

She'd taken Dr. Sharp's advice and called Miri right after their session to confirm that she was coming. Her anxiety hadn't dissipated much, but she was bolstered by a certain resolve to see this through. She'd do as her therapist advised and try to view the interactions she had with these new people through clear, discerning eyes. Aja just hoped she didn't end up seeing something that made her regret the entire thing.

When she arrived, she sat in her car for a few minutes, gathering herself. Once she finally worked up the nerve to get out, she checked to make sure her car door was locked three times, to buy herself a little more time.

Miri's smile was bright white against her dark skin and just as infectious as it always was when she answered the door.

"Hey, girl! Come on in, you're lettin' all the cold air out." She motioned for Aja to step inside the house, closing the door behind her.

Aja was immediately greeted by the smiles of the two other people in the room.

"Aja, these are my two best friends and also my two worst enemies. Jade"—she pointed to the light-skinned Black woman

sitting on the floor between the couch and the glass coffee table—
"and Olivia"—she gestured to the red-haired white woman on the
left side of the couch, closest to the door.

"Y'all, this is Aja. She came into Fresh Coat on Monday and
was sweet as sugar. I figured we could use a little more of that,
since y'all are so damn sour all the time."

Aja's face heated. The words made her feel like a lost little
puppy, picked up off the street and brought in from the cold. Perhaps she was.

"Nice to meet you." She swallowed, trying not to let her smile
turn into a grimace.

Olivia and Jade smiled back at her as warmly as Miri had.

"Here, Aja, we left the love seat open for you," Miri said,
throwing herself down on the other side of the couch from Olivia.
"I figured you might not want to be squished together with three
people you barely know."

"Plus, Jade smells like her man's cologne, and that shit is awful," Olivia commented, smiling into a glass of white wine.

Jade reached back and pinched Olivia's knee. "You're just mad
that the only smell you carry around with you is the scent of your
cat's loathin'."

Olivia's mouth dropped open. "Fuck you!" she said. "Buffy
loves me!"

Both Miri and Jade snorted into their glasses, leaving Olivia to
press her back into the couch, looking affronted.

Their banter made Aja feel comforted. It was funny and familiar and reminded her of the conversations she had with Reniece.
Aja was of the opinion that a friendship reached true intimacy
once you felt comfortable enough to lightly drag each other now

and then. She didn't know how long Miri's group had been together, but she could tell the roots were deep.

Toeing her shoes off and leaving them by the door, she parked herself in the love seat and took in her surroundings. Much like with Fresh Coat, Aja had a hard time picturing Miri picking out any of the furnishings in her home. Everything was nice and plush and older but well-kept, that exact same "auntie chic" aesthetic that made her nostalgic, right down to the '80s-era Afrocentric art that hung on the walls.

"This is my mom's spot," Miri said, smiling over at her. "I mean, I live here too, but you know how they are—if I don't own it, it's still hers." She rolled her eyes playfully. "Whenever she and my auntie go to the casino in Little River, I have the girls over."

Aja nodded. "My mama has that print too." She pointed to one hung next to the doorway to the kitchen. It was called *The Sugar Shack*, originally painted by Ernie Barnes. It depicted a bunch of Black people in an unassuming juke joint, their bodies bent and twisted, forever in motion, joyous in the freedom of their dancing. She'd seen the exact same painting in countless homes, beauty salons, and barber shops in her life. And she never got tired of seeing it. In her childhood home, the print hung in the dining room. Every time she saw it, wherever she happened to be, whoever she happened to be with, it filled her with warmth. This time was no different.

"I think my granny has that one too," Jade laughed.

"I swear to God every Black person in the country gets a free print of that paintin' when they're born," Miri said. "There's no other explanation."

"I'd believe it." Aja settled into her seat more, her shoulders relaxed. "I have no idea where all the aunties and grannies are getting them from otherwise. I've never seen one for sale in any store I've ever been in."

"It's a conspiracy!" Jade giggled.

"Anyway, where are you from, Aja? I know you're not from around here. My mama makes it a point to know every Black family in Greenbelt, and we haven't had any Owens in town for as far back as I can remember, at least," Miri asked.

All three pairs of eyes were trained on Aja, but she didn't feel like she was under a spotlight the way she normally would.

"Uhm . . . I'm from DC actually."

The shock on their faces was one Aja had grown accustomed to since moving to Greenbelt. Growing up, DC was simply home; she'd saved all her wonder for places like New York or Los Angeles. She tended to forget that it was one of the most popular cities in the country.

"You moved from Washington, DC, to *Greenbelt*?" Olivia spat out the name of her town like it had personally offended her. "For what?"

That was another reaction she'd gotten a lot—so much so that she had a ready-made reply that revealed just enough truth without giving too much away. "I needed a change of pace. I work from home, so I can do that anywhere, and I wanted to get out of the city, go someplace where things moved a little slower."

"So why didn't you choose somewhere like Hilton Head?" Jade asked. "I mean, you'd be surrounded by all those rich, racist assholes, but at least the beach is there. Here, you still get the racist assholes but none of the view."

"I actually didn't know Greenbelt even existed a little over a year ago," Aja admitted. "But I stumbled across it online, and it seemed so peaceful. I felt this kind of immediate connection with it and knew I had to come. Plus . . . I sort of hate the beach. The sand always gets *everywhere*, and it's disgusting."

"Now that I agree with." Miri leaned forward, grabbing the wine bottle off the table and shaking it at Aja. When she declined with a shake of her head, Miri topped herself off. "Give me some snowy mountains any damn day."

"And what would you know about snow, Miriam?" Jade pursed her lips. "You've never seen more than an inch of snow in your life."

"I still know that shit is better than sand all up through my labia."

"Y'all are so fu—" Olivia stopped her sentence abruptly, then gasped, making all of them look at her in alarm. "I fuckin' forgot to tell y'all. Guess who I saw at the Piggly Wiggly the other day?"

"I swear if this is about that raggedy-ass ex of yours . . ." Miri muttered into her glass.

"I'm ignoring that. . . . You remember Wally Abbott? From high school?"

The comfortable bubble Aja had found herself in disappeared with a pop that left her ears ringing. Hearing Walker's name come out of Olivia's mouth was so shocking that it made her head rush.

"Wally Abbott . . ." Miri's face contorted in confusion. "Abbott . . . Abbott . . . Abbott . . ."

"You remember!" Olivia insisted, brushing her long red hair over one shoulder. "Tall white boy, quiet, blond. He used to eat lunch every day at the table right near the boy's bathroom."

"Wait . . ." Jade put her wineglass down on the table. "You mean the one who beat the fuck out of Spencer Bell that one time?"

Miri gasped. "Oh yeah! That was senior year, right? Ol' boy

who worked Spence over in the teacher's parking lot because he talked spicy about his daddy or somethin'?"

"Yes!" Olivia cackled.

"I haven't seen him in years," Jade said thoughtfully.

Olivia nodded. "Well, he's back, and he's fuckin' gorgeous."

That made Aja's throat tighten up. Was that . . . jealousy? She thought on it and decided that yes, it was. She also decided that there was absolutely no reason for her to be feeling it. Not a logical one. Walker wasn't hers. He was barely her friend. She had no claim to him, and whatever bizarre level of possessiveness she felt at other people finding him attractive was ridiculous.

He was leaving in six weeks and their friendship would be going out the door right along with him. Aja would be left in Greenbelt, though with what she hoped would be the friendships of people other than him. If she was lucky, Olivia might become one of those friends. Allowing some misplaced jealousy to mess that up was completely out of the question.

"I mean, you know I have that thing going with Ivy right now so I'm not exactly on the market, but if I was, and I was *ever* willing to date another straight cis dude again, I would have jumped at that shit. Y'all should have seen those shoulders of his," Olivia moaned into her fist.

Neither Miri nor Jade seemed very interested in the comments about his looks, which Aja counted as a blessing. She would push down the jealousy as much as she physically could, but her self-control only extended so far.

"I wonder why he's back . . ." Miri said aloud.

Before she could hold herself back, Aja spoke. "He's taking care of his grandmother. She fell and broke both her arms a few weeks ago."

All three women damn near snapped their necks turning to look at her, their eyes varied in shape and size and color but equally unwavering in their gazes.

"We met at bingo." Her explanation sounded insufficient, even to herself. "He's nice."

It was almost cartoonish the way grins spread across their faces slowly and in tandem.

"You let me do all that talkin' about Wally without tellin' us that you were messin' around with him?" Olivia asked.

"He prefers to be called Walker." Aja cut her eyes to the ceiling. "And I'm not messing around with him. Like I said, we're friends."

"As attractive as you both are, you expect me to believe that you don't have any kind of hokeypokey? Not even a piece of a chunk of a smidgen?"

"Hokey . . . pokey . . . ?" Aja was glad, not for the first time, that she was a master of avoidance.

Miri made a crude hand gesture, pressing her index and middle fingers together and swirling them around in the air before making a "come hither" motion.

"Hokeypokey." Jade pointed at Miri's action.

"No hokeypokey at all." Aja put a hand to her heart. "I swear."

"That's a shame." Miri took a slow sip of her wine. "If he's as fine as Olivia says, some hokeypokey might be good for you. It might loosen those shoulders up some."

"I doubt they'd be very happy about us having . . . hokeypokey on one of the tables at bingo." Aja snorted at the thought, then heated. "Not that we'd be having any anyway because like I said, we are just—"

"Friends," the three others chimed in along with her. None of them, not even Aja, sounded entirely convinced.

"Exactly," she said anyway.

"Well." Olivia turned her face back into her wineglass. "If you and Walker ever become more than friends, promise you'll let us know. I need details about whether or not that little ass of his is actually as tight as it looked in those jeans he had on."

●●●

She was walking up the steps to her apartment when the call came. The phone's ring was so loud, even from inside her purse, that she jumped, then struggled to retrieve it. It was late, nearly midnight, and it was unlikely to be one of the many scam calls that came through over the course of the day. So she answered without looking at the screen.

"Hello?"

"What are you doing?" Hearing Walker's voice was such a shock that her key missed the lock entirely, the ring slipping from her hand and onto the floor. "You sound like you're out of breath."

"I was just coming up the stairs," she said, more breathless from him than anything else. She took her time getting her door unlocked, hands shaking as she put her keys and purse on the little hooks next to her front door.

"You're just gettin' in? You have a hot date or somethin'?" It was clear his words were meant to be lighthearted, a joke, but they didn't sound that way. Not completely.

"I was with some friends." Aja didn't know whether she had the right to call them that yet, but she did anyway.

He hummed, the sound rumbling through her. "And did you have a good time with your friends?"

For a second, she considered telling him that she'd been with three people who knew him. But she didn't know to what end—what would she even say? That Olivia had recognized him from high school and then had proceeded to ask her if they were fucking around? Aja had no idea how that conversation with Walker would go over, especially since the man seemed to hate everything about Greenbelt. It was understandable, honestly. She'd heard Miri and the girls talk a little about what high school had been like for him. Years of solitude culminating in an awful fight. If she'd been in his shoes, she would have hated Greenbelt too. But she didn't want to upset or trigger him by needlessly bringing up unpleasant things so she didn't.

"I did. We just sat around not doing much, but it was nice to get out and be around people. What did you do today?"

Aja held her phone between her ear and her shoulder as she took off her outside clothes, ridding herself of her socks and leggings, then put the phone on speaker so she could take off the things up top.

"I hung out with Gram," he grunted softly into the phone, probably just switching positions, but she got flustered anyway. "We went for a walk. . . ."

"That's nice, it's always good to get some fresh air," she murmured absently, shoving her clothes into her hamper. "Walker . . . why did you call me?"

The other end of the line went so silent that she had to look at her phone to make sure he hadn't hung up.

"To be honest, I don't know. I was just thinkin' about you, thinkin' about how kind you were to me the other night, all understandin' and shit. And I wanted to hear your voice."

She collapsed back on her bed, her hand immediately going to clutch at her stomach like she was afraid something might fall out of her if she didn't physically hold it together.

"I like hearin' your voice," he continued. "It's light and a little—shit, what's the word?—breathy. Sweet. I can always tell that you've thought about what exactly you want to say before you say it."

Her fingernails glided along her skin, heat pooling in her lower belly. "Are you drunk?"

Walker laughed quietly, like he was keeping a secret. "I'm completely sober. I feel good is all. Better than I have in weeks."

"Oh, that's good. I'm glad to hear that you're happy. I was worried about you after Wednesday night."

"You're sweet to worry about me, Aja." His voice went deep again. "Real fuckin' sweet." He cleared his throat. "Sorry, I need to watch my mouth."

It was her turn to laugh. "I'm a grown woman, sir. I can handle an errant fuck or two."

Was that a groan? She came incredibly close to asking him to repeat it, wanting to confirm his groan, and to recreate the throb that had pulsed between her thighs when she'd heard the low, rough sound. Aja had never claimed to have any kind of foresight, but she could see their conversation was close to taking a turn. Part of her wanted it to, craved him growling softly in her ear while she got herself off. The other part of her knew it was a bad idea. Walker was supposed to be her friend. It was bad enough that she masturbated thinking about him sometimes; she didn't need to cross an even bigger line by masturbating *with* him.

It pained her, but she turned the conversation around. "Any-way," she cleared her throat. "Of course I worry about you. It was obvious that something was up. I know I couldn't really do anything to fix the problem, but I wanted to help you the way you helped me."

"You did help me. You just being there helped. I know you know how that feels." She heard him move around, the sound of something opening, then the chirping of crickets. "Gram and I talked about it this afternoon. We're goin' to work on our relationship, I guess."

"That's amazing, Walker. I'm glad you guys were able to talk. I know it must have been hard, but I can tell how much you love her. It's the most obvious thing about you."

"The most obvious, huh?" He chuckled warmly.

"Nothing is more obvious than a country boy who loves his granny."

They were quiet for a while. Aja wasn't sure how long the silence stretched, but she could hear him breathing on the other end of the line. Slow and steady and deep, the rhythm lulled her so much that her eyes closed in response.

"Thank you for talkin' to me tonight, Aja."

She shivered as if a window had been opened in her room. "You don't need to thank me. We're friends, friends talk. That's the whole point."

"Right . . . friends." He paused. "Well, I'd better let you go. I don't want to keep you up too late."

Instead of reminding him, yet again, that she was a grown woman, capable of instituting her own bedtime, she let it slide. It was time to get off of the phone anyway, before her ridiculous horny lizard brain circled back around to that phone-sex craving. "I'll see you Monday, right? For bingo?"

"Nothing could keep me away."

Chapter 11

She was wearing a dress again. And it was a fucking problem.

The dress was yellow, printed with white flowers that had long green stems. The short sleeves touched just above her elbows, and the little white buttons up the front holding it together were nothing short of a tease. All things considered, the dress was pretty, but unassuming. It didn't show any cleavage and was too loose fitting to allow him to make out the shape of her body. Even the coloring was more sweet than tantalizing. But he was so thirsty it might as well have been lingerie.

The neckline displayed a collarbone that made his tongue heavy with the need to lick. The hemline fell about mid-thigh, longer than the shorts she'd worn last week. But every time she moved or shifted, it adjusted with her, revealing supple brown skin that made other parts of him feel heavy. Aja was a vision, from the braids that cascaded over her shoulder to the white toenails peeking out of her sandals.

Walker hadn't known he had so much restraint until he'd met

her. He was also positive he had never experienced true desperation before either. And fuck, did he feel desperate. Every time he
laid eyes on her, he felt desperate to touch and taste and hold. Those
were dangerous things to feel desperate for. Especially when he
was trying to keep from making a mess out of things by catching
feelings for a woman he couldn't be with.

But he would have given anything to run the tip of his nose along
that exposed neck, smelling her perfume at the source instead of in
the air. She was sitting next to him again, close enough that their
thighs were only about an inch apart. They hadn't spoken much before they'd come in; after the phone call there was an awkwardness
even more potent than their first meeting. Nothing had happened
during the call. Nothing untoward or explicit had been said, but
the energy had been there. Clear as day as it lit up behind his eyelids. And it was still there, making the hair on his forearms stand
on end every time some part of their bodies accidentally brushed.

"I'm finally getting' the hang of this," he whispered to her,
purple dauber hovering over his sheets.

"Don't get too cocky too soon," Aja joked. "You'll call a false
bingo, and you'll never live it down."

"The thought keeps me up at night."

She kept her face forward, but her grin made his throat tight.
This Monday was even more sparse than the last. There were only
about fifteen other people in the hall. The room was so quiet that
he and Aja had been keeping their talking to a minimum because it
felt more polite. Walker didn't like that they'd already been there
for over an hour and had barely had a full conversation. Being so
close but not talking made him anxious and unsettled. If he was
going to push down his growing feelings and keep things between

them uncomplicated, he needed *something*. The sweet sound of her voice was his reward for being a good boy. Without it, he was barely hanging on.

"You want to get out of here early?" He was almost surprised at his boldness. "We could grab a bite . . . maybe at a place where the waitress won't make me have a fuckin' emotional breakdown."

He got caught up in the heaviness of her long eyelashes when she looked at him. "I can't stay out too late. I have work to do in the morning."

"Swear I'll have you home at a reasonable hour. More than enough time to get all the beauty sleep you need."

She pursed her lips and looked at him like she didn't believe him but nodded. "All right. I guess I can let you buy me dinner again."

In his triumph, Walker silently remarked that he would buy her dinner every night if she'd just keep those eyes on him for a little longer.

It wasn't until he turned back to his sheets that he noticed he was one square away from a diagonal bingo.

"Wait . . ." His heart rate increased immediately. This was the closest he'd ever been to having a bingo. He still didn't expect to get one, but he hadn't expected that being so near the possibility would have him this excited. If someone had come to him a few weeks ago and told him that the spike of adrenaline he'd get over possibly winning bingo would rival seeing the Braves in the World Series, he would have told them to go fuck themselves. But here he was, suddenly less concerned with leaving, his fingers tight around a dauber, forehead dotted with sweat as he listened intently to the balls being called.

"What's wrong?" Aja whispered, the lines in her forehead

deepening. Walker shook his head and swallowed, his tongue unable to form words.

When it came, his head tilted back to control the rush. Mrs. Schofield's voice was as relaxed as ever. That slow, steady drawl called out "G46—up to tricks," sending Walker out of his chair and up into the air.

"Bingo!" His voice was so loud that everyone in the hall turned to look at him. "I have a bingo." He felt the need to repeat it, to confirm it for himself.

"Oh my God," he heard Aja breathe softly. "Oh my God."

The grin he threw her way felt unhinged.

He sat down when he saw one of the attendants approaching him. Once the man was behind him, looking down at his sheets, Walker found that his hands were shaking.

"Show me." The man's voice held a seriousness that would have been more in place behind the judge's bench in a courthouse.

Walker pointed his finger along the line of numbers.

"BI3, I36, N4, G46, O92," the man read off the numbers, cross-checking them with the numbers that had been called over the course of the game. Then, he nodded his head once. "That's a bingo."

The confirmation sent Walker soaring. He had to hold himself back from jumping out of his seat, stripping his shirt off, and running around the room, waving it like a flag. On the inside, he was pumped, fists waving, face contorted in happiness. On the outside, he schooled his features enough to give the man a wide smile and a firm nod.

Then, within moments of the man handing him a paper of proof so he could claim his money, everything was back to normal. For everyone else at least. His heart still thundered, his cheeks stayed flushed. Goddamn. He finally realized why people did this—

subjected themselves to the flat voices of disinterested bingo callers calling out a truly mind-numbing string of numbers and letters for hours on end. Winning felt incredible. If the feeling could be bottled, he would be first in line to shell out cash for it. He understood now why gambling was so dangerous for so many people. If this was how he was over a small win in small-town bingo, he couldn't imagine how he'd be after a winning streak at the craps table.

When he finally got his breath back, he looked at Aja. Her eyes were on him, like she'd just been waiting for him to get himself together and turn to her before anyone else.

"Congratulations, Walker." It was a genuine compliment, he could tell.

"Thank you," he gushed. "This feels fucking amazing."

Aja giggled—the twist in his chest started feeling familiar. "I bet it does. You shot up out of that seat like you'd just won the lottery."

"Getting that bingo might be the best thing I've ever felt." It was an exaggeration—kind of, maybe—but he was dazed.

She raised her eyebrows, surprised stamped on her face. But she made no comment.

"You want to get out of here then?" she asked him. "Or did you want to stick around and see if you can get another win?"

Walker looked at his watch; it was already nearing half past eight. Even in his excitement, he wanted to be around her—maybe even especially in his excitement. He still needed to get her home at a reasonable hour, and the odds of him getting two bingos on the same night were incredibly slim.

"Yeah." He started gathering up his sheets. "Let's get out of here."

It only took a few minutes to collect Walker's winnings, all three hundred dollars of it. And when they stepped outside into the thick summer air, his body hummed with satisfaction.

Their cars were parked right next to each other in the back of the sparsely populated parking lot. Aja leaned against the back door of her car, arms crossed as she looked at him.

"Where do you want to go eat?" She spoke softly, like she was scared of disturbing the peace around her. Aside from the crickets, it was quieter outside than it was indoors.

Staring at her, his mind went blank. How was he supposed to think about food when his already persistent elation was bolstered by everything about her—sight, sound, even just the possibility of her?

His legs propelled him forward until he was standing so close that he could make out the tiny, dark mole on the underside of her chin. Her eyes widened in surprise, and her chest expanded as her breaths drew in deeper.

His resolution to stay her friend be damned—Walker felt bold. Not bold like some asshole guy in a movie who kisses a woman without her permission. But bold like a different kind of guy, in a different kind of movie, who was about to tell a woman that he wanted her. Who was ready to put his desires on Front Street, knowing she could crash those desires with one quick flick of her tongue.

"I don't know if I'm feelin' hungry anymore." Not for food anyway, which he didn't dare tell her—not yet, not until he was positive that she wanted to hear it from him.

"Oh." Her brows furrowed. "Well, that's all right, I have food at home. . . ."

"Are you hungry right now, Aja? Like *right* now?"

If she was, he'd take her to get whatever the hell she wanted. Sit across from her while she ate her fill, send her on her way, and be content with it. Sure, he'd go home and jerk his dick until it was sore at the thought of her, but what else was new? But if she wasn't hungry, if she was open to something else . . . that was different.

"I mean, I'm not starving or anything yet. But I thought . . ." she trailed off.

"I am hungry," he assured her. "I'm just not hungry for food."

He could see the exact moment the realization dawned on her. His breath stuck in his chest as he waited for her reaction.

It was dark, but the sky was lit up with twinkling stars that, paired with the streetlamps, illuminated her perfectly. The round- ness of her face, the slope of her nose, the weight in her eyelids. Everything about her was clear and open for him to take in.

She drew her top lip into her mouth, gnashing her teeth into it before releasing it again, wetter and more swollen. Her eyes were as dark and alluring as ever, but Walker could see something else in their depths. Something he knew was reflected in his own gaze—need, longing, good old-fashioned *want*.

"What are you hungry for, exactly?" she asked in that sweet way of hers. Voice soft and floaty.

He stepped even nearer, until his sneakers were toe-to-toe with her sandals. He made sure not to step on her pretty little toes, but even this felt good. Touching her but not touching her—being close. It wasn't enough, not nearly, but it could be. If it ended up being the closest she ever allowed him to be, he could make some- thing of it. His dreams would still be filled with her. Thoughts of his hands on her soft skin, of her body pressed up against him, of the sweet, wet grip of her around him. If these things could only ever come to fruition in his fantasies, he could live with that. So long as he had this to feed it. The type of tension that could only exist between people who wanted madly, desperately, but couldn't—shouldn't—act on it. So, they settled for sitting a little too close or looking a little too long.

That was part of the fun, wasn't it? Walker had never considered himself an expert in this department. But he figured sexual tension was more poetic when it was unresolved anyway. At least that was what he told himself in preparation for rejection.

Aja might be turned on by him, might walk on the same horny tightrope he found himself on whenever he was around her. But that didn't mean she didn't also understand why flipping the switch on their friendship might not be the best idea. Aja was smart. Maybe—almost certainly—smarter than him. And maybe she didn't find herself as overcome as he did.

"I'm hungry for you." The words were ragged, born completely out of the burning inside him.

She blew out the breath of someone who had been sucker punched in the gut.

"Are you hungry for me?" He was unable to stop himself from asking.

"Oh God. . . ." She shut her eyes, her shoulders falling back against her car, steadying herself. "Remember when we were at Kenny Mack's, and I said that thing about you claiming me as your winner's prize?"

Of course he remembered. The conversation had replayed in his mind countless times. "Yeah, I remember."

"Was that a joke? Or were we being serious?"

He swallowed. "I don't know if I'd call what I want to do to you a claimin'. In my mind you'd play a much more active role in the whole thing . . . but . . . yes, Aja. I think we were bein' serious."

He noted the exact moment when she started trembling and he clenched his fingers to keep from putting hands on her. He wouldn't do that until he had express permission to.

She blinked up at him slowly. "I know it's not cool or sponta-neous or whatever to talk about all this . . . before . . . but I need to be clear about what we're getting into, so I don't drive myself up a wall overanalyzing everything. Are we doing this just the once?"

Walker hadn't so much as kissed her yet and already he knew that he wouldn't be satisfied with only having her the one time. Something about Aja told him that her touch had addictive qualities.

"If that's what you want," he told her, letting her know that he would follow her lead. "But I don't want you to miss out on claimin' your prize either."

The moment was thick with suspense, but Aja's cheek dimpled as she smiled. "Yeah, we definitely wouldn't want that . . . so . . . twice then?"

He screwed his lips up. "We could make it a kind of tradition," he said. "Any time one of us wins a bingo game."

"It's also a way for us to get out this obvious sexual tension without risking falling into something neither of us wants or needs right now."

"A two birds—one stone kind of thing."

"Exactly."

Aja stared at him before finally she closed her eyes and let out a wry chuckle. "I cannot believe we're doing this in the bingo hall parking lot. I thought—" She stopped and released another breath.

"What did you think?"

Aja opened her eyes slowly. The right one first, peeking at him, then the left.

"I thought maybe we would wait until the night before you left to acknowledge it. Whatever the hell this is"—she gestured between them—"I thought we'd do it one time and you'd leave and that would be it. I definitely didn't think we'd try to make some kind of sex arrangement like we're in a dirty '80s movie or something."

"I had more faith than that," he chuckled. "I thought I'd be strong enough to deny it entirely. Still don't know how the fuck I ever thought I stood a chance when you . . ." He trailed his gaze over her, trying to narrow down words for what she was but coming up short. "When you're *everythin'*."

Another breath, but this time, she followed it by leaning towards him and resting her forehead against his shoulder. His hand went to her back, resting in the center, waiting for her reaction. When she snuggled a little closer, he stroked his hand along the expanse.

"I'm hungry for you too, Walker," she whispered into his shirt. "So, so hungry. There's so much of it inside me, I don't even know what to do with it all."

He touched the shell of her ear, trailing the pad of his fingers along the warm skin all the way down to her jaw, cupping there as he made her look at him.

"Let me take care of it then." He leaned close until their noses touched. "I can make sure you get that hunger satiated plenty, and then some."

She bit down on her lip. "We are so ridiculous," she said, seconds before she brushed her mouth over his.

"Absolute fuckin' fools," he agreed.

Theirs had all the exhilaration of a first kiss after a period of tension-filled waiting. There was an urgency to the way their mouths moved. Wet and rough, and a little sloppy in the best way possible. Aja pressed her body up against his, grinding their hips together.

"You really are hungry, huh?" He nibbled gently at her bottom lip. "Rubbin' yourself against me like you're desperate for whatever I want to give you."

She whined. "I didn't think you'd be the type to tease."

"I'm not teasin', I just want to make it last for as long as possible."

Her tongue went to his neck, licking over his birthmark, making his eyes roll up into the back of his head. She had the same urgency she'd had when kissing his mouth. Wet and warm and insistent, so fucking overwhelming that it made his dick pressing against his zipper almost painful.

"I don't want to wait," she whispered into his skin. "I just want you."

He could already feel her hard nipples pressed against his chest, feel the slight trembling of her body. Slowly, he walked them forward until her back rested against her car again. She raised her left leg all on her own, that luscious thigh wrapped tight around his waist.

"Right here?" Walker nuzzled the sweet-smelling skin of her neck. "Right where anybody could come out those doors and see what we're doin'?"

Her breath fanned across his cheek as she shuddered. "We could get in the car."

"I think the rockin' might give us away, honey," he chuckled.

"I don't care," her words were stressed and strong and he knew immediately that she meant every last one. He was also incredibly relieved to hear them.

"Me either."

The yellow in her dress seemed to glow as he inched his fingers up the hemline like he'd imagined doing earlier. He made the glide up her thigh a slow march, her supple skin growing hotter the closer he got to the center of her.

Aja sucked in a gasp when he grazed the edge of her panties. He couldn't see them, couldn't assess style or color, but he could tell they were cotton. No frills, probably chosen for the sake of comfort. That only made him harder. Walker wasn't the type of man who needed to be dressed up for, impressed. Not that he wouldn't enjoy seeing her in some barely there scraps of lace and silk. But more often than not, when he thought of Aja this way, he thought of her naked. Open and exposed, comfortable in the fact that she trusted him to be good to her. Plus, cotton panties were easier to rip off; you didn't have to be careful like you did with the fancy stuff.

Desperate as they both seemed for relief, Walker had no interest in rushing. His fingers danced along the edge, in that space where her thigh met her pussy. He could feel the quiver there, the way her muscle stretched and strained to keep her thigh around him.

His thumb dragged up the gusset, working slow from the bottom, near where her entrance was, to the top, stopping around her clit when he finally felt the wet spot.

"Mmmm." His thumb circled, rubbing her, feeling the evidence of how he'd made her feel. "There it is."

"Yes," she hissed, gently rocking her hips forward. "Right there."

There was nothing in him that wanted to deny her. Even his apprehension about how this would change things wasn't enough to keep him from pushing her panties to the side and running his fingers over her.

Both of them shuddered, already sweat-slicked and sensitive. Aja was soaked, dripping onto his fingers.

"You have no idea how many times I've thought about this," Aja panted, hips still rocking, thigh locked. "You feel ever better than I thought you would."

"You have no fuckin' idea how good you feel." Thumb still poised, circling her clit, he slid a finger into her heat. Her walls scorched then soothed him with the rush of wetness.

"Tell me," she demanded through her clenched jaw.

That, he had no problem with. "You're clutchin' at my fingers like you don't want me to leave."

"I don't," she bit out. "I feel like I might die if you do."

He chuckled against her cheek. "I have no intention on stopping until I make you come. Relax, Aja. Let yourself feel good and come for me."

Aja moved her lower body a little faster, her wide hips moving with his fingers, giving him no choice but to fuck her faster with them. He focused on his movements, eager to get her off. Thrusting and circling, feeling her grow wetter and wetter.

Instead of the breathy moans or sighs he'd come to expect from her, she was guttural when she came. Tucking her face into his neck and biting down on his shoulder as he petted her through her orgasm.

Breath heavy, her leg fell from around him, her body heaved backwards, chest thumping. Walker slid his fingers from her slowly, watching her teeth clamp together once he was finally out. They were soft, wrinkly at the pads, and fucking soaked with her.

He raised his fingers to his mouth, licking them like he was tasting the first sustenance he'd had in weeks. Aja watched him with hooded, hungry eyes that he couldn't bear to look away from.

"It might be the lust talkin'," he told her. "But you might just taste better than peach cobbler, woman."

"Oh God." She knocked her head gently back against the car.

"I mean it too," he laughed. "I should start callin' you Peaches. You're juicy like one."

Aja giggled and he was on her again, hand at her waist, drawing her close, mouth next to her ear. "You wouldn't mind that would you?"

"You can call me anything you want as long as you fuck me," she offered.

He pulled his mouth off of her long enough to flash her one of his signature grins. "Get in," he said, tapping on her back window, pleased as goddamn punch when she fumbled with her keys to follow his order.

Chapter 12

Walker Abbott was apparently the type of man who kept condoms in the glove compartment of his truck. Laid out on the back seat of her car with her panties already somewhere underneath one of the seats, Aja realized the only thing she felt about this was relief. She didn't even have condoms at home. If he hadn't been prepared, they would have had to stop at the drugstore before going back to her place, because they definitely couldn't go to Ms. May's place. She was desperate for him, but not desperate enough to let his grand-mother listen to her screaming out his name as she came.

If they even got that far—who knew if the moment would still be there? If given time, they might have come to their senses and realized that what they were doing wasn't a great idea.

She also knew how she felt though. Knew that it wasn't but-terflies she felt in her belly when she was with him, but calm, quiet contentment. Knew that it felt incredible when he smiled at her. Knew that she'd met him only a few weeks ago, but she would sure as hell miss him when he was gone. And he would be gone.

If there was only one thing that he had made clear, it was how he couldn't wait to put Greenbelt behind him. Which meant he would eventually be putting her behind him. Soon all she would have left of him were her memories.

That was why, bad decision or no, she was going to sleep with him. So long as he was ready, willing, and able to have her, she was going to let him. And she was going to enjoy the hell out of it, every single time they did it. So that when it was all over, when he was back to his life in Charleston, and she was still here in Greenbelt, alone in the quiet of her apartment, fingers frantic as she rubbed herself off, her fantasies could be based on more than just an imaginary version of him.

When he opened her car door, she looked up at him, trying to convey every bit of thirst and eagerness she felt for him, for what they were about to do.

"You're so beautiful," he breathed, climbing in over her and shutting the door behind him.

Her car wasn't very large. Aja was fat and Walker was tall and that made the back seat seem even smaller. She maneuvered her thighs so he could rest between them. It helped them utilize the space they had a little better, but it still wasn't ideal. Their limbs were compacted and bent at awkward angles, their bodies pressed together a little too tightly to be completely erotic. They probably would have had a better go of it in his truck, in the bed or on the bench. But it was too late for that, and she feared that if they had any more delays, this thing might never happen.

"Walker, can you sit up for a minute?" He gave her a questioning look but did as she asked, folding his body into the seat as if sitting there properly.

She sat up, standing as much as she could and reaching around the front for the little lever under the driver's side, pulling it and pushing the seat up at the same time. Walker caught on quickly, doing as she'd done with the other seat until they had more room.

Now that the stars were hidden, all she had was the distant glow of the streetlights to see him by. His handsome face was shadowed, but she could make out the hard bridge of his nose and pink of his lips. He was gorgeous, and the only thing she wanted was to have him inside of her.

She started with his tongue. Beginning with brushing her lips against his. Feeling playful and daring, she teased him with a flick of her tongue, making him growl and draw her closer until they were kissing in earnest. If what she'd been desiring was a back seat make-out session, this would have satisfied her. But that wasn't enough to remember him by. Slowly and with great reluctance, she pulled back. Licking the taste of his mouth from her own.

"I want to ride you," she told him. "Is that OK?

He groaned, head thrown back against the seat. "I honestly can't think of anything I'd like more in the world right now."

She shuddered. "Me either."

He leaned against the seat, widening his thighs. "Go on then, take what you want from me, Peaches."

She didn't waste time trying to get them naked. It wasn't that she didn't want to see him, or have him see her, it just wasn't the priority. The thing that mattered most right then was having him inside her, and if they had to stay fully dressed to make that happen quicker, she was willing to make the sacrifice.

Aja stroked over the hardness behind his jeans, rubbing and petting until Walker raised his hips in a silent plea for her to take him out. She worked his zipper down slowly, pushing his boxer briefs low enough so she could reach inside. He was hot as she wrapped her hand around him, and even hotter as she pulled him out.

She had the condom on him in a stroke. But instead of straddling him in the traditional way, she turned with her back to him, throwing her right leg over his. She did it so fast that she didn't get a chance to see the surprise on his face, but his hotly muttered curse clued her in that he was very much unopposed to the position.

Hopefully it would be easier this way. Not only on a logistical level, but from an emotional standpoint too. If she could focus on the feelings and sensations of the sex without having to look at his face, it might make things easier for her when it was all over. Plus, she'd always wanted to try it this way.

Walker's hands immediately went to her ass, raising her dress up over it and hissing once she was revealed.

"God, this ass." His tone was almost dreamlike. "I've spent a lot of time thinkin' about this ass."

"Does it live up to the hype?" Her confidence seemed to come out of nowhere, but she refused to question it.

"It's better," he said. "So much fucking better. Can you lean forward? I want to see more of you."

Aja did as he asked, moving until her forearms were resting on the center console and she could feel a slight draft on her center. She knew that he was just looking at her, staring at where she was hungriest for him. It was a heady feeling. It made her feel free and powerful—and so, so hot.

She immediately clenched around his length when he finally

slid inside her, shivering at the feeling of being stretched so wide by something real for the first time in a long time.

It was her job to move the rest of the way, moving her ass back until he was in her to the hilt.

"Oh fuck," Walker muttered. "Oh my fucking God."

She kept silent but smiled, that powerful feeling swelling in her chest. Riding him in this position was easier than she'd thought. Having her upper body leaned forward gave her more leverage to bounce her ass in his lap without getting tired.

Their breath and bodies made the car hot, and she didn't take the time to open her eyes and look, but she would have bet the windows were fogged. She was also positive that the car was rocking—even if only a little bit—with the force of their fucking. Should she have been embarrassed? Probably. Was she? Absolutely not. She was too caught up in the way his dick curved to her so perfectly to care about anything else.

"I swear you're goin' to kill me, Peaches." The nickname made Aja tighten around him. "I don't think I've ever felt anything as good as you."

She whimpered; the feel of him had her unable to speak. He was mouthy during, and even when she didn't have the words to reply, she realized that she liked that. A lot.

He gripped her hips, helping her ride him, but managed, some-how, to keep his own hips relatively still.

Fire traveled from her toes, up to her knees and thighs, which burned slightly from the lack of this particular kind of use. When the heat reached her pussy, she bounced on him faster. Then Walker was touching her all over. Rubbing the insides of her thighs, squeezing her hips, reaching around to rub her nipples through her dress. He was *everywhere*, inside her, outside her, all around her. She could smell his cologne mixed with the sweet summer sweat on his skin, feel the weight of him entering and leaving her, hear his nasty coaxing words of encouragement. The only thing she couldn't do was see him, but even then, she could picture his face perfectly behind her eyelids.

"I want to feel you come, Aja," he growled. There was desperation there, so deeply rooted that it felt like he'd been yearning to say the words for a long time.

She couldn't compel her mouth to work, words refused to form even in her brain. But her hips had a mind of their own and the only thing they wanted was to get them both off.

She cried out when she felt his fingers graze her clit. Soft and a little dry, like always, they sent a jolt of pure ecstasy through her body. His fingers circled her, bringing her closer and closer.

She ran into her orgasm like a brick wall. So hard and fast, it sent her reeling. Her head went heavy, and her toes curled. Her stomach flip-flopped as she fell deep into her pleasure. Body shivering, she fell forward even more, giving Walker room to fuck at his leisure.

Hers hadn't even subsided before his hips stilled and the hands on her hips gripped tighter. She tightened around him, and he let out a shuddering breath, then a low moan. He kept his grip tight on her hips as he came down. She could feel him bend forward some, pressing his head into the center of her back. When the whisper of his lips hit her skin, she nearly bit down on her tongue.

"Turn around, Aja." Walker was the first to speak. "Let me see you, let me kiss you. Please."

She rose up off him slowly. He still felt so unbelievably good, and she was regretful that she couldn't hold on to him a little longer. Walker had his arms around her as soon as she turned.

"There's that beautiful face," he whispered against her lips. "The only part of that I even slightly regret is how I didn't get to see your face when you came."

She kissed him, hoping her mouth said everything she couldn't say out loud. Conveying every bit of longing and happiness she felt. And when they pulled away from each other, she felt lighter—she felt good.

Walker smiled at her, lips stretched, teeth gleaming white, eyes burning even in the dark. She was helpless to do anything but smile back.

●●●

Walker had insisted on following her home in his truck. She'd had no problem with it, content to let him be the sweet Southern gentleman he was so eager to be in the absence of a more . . . traditional . . . first time. Had they been in her apartment, Aja had no doubt that he would have stayed over. Curled around her as they slept, big hands on her belly and hips. And when they woke up, he probably would have made them pancakes. Then he'd have flashed her one of those smooth, charming grins before he went on his way.

Because that was the kind of man he was. The kind who didn't need to lie or scheme to get women into bed. The kind who didn't try to coax out physical attraction with promises of the love of a lifetime or happily ever after. All those things were unnecessary when held up against the sheer reality of him.

She'd been bold, leaning into the window of his truck and giving him a long, hungry kiss before pulling away and running up-stairs. She could still taste him when she got inside, so much so that she seriously contemplated not brushing her teeth before bed. She decided against that ultimately, on the grounds that doing so might mean she was on a whole 'nother level of sprung.

It was just after eleven when she got home; around the time she normally would have gotten into bed. She was going to need rest if she expected to focus on work tomorrow. But she was so damned wired. Her skin felt alive, and her brain buzzed, and she was ri-diculously close to spinning around in some kind of lovesick circle. She felt at a loss for what she was supposed to do now. She also felt the deep, aching need to tell someone about it.

One moment she was leaning against her door and the next she was calling Reniece, hoping and wishing that her best friend was awake.

"Your brother says you need to stop calling us while we're watching *The Bachelor*." Reniece didn't bother with pleasantries, so Aja decided not to either.

"Niecy, I just had sex."

"Hold up."

The silence on the other end seemed to stretch on forever. Then she heard movement followed by an annoyed objection from Tyson. When Reniece spoke again, it was quiet in the background, and her voice was a whisper.

"Can you repeat that for me, please?"

"I. Just. Had. Sex." Aja hoped her eye roll could be detected over the phone.

"With who?" Her best friend's voice got a little louder.

Aja realized then that she hadn't mentioned Walker in any of their conversations. She hadn't known how to. It wasn't like he was her man, or even her prospective man. But it had also never felt totally right to bring him up as a new friend. That was what he was, technically. But she'd known that wasn't all he was to her.

"J-just this guy," the words stumbled out and Aja silently begged Reniece to keep it moving without forcing her to expand on that.

"What guy? I didn't know you were seeing somebody."

"I'm not."

"Oh, so it's a one-night stand?" Reniece sounded impressed. "You had a one-night stand on a Monday? Damn, girl. When I told you to get out there, I didn't think you'd go all out like this."

"It just happened." Aja put the phone on speaker, using one of the hair ties on her wrist to put her braids in a low bun. "I really didn't plan it."

"But you used protection, right? You were safe?"

"Yes, Reniece, of course. I was impulsive, not reckless."

"Hey, we've all been there. I'm just making sure we don't have any surprises in a few months—in any form."

Suddenly Aja felt the need to roll back her previous statement. She and Walker had used protection, but they hadn't had the full talk. The one where they discussed the existence or statuses of their latest STI tests. Her last test had been over a year ago, before she'd moved to Greenbelt—and long after the last time she'd had sex with anyone other than herself. She supposed that had been reckless. Even if she and Walker never had sex again, she made a mental note to get tested, and to remind him that he probably should too.

"I'm fine," Aja stressed.

"Good," Reniece breathed. "Now tell me what happened. Did you do it in your place? Is he still there? Put him on!"

"Girl, no! He's not here. And if he were, I sure as hell wouldn't let him talk to you." She laughed at the absurdity of it. "We, uh . . . we actually did it in the Honda."

"Excuse me?" Her tone was deadpan.

"Yep. I rode his dick right there in the back seat."

Reniece released a sound that at first sounded like a wounded animal. Then she squealed. Aja could picture her sitting downstairs on the couch in the dark, trying not to disturb Tyson or wake Justin up and failing spectacularly.

"That's what the fuck I'm talking about," she stressed, sounding like her teeth were gritted. "I knew you had some of my bad-bitch energy in you."

"Oh please." Aja pulled her dress off, laying it over a chair. "You act like I'm some innocent little virgin. My anxiety didn't always get in the way of me getting dick, you know. That's a recent development."

"Even when you were out here doing your thing, you never had stories like this. They were always pretty tame."

She wasn't wrong. Aja hadn't had a bad sex life—not by a long shot. She actually considered herself lucky; the string of boyfriends and flings and one-nighters and *situations* she'd had in her life had been pretty good. Better than most straight women had, she figured. The majority of them had even managed to make her come most of the time. What they hadn't been though, was very adventurous.

Sure, her encounter with Walker had probably been tame by other people's standards, but it was the hottest thing she'd ever done. Spontaneous dick riding in the back seat of her car? Aja of a few weeks ago would have laughed in the face of the Aja of today if she'd been fed that story. It had happened though. The experience was real, and she could hardly fucking believe it.

"It was the best sex I've ever had, Niecy." Aja put a hand to her chest to calm the fluttering. "I don't know how I'm supposed to go back after this."

"Why do you have to? You can't just call him up again?"

Aja sighed. There was the rub. She didn't know where the hell she and Walker stood. She felt certain that they weren't together, but uncertain about everything else. Was he going to call her in the morning? When they saw each other on Wednesday, were they supposed to behave like they hadn't gotten hot and heavy? Were their Monday-night bingo games still on? Perhaps they should have discussed all of that before they'd fallen into bed—or back seat, rather.

Now she was left with warring emotions. Elation for what had happened and apprehension for what was to come. She was incredibly familiar with the latter. Sometimes the anxiety even felt comfortable when she was faced with the parts of life that she found more difficult. She had no idea what to do with the elation. Tuck it away? Fold it into some hidden place in her head until she needed it most? Maybe she wasn't supposed to be feeling it at all. It was highly likely that Walker was lying in bed right now, satisfied and content with the state of his orgasm without any of the extra shit. She knew that was a big possibility, and she desperately didn't want it to be.

"I didn't get his number," Aja lied, listening as her best friend cackled. "But that's all right—on to the next one, right?"

That was a lie too. She had no other men on her roster, nor the desire to add any. But Reniece didn't need to know that. Aja didn't feel like explaining feelings that she hadn't entirely worked through yet. She didn't feel like hearing the pity or the lecture. This was just for her to wallow in. Maybe once it was over, when he was gone and she was forgotten, she'd cry in her best friend's lap. Not now though. Now she needed to shower to wash his scent off so she wouldn't stay up all night trying to catch traces of it on her skin.

"I have to go," she rushed out. "It's late and I have to work in the morning, but I wanted to tell you. I thought you'd be proud of me."

"I am! I'm glad you had a good time, and I'm happy you told me. I like knowing what's going on in your life."

"When it's not so fucking sad . . ."

"Even when it is."

Both of them let out shaky breaths, and Reniece, probably sensing that Aja was at the end of her emotional rope, wrapped things up.

"All right let me get off this phone and get back to my man then. Tyson always gets horny after the rose ceremony," she whispered. "Maybe I can do some dick riding of my own."

"Reniece, gross. What the fuck?"

Chapter 13

About a year or so after moving into Gram's, he'd come home from school crying about how the D.A.R.E program lady had told him that the cigarettes Gram smoked could kill her. He'd been terrified. Neither of them knew where his father was at any given time, and they had very little else by the way of family. She'd been the only person he'd had—in certain ways, she still was—and because of that, he'd refused to lose her to something as silly as those "cancer sticks."

It had taken him months to convince her to quit smoking. With enough crying and begging and home-based book reports about the dangerous long-term effects, he's persuaded her to give it up. But May Abbott had been smoking since she was twelve, and kicking a habit that deep was not an easy feat. So she'd taken up cooking to distract herself. She'd gathered all of her mother's old cookbooks from the crawl space above the stairs and set her heart on making everything in them.

Walker had been forced to eat all manner of dry chicken and

overcooked beef. Their kitchen saw a bevy of mushy pasta and horrendous cream-based sauces for months. But she got better over time—so good that he'd started looking forward to eating dinner at home. He'd braved it all, sometimes with a sore stomach, and he'd come out the other side with a nonsmoking grandmother and a delicious meal every day.

His absolute favorite was her French toast. She didn't use any fancy brioche, just thick-sliced white bread. She waited until the bread was a little stale and hard enough that the milk and eggs and cinnamon stuck to it perfectly. And then she fried it up in the cast-iron skillet until each slice was dark and crispy along the crusts and golden brown in the middle. Finished simply with a dusting of powdered sugar and a side of maple syrup, it was the perfect breakfast. He didn't need anything else either. No eggs or bacon or sausage; he was always perfectly satisfied with the toast.

Walker came downstairs that Tuesday morning, hoping to find something to throw together for them to eat, only to find Gram already in front of the stove. He was stumped silent for a few moments, standing in the doorway as he watched her struggle to whisk milk and eggs together.

"Uhh . . ." His jaw flapped. "Gram, what are you doing?"

She jumped and turned to face him with a surprised look on her face. "You're up early."

He looked at the time on the microwave. "It's ten . . ."

Working from home had been a godsend. He didn't have to be in the office by nine and stick around until six even if he had no work. Without anyone breathing down his neck, he woke up when he wanted, stopped working when he wanted, and got more done as a result. The arrangement was amazing. It was probably the only thing he'd miss when he returned to Charleston. Well . . . now, that wasn't true, was it? Not by a fucking long shot.

Still, he hadn't been sleeping in *that* late. Not late enough to warrant any side-eye anyway. Old people might love waking up with the sun, but that didn't mean he was some kind of lazy bum for wanting to luxuriate while he had the chance.

Gram made a face at him before turning back to her task, accidentally spilling some egg and milk over the side of the bowl.

"I figured I'd make your favorite breakfast," she said absently. "You've been cookin' all the food around here, makin' sure I get around OK. I thought you deserved a treat."

He didn't think he deserved any kind of special treatment for helping his grandmother, but he wasn't about to turn that French toast down. He took a seat at the table, close enough to quickly hop up and help if she needed it.

"How are you feelin' this mornin', Gram?"

"These damned things itch like the devil." She lifted both of her elbows. "I had to stick an old wire hanger down there this morning."

The image was so hilarious he couldn't help but laugh. Gram harrumphed but turned a fond look on him anyway.

"Your father called me last night."

The news nearly bowled him over. He hadn't spoken to his father in years. The last time he and Benny had exchanged words was a week or so before his high school graduation. Benny had called the house, his voice somber and broken, to tell Walker that he wasn't going to be able to come. He hadn't given a real reason why, just some mumbled words about driving and work. Neither he nor Gram challenged him on it, but they all knew it was his lack of sobriety that kept him away. Walking across that stage, with only Gram there to clap for him, Walker had felt nothing short of humiliation and rage. Hands shaking, he'd promised himself that he wasn't going to allow Benny to let him down ever again. No more calls, no more sporadic, days-long visits that left his head spinning. As far as Walker was concerned, he didn't have a father.

The silence between the two men had lasted so long that Gram had been the one to tell Walker that his father had finally gotten sober five years ago. There had been no relapses since, but there also hadn't been any more contact.

He knew Gram and Benny spoke from time to time. He didn't know how often or for how long, but sometimes Gram would mention some news about his father and Walker's chest would tighten up.

Sometimes, in the dead of night, when he was in bed reminiscing—or being triggered by childhood memories—he'd briefly consider reaching out to Benny. It would be nothing to get his number from Gram. But that was always as far as he got with that particular thought. He didn't know what he'd say to the man. What they'd have to talk about. Hell, he wasn't even sure if he *wanted* to speak to his father. So instead of examining any of those questions, he left them alone.

Anxiety settled in the pit of his stomach as he contemplated why Gram was telling him this bit of information. Her voice held a slightly grim note, like she knew whatever she was going to relay was going to rock his world in the worst way.

"Uh . . . did somethin' happen?" The last thing he needed was for his father to need some kind of help. It was awful, but he honestly didn't know if he had it in himself to lend it.

Gram waved him off. "Nothin' like that, he's fine. He didn't say much, actually. Just that he was sorry I'd gotten hurt and to call if I needed money or anythin'."

That sounded about right. Benny was always sending Gram money. In the beginning, even before he'd gotten sober, he'd sent cash for Walker too. Fat envelopes stuffed with crisp bills that Gram was always trying to push onto him. He never wanted it though. It didn't feel right to take money from a man he wouldn't even talk to. Whether his grandmother had stopped trying or Benny had stopped sending he didn't know, but it was another thing he was glad he didn't have to decipher.

"Well, what did he want?" He kept his tone light, still not knowing exactly why Gram felt the need to bring Benny up.

"Not much," she said, her voice filled with obvious false levity. "I told him I'd been draggin' you to bingo the same way I used to drag him with me when he was a little boy. He got a kick out of that."

Walker's jaw clenched. There she went, doing that thing she did when she had bad news to give him but wasn't quite ready to watch him break into pieces. He wished she'd get it over with. If he was going to shatter, he didn't want to break out into an anticipatory sweat first and ruin one of his favorite shirts.

Gram kept going. "And uhm . . . he said he'd probably be drivin' the truck through here for work sometime in September. He mentioned droppin' by to see me. He . . . he said he's thinkin' about movin' back to Greenbelt."

Now his heart dropped into his stomach. He didn't know what he'd been expecting, but it sure as hell wasn't this. A thousand things rushed into his head at once. The overwhelming number of feelings made his head spin. Terror. Anger. Shock. Anxiety. He should be happy for Gram. She was finally getting something she'd wanted for years—the possibility of having her only child back in her life. Walker couldn't imagine how she felt. But he had to think of himself too. How was he supposed to go from not speaking a word to Benny in over a decade to knowing that he was less than two hours away at any given time? What would happen if he called to speak to Gram and Benny picked up? Even if he spent the rest of his life avoiding Greenbelt, he wouldn't be able to avoid his father now. Not completely.

It wasn't even that he didn't want a relationship with Benny. Maybe that was a small part of it. But mostly he didn't know how a relationship between them could even be possible. They had so much baggage. And beyond that, they knew next to nothing about one another. Walker and Gram had their problems, but they were close in a way he and Benny hadn't gotten the chance to be. He and Gram knew each other's favorite meals, they knew how the other reacted when a spider was found—hell, they'd even known each other's bathroom habits at one point. There were times when Walker blanked on what Benny's voice sounded like.

There was so much shit between them that Walker was afraid they didn't have a chance of having a healthy relationship. He figured Benny felt the same. That was why it had been so easy to stay away from each other for so long.

There was also that little boy inside of him. The one who cried for his father at night. Who spent long nights lying awake, begging someone, anyone, to make sure he was all right. The little boy and the grown man both found themselves torn between excitement and anxiety at the promise of seeing their father.

He turned his eyes to Gram and saw her looking at him, apprehensive. How was he supposed to tell her his fears? Especially when, for her, this meant getting her son back.

"That's . . ." He stopped, completely devoid of words he thought wise to express externally, but he knew she could read every emotion running across his face. "That's . . ."

His breaths came faster, and he touched a hand to his forehead, feeling the heated skin.

Gram didn't say anything and neither did he, but they could both hear his panting as they each waited for the other to say what they were feeling.

"I know you're probably . . ." She shook her head. "I know this is probably a lot for you. I know you boys aren't close—"

"We haven't spoken since I was seventeen, Gram," he interrupted.

She let out a shaky breath. "It's not for me to decide whether you have a relationship with your father, Wally. It would be wrong for me to even give my opinion on that."

"I already know what you think."

She wanted her family. It was obvious in every word out of her mouth and look on her face. In a perfect world, she never would have lost it in the first place. But this world wasn't perfect, and what she had was a family that was so fractured, it made gluing the pieces together feel like an impossible task.

"Well, if you know me so well, you know that I think you should at least consider seeing your father. He'd like to see you."

"Did he say that?" Walker swallowed.

Gram paused. "No, but I can tell."

He shook his head. He didn't know nearly enough about his fa-

ther to assume anything about his wants. Honestly, he wasn't sure
Gram did either. The entire conversation was setting him on edge.
His jaw clenched tight and his heart beat hard against his chest.

"Did he say exactly when he was comin' through?" He wanted
to know so he could prepare himself.

"He doesn't know for sure yet. Said he'd give me a call when
he knows for sure. You might already be back in Charleston." She
looked at him with imploring eyes. "Think you'd be willin' to
come back to see him? Talk to him?"

"I don't know."

He ran a hand through his hair, suddenly feeling haggard and
aged. His mind had been completely made up about leaving Greenbelt and not returning. Now everything was getting all jumbled.
Before, his desire to stay away had gone relatively untested in his
mind. He'd gotten flack for it, but his conviction to stay away had
stayed strong. But his relationship with Gram was shifting, he
could feel it even only a few days after their talk. There was also
Aja and the feelings for her that grew by the second—especially
after they'd had sex. Now, finally, his father. The chance to see the
man face-to-face, even amidst all his fears of doing so, was already
weighing heavily on his heart.

He'd spent so much time thinking about the people who kept
him away from Greenbelt that he hadn't stopped to consider there
might be people who could make him want to stay. This made his
head hurt. How could he hate and not hate a place at the same time?
How did he both long to leave and feel compelled to stay? None
of it made sense, but it all made him want to run somewhere and
hide away. Suddenly the little clear space in the back of his closet
sounded mighty appealing. It was small and dark and quiet—it

had the ability to calm all of his senses. It would be hard to fold his long legs and broad shoulders into it, but the discomfort would be worth it, as long as it reduced the anxiety he was feeling.

Thankfully, Gram accepted his answer easily, even if she didn't like it. They were silent, her pressing the toast into the butter-coated skillet and him trying to calm down. He wasn't sure how he'd managed to hold it off for so long, but now he could feel the anxiety building. Creating pain between his shoulder blades as he stiffened, putting pressure on his calves as his knees bounced, and making his jaw hurt from his grinding teeth.

It never failed to surprise him how he could be fine one minute and completely off the rails the next. He'd grown familiar with the telltale signs of a panic attack. This wasn't that. This was straight anxiety, the kind that threatened to stick around for however long it wanted. Minutes, hours, days—it had a mind of its own.

He preferred the panic attacks. The short bursts of fear and emotion were almost comfortable. He knew they would pass relatively quickly, and after he could crawl into bed, let his emotional exhaustion drag him into a deep sleep, and wake up the next day to only a slight headache. The anxiety stuck around too long for his liking. It followed him to work, to the bar, it even slept right next to him every night. It was still there in the morning too, up bright and early to make him breakfast and remind him that he was never, ever truly safe.

He wasn't going to run upstairs and hide though. Mostly because that wouldn't serve him, but also because he still wanted that French toast. He'd been in therapy for ten years, and he had the calming techniques to show for it. He worked through the ones he knew, trying to think of one that would allow him to do most of the coping work inside his own head. The last thing he needed this morning was to slip into a mindfulness meditation in the middle of the kitchen and spend the rest of the day fielding questions he didn't want to answer from Gram.

Progressive muscle relaxation exercises had always been his favorite. He could complete them quickly, anywhere he needed. At work, in the car, in a strange woman's bathroom the morning after some aggressively mediocre sex. With this exercise, ten minutes was all he needed to start reducing his anxiety.

He started by relaxing in his chair as much as he could. The old wooden furniture wasn't nearly as comfortable as the couch would have been, but it was all he had. He focused his attention on slouching his shoulders some and spreading his legs and thighs until his body felt less like it was being held together by safety pins. Then he fixed his breathing. Deep, heavy breaths in his nose and out his mouth that helped build awareness of his calm surroundings and steady his heart. Starting from the bottom of his body, he worked his ankles, tensing and rolling them, flexing his feet upwards. Creating tension, then releasing it. He continued these actions with the other parts of his body, his calves and shins, his thighs, his ass. Isolating muscles, making them rigid, then soothing the strain.

He became aware of nothing but his body. The way it moved and shifted as he manipulated himself. Everything else faded, even the things happening around him. His ears were too busy being brushed by his rolling shoulders to hear the French toast frying. His brain was too busy focusing on his body to think about the uncertainty of the future.

By the time Gram set their food on the table, his body was

floating, and his brain had calmed. The anxiety surrounding the choices he would soon have to make wasn't going to disappear completely. It would come back, and it likely wouldn't leave until his decisions—whatever they turned out to be—were made. But for now, he felt OK. He would take some time to enjoy his breakfast and his grandmother's company and try to feel comfortable and at home in his body and mind—those things *did* serve him.

Chapter 14

"Did you know there are only three drive-in movie theaters left in South Carolina?"

"Uhm . . . no . . ."

"Well, there are," Walker held the phone between his shoulder and his ear, taking his baseball cap off to comb his hair back with his fingers before putting it back on. "One in Greenwood, one in Monetta, and the other in Beaufort."

"That's . . . great, Walker." Aja's voice was a little far away, like she was focusing on something else.

"Obviously, the ones in Greenwood and Monetta are a few hours' drive away, but Beaufort . . . that's practically next door. A half hour if there's no traffic. Which there shouldn't be on a Saturday afternoon."

"Walker, is this another one of your roundabout ways of asking me out?"

"They're playin' all the new movies. Even that one with Lucy Liu that just hit theaters."

She paused. "The one where she beats the crap out of all of those men?"

"The very one."

"Hmm . . ."

His heart was stuck in his throat as she made him wait on her answer. On Tuesday, the day after their romp in the bingo hall parking lot, Aja had been dealing with some work emergency. Then he and Gram had missed Wednesday-night bingo because one of Gram's friends had been hospitalized in Orangeburg that morning and they'd had to make the hours-long drive through the state to see her. On Thursday, his own work had gotten the better of him. All this meant they hadn't had the chance to talk about what had gone down. The only real acknowledgment was Aja mentioning she'd made an appointment at the closest Planned Parenthood to get an STI test and thought it would be smart for him to get one too. He'd agreed, making an appointment of his own a few minutes after their call. Other than that, there had been no mention that anything sexual had happened between them at all.

He didn't want to push, but they needed to have the discussion. They could only go so long not bringing it up, pretending like it hadn't happened before something exploded. Walker had no clue what the hell the outcome would be, but whatever it was, he was ready. He was done waiting.

"OK."

He breathed a sigh of relief, not caring if she heard.

"But we're taking your truck *and* you have to buy the snacks."

"I was already doin' both those things anyway."

"Well, good . . . Then I'll see you this evening."

"Six," he told her.

"Right, six."

It wasn't until hours later that Walker realized what a colossal fucking mistake he'd made. Maybe "mistake" wasn't the best word for it, but once Aja answered her door in a pair of cuffed denim shorts and a white T-shirt so thin that he could see the color of her bra underneath, he had to keep from biting down on his fist. When he saw the way the hem of her shorts pinched at her big thighs, it finally dawned on him that he would be sitting next to her for a few hours. Alone, close together, in a place that was notorious for being a sexy hookup spot. Walker got the feeling that he was in for a world of trouble.

"We match," he told her lamely.

"A tiny bit." She turned to lock the door behind her, and his mouth watered at the way the shorts molded to her ass. "I see you weren't bold enough to show off a little more leg like me though. Shame."

"If I had a pair of big pretty legs like that, trust me, I would. But these pale, scrawny motherfuckers simply can't measure up."

"I don't know . . . I see some strength in those thighs of yours. A little more sunlight and you might be surprised."

"They still wouldn't be as incredible as yours though," he said, opening the truck door for her to climb inside.

"Well, everything isn't a competition, Walker."

Arguing with her—even in jest—was fruitless. Even if he refused to believe her, the woman still made a great argument. Once they were secure in his truck, he plopped a full grocery-store bag in her lap before starting the engine and pulling out.

"I got a few things on the way over. I wasn't sure what you liked, and I didn't want to bug you with tons of texts, so I just got a little of everythin'. But if there's somethin' you want that I didn't get, I'm sure the drive-in has a concession stand."

Aja rummaged through the bag before she made a triumphant little grunt.

"I love Hot Tamales!"

"Really? I got those on a whim, figured I'd end up havin' to take them back to Gram."

"Nope." She clutched the box to her chest. "I love these. They're hard but soft, sweet but hot. They're perfectly balanced in every way. And they're my favorite candy."

"So . . . you seem to have thought about this a lot," he said, endlessly amused.

"I have." Her matter-of-fact tone didn't surprise him in the least. "I have a definitive ranking of every single one of my favorite candies, and Hot Tamales are absolutely number one."

He turned onto the highway then, the road open, the sun still a couple hours from setting. Knowing that he was heading out of Greenbelt, even if only for a few hours, made him feel free. If he'd been alone, he would have leaned his head out the window and released a giant "whoop" in celebration.

"I need to hear this ranking," he said instead, pure delight bubbling up in his belly.

"I *literally* thought you'd never ask."

By the time they pulled into the Highway 21 Drive-In, he'd sat through—and thoroughly enjoyed—Aja's candy ranking. As it went, Hot Tamales were at the top, Sour Patch Kids were at the bottom, and Skittles, which were his personal favorite, were far too deep in the middle for his liking. He'd managed to only argue with her a little, and she hadn't been afraid of pushing back, pro-testing until the very second they arrived at their destination.

Cars were still filing in when they got there. The first movie wasn't set to start until nine, well after the sun went down and the giant movie screen could be seen clearly by everyone. They picked an optimal spot in the center of the field—close enough to the concession stand that Walker wouldn't have to walk too far but far enough from the screen that they wouldn't have to crane their necks to watch the movie.

He backed the truck in, making sure the bed was facing the front, then turned to Aja.

"You ready?" He patted the large tote bag full of old blankets he had sitting on the floor between them.

Her nod was enthusiastic.

"Did you clean the truck?" She ran her hand over the edge of the truck bed. "I didn't notice earlier."

"Sure did. Gave the bed a deep scrubbin' and everything. You didn't think I was goin' to let you hang out in a dirty truck bed all night, did you?"

"I didn't think about it, honestly."

"Well, I wouldn't. You deserve only the most spotless of truck beds in which to luxuriate."

"You're ridiculous." She rolled her eyes, grabbing one of the blankets out of the bag. "What I really deserve is a soft place to rest my behind, so let's get these blankets together."

Walker watched as she parachuted one of them, straightening it out when it landed on his side. "You know, I've been told my lap is a pretty soft place to rest."

"Have you now?" She kept her attention on releasing the second blanket.

"Yep. These thighs might not be much, but they make a pretty sturdy seat."

Aja shot him a look, lips pursed, and an eyebrow raised. She muttered something under her breath that he couldn't understand.

"What was that?" he asked playfully.

"Hmm?" Her eyes were wide with fake innocence when she turned them on him. "I didn't say anything."

He heard her scoff at his answering smirk, and that just made his smile bigger.

Once they got the blankets situated, Walker helped Aja climb up and settle into the bed before he went back to the front, grabbed his keys and the snacks, then locked the doors. He made sure to situate the little corded speakers on the edges of the bed before he climbed in.

They'd made a cozy little space. It was soft and comfortable, and the evening air was warm enough that they didn't have to tuck themselves in but cool enough that they didn't sweat on top of all the fabric.

"This is really nice." Aja looked around at the wide-open space. "I've never been to a drive-in before. To be honest, I kind of forgot they existed. I think there's one a few hours outside of DC, but I don't know anyone who's been."

"This is my first time too, actually."

She looked shocked. "What made you want to come then?"

"It's more . . ." He tried to search for words as far away from "romantic" and "intimate" as possible. "It's more fun, I guess. Less stuffy than a movie theater, we can talk if we want to, and we got to take a baby road trip."

"Oh, it was definitely worth it. I just feel like everyone here is either a family of five or a couple."

Walker made a show of looking around at the darkening area. "You mean you don't think there are any other bingo buddies who have had wildly good sex exactly one time in the back seat of a Honda Civic around here?"

"Somehow, I doubt it." Aja's chuckle was tight. "That particular level of ridiculousness can only exist in two people at a time, I bet."

"I don't know. . . . All things considered, it's not that ridiculous. A buddy of mine slept with a woman who also turned out to be the person his older brother was having an affair with."

"Damn. . . ."

"Yep, that next-level Jerry Springer shit is way worse than our situation."

"That's true." Aja's voice lightened up. "I can pretty much guarantee that I'm a one-sibling kind of girl. Plus, my brother would never sleep with a Braves fan."

Even in the large, grassy lot, with plenty of space between them and the nearest car, Walker's laugh was loud. "And I'd never debase myself with a Nationals fan, so yes, you can be sure of that."

"It's a good thing I don't care about baseball then, huh?"

"Absolutely."

For the next half hour, they were relatively quiet as they got situated, both making a point of taking in their unfamiliar surroundings as showtime moved closer. Walker wasn't sure when or if he'd ever make it back to the drive-in, and he wanted to soak in the experience as much as possible. The low hum of voices, the engines of cars driving in, even the slight breeze making the tree limbs shake and shiver. There was movement everywhere, something to see at every turn. Instead of making him anxious, it almost soothed him.

It felt like they were in the center of it all, watching without being watched. There, but still apart. It was only made better by Aja being there with him. Even when they weren't speaking, her presence made him happy. Her scent, her knee touching his, the knowledge that she wanted to be there just as much as he did. She surrounded him in a way that probably should have been more concerning than it was.

When the movie started, they had settled their backs against where the truck bed met the cabin. Unlike at a traditional movie theater, there were no previews first. A hush fell over the large field when Lucy Liu appeared on-screen clad in a pair of yellow leather pants with brass knuckles on her fingers. The man on-screen was tied to a chair, struggling and spitting in her direction. The second she brought the knuckles down on his face, sending him reeling backwards and onto the floor, Walker was hooked.

About a quarter of the way into the movie, there was a lull when the obviously shoehorned-in romantic subplot began to take hold. Walker turned to Aja, noticing that she'd made her way through half of her box of Hot Tamales.

"You hungry?" he whispered.

"Uhm . . ." She tore her eyes away from the movie reluctantly. "Yes, actually."

"Me too. I'm goin' to get us somethin'. Did you have anything specific in mind?"

"I could go for a hot dog. Ketchup, mustard, and relish. Oh, and some fries if they have them. Oh, and some water."

She was all but licking her chops when he got back with her

hot dog and his nachos. He could barely get comfortable in the truck bed before he was watching her devour her hot dog. There was no room for talking while they stuffed their faces. When they were finished, only the bare remnants of their meal were scattered around them. Condiment stains on cardboard, a couple of particularly mushy fries. All evidence they'd been sufficiently satisfied.

Afterwards, Aja scooted closer to him, her legs crossed at the ankle as she laid her head on his shoulder. Her braids smelled sweet as they pressed into the skin of his neck.

"Tired?" His voice was soft.

"No, just getting comfortable."

He threw an arm around her shoulder, allowing her to cuddle up even closer.

"Feel free to use me as your human body pillow, then." Insincere sarcasm dripped from his tongue.

"Stop being so damned comfortable and I will."

"Nah, it's all right. I happen to like your cuddles, Peaches."

Aja groaned. "You and that damned nickname."

"What? You don't like it?"

"I like it a little too much, honestly."

"No such thing."

"Oh yes there is." She moved back to look him in the eyes, and he immediately felt bereft. "Especially when it makes me feel all . . . tingly."

"On the list of all of the sensations a human being can feel, I'd say tingly is near the top."

Aja shook her head. "Not when it comes to you. I thought having sex Monday night would make things feel a little less intense but . . ."

"But it just made shit even harder to ignore?" He brushed his nose against hers, then bumped the tips together.

"Exactly. And that's not a good thing. I don't have a ton of experience with casual sex, but I think I have a limit. I'm too high-strung to really enjoy tons of it without overthinking things. And you're leaving in a few weeks and—"

"And that's not exactly optimal for exploring any kind of feelings we may or may not have."

"Exactly." It was her turn to bump their noses together. "Which is why our little pact should work so well. If we keep our encounters contained and treat them like rewards, we won't have the chance to get so attached. It'll be easier when they're done."

Their mouths were so close that all it would take was a slight movement for them to brush. Walker could smell the gum she'd started chewing after her food. Her breath was cool and minty against his face and made him want to press his lips to hers. He held back though. His wants couldn't supersede their need to have this conversation.

"Maybe we should come up with some rules," he said. "Make sure we're as smart about this as possible."

It was honestly the last thing he wanted to say. Almost everything in him wanted to run into this thing with her with as few limitations as possible. To feel the full force of whatever was about to happen and suffer the consequences later. But Aja was obviously concerned, and while he was willing to risk his own feelings, he wasn't about to risk hers.

"Rules?" Her tone was thoughtful. "Like maybe we don't do anything sexual outside of when we're fulfilling the pact? Like not even kiss?"

He clenched his jaw. "Yeah, that sounds smart. Maybe we shouldn't talk about sex too much either. Keep the temptation as low as possible."

Aja nodded. "And we don't tell anybody. Especially not your Gram. I don't want her looking at me funny when you're gone because she knows her grandson has been inside me."

"Jesus, Aja." His voice was strained with his attempt to hold back his laughter.

"I'm serious. I don't want her to look at me weird."

"She wouldn't," he argued, trying to soothe her. "If anything, she'd be wonderin' what the hell you were doin' with me."

Her expression was dubious, but she didn't say anything.

Walker moved away slightly. It was damn near impossible for him to get his bearings back when they were so close that he could almost taste her.

"I can't think of anything else," he said. "Which is weird because I feel like there should be a million rules for a situation like this."

"I'm sure we'll think of some." She leaned back against the window and closed her eyes briefly. "Maybe I'll make a list when I get home and send it to you."

"I think we'll be OK as long as we remember the most important rule."

"No sex unless either of us wins a game." Aja said the words softly.

"No exceptions." He mirrored her position, needing to get his eyes off her so he could focus. "We can do this." He was clearly trying to convince them both. "It's just sex. It should be easy enough."

"Yeah," she whispered, resting her head on his shoulder. "Easy."

●●●

The ride home was almost silent except for the soft music playing from the truck's radio. Walker spent the entire half hour trying to find ways to ask Aja what she was thinking as she stared out the window. Every time he came up with something halfway decent, he decided against it. He didn't want to disturb the peaceful silence they'd created. Plus, he wasn't sure he wanted to know the answer.

Neither of them made an immediate move to get out of the truck when he pulled into the parking lot of Aja's apartment building. They sat there, perfectly still, listening to the crickets chirp like they couldn't bear for their time together to end.

Aja turned to him after a few minutes. He could barely see her face in the darkness, but he caught the outline of her, the little glimpses of her eyes and lips and cheeks he could make out in the moonlight.

"I should go in."

"Yeah, I should probably be gettin' home to check on Gram," he agreed. "Just hold up a second."

He shot out of the truck, jogging to her side so he could open the door and help her step out. "This may not have been a real date, but I'd still like to walk you to your door if that's all right."

"I'd like that too." She smiled, linking her arm in his.

When they got to her door, things turned slightly awkward. Walker knew what he wanted to do and say, but he didn't know if she'd be open to them. He watched as she unlocked her door, then turned to him. Her gaze was soft and open, and he knew then that he had to at least try, or he'd regret it forever.

"One more thing," he said quietly, linking their fingers together. "Before you go?"

"What is it?"

He paused. "I'd like to kiss you one more time. Before the rules really go into effect."

Aja swallowed, then her mouth dropped open a little. He watched as her breathing deepened.

"Yes." It was emphatic—and it was all he needed.

His hands went to her waist, pressing her back against the door. If this was the last kiss that he was ever going to get from her, he was going to make it memorable.

The slide of their lips was hot and wet, and when her tongue touched his, his dick pulsed. His fingers clutched her full hips, digging into the fleshy parts of her, trying to hold on, aching to *take*. It was overwhelming how much he wanted her, how much something as simple as a kiss had him teetering on the edge of control. Had he ever felt like this before? He didn't think he had.

He forced himself to pull back before he broke their pact only hours after they'd made it. Their mouths clung together, spit-slick and swollen. Aja's eyes were blown wide, darker than they usually were. He was sure that his reflected the same darkness.

"I should go." His voice was completely wrecked. "Before . . ."

"Right." She nodded. "Yeah, definitely."

"OK, well, I'll see you Monday, right?"

"Mmhm."

He started walking away backwards, trying to keep his eyes on her for as long as possible. "Bye, Peaches."

"Walker . . ." Her tone was half warning, half lust.

"I just needed to." He laughed. "One last time."

"Leave, boy!" She rolled her eyes, opening her door. "Text me to let me know you got home all right, please?"

"Yes, ma'am."

Chapter 15

Aja wasn't sure how long it was going to take her to get used to people wanting to hang out with her. The footing she'd found with Walker, and Miri and her friends was still new, unsteady. The other shoe hadn't dropped, but she waited anyway. When she woke up late Saturday morning to a text from Miri, asking if she wanted to hang out, she had to swallow down the surprise and read it two more times.

Miri told her that she, Jade, and Olivia were going to one of the bars in town that night. Even through text, Aja could tell Miri was a little cautious about inviting her. She made sure to mention that they definitely wanted her there, but that she shouldn't feel pressure to come if it wasn't her scene. There would be plenty of other times for them to get together.

In truth, bars weren't her scene—at least, she didn't think they were. But it had been more than a week since she'd hung out with them, and she was dying to see them again. Which was how she found herself walking into a crowded bar downtown with her ass cheeks nearly peeking out the bottom of a tiny black romper.

The Garage was half opened to the street outside thanks to an oversize retractable garage door with frosted windows. She didn't know how many bars Greenbelt had, but this one clearly catered to its younger citizens. The decor was hip without being too modern and the music was fun without being too Top 40, it was . . . nice. Even if it was nearly packed to the gills with people, none of them were too rowdy. And the open concept of the bar filtered plenty of fresh air through the space, allowing her to gulp as much down as she needed. That would do wonders for keeping her anxiety as under control as possible. Even still, the amount of people made her brain buzz with it.

For a moment, deep regret settled behind her ribs. She'd been so eager to hang out, but she wasn't sure she could do this: be in a room full of loud, moving bodies. Have people accidentally touch her, hear all manner of loud sounds in her ears. She wanted this desperately but also ached to run. She resigned herself to the fact that she might have to give in to the latter at some point. That was nothing to be ashamed of. She promised herself to only stay for as long as she could handle it without causing harm to herself. The second it became too much, she would leave. And she would force herself to not feel bad about it.

Miri, Jade, and Olivia were sitting close together at a small table a few feet away from the long bar. Olivia saw her first, rising halfway out of her seat to beckon her over with flailing arms. When the other two women became aware of her, they smiled, excitement practically dripping off of them. Seeing such obvious displays of enthusiasm at her presence eased Aja a little. But her body was still tense as she waded through the crowd, getting tighter and tighter each time someone bumped or brushed against her. But the small part of her that had been nervous that Miri had only invited her because of pity had eased.

She knew pity had been the catalyst behind Miri's first invitation. But Aja had been so overcome with the need for companionship that she hadn't cared. She still was, honestly, or else she likely wouldn't have stepped foot in a bar just for the promise of it.

"Hey," she greeted them shyly once she reached the table.

"Hey, girl!" Jade grinned. "You look cute."

"Come on, legs!" Miri's face was impressed as she looked her up and down.

Aja's face heated at the compliment. She'd bought the romper months ago while drunk on cheap wine and fantasizing about being sexy. She'd been sober when she got it in the mail and tried it on. But it had showed off her thighs and clung to her body in a way that satisfied her until she'd realized that she didn't have anywhere to wear it. Getting dressed for this night, she'd figured that if she was going out of her comfort zone, she could at least look good while doing it. Even if she had ended up slightly overdressed in comparison to the other three women, who all had on some combination of jeans and tanks or cropped T-shirts.

"Thank you." She smiled at them, settling into the open chair next to Miri. "And thank you for inviting me out."

Olivia waved a dismissive hand. "Please. We had a good time with you last week. Plus, I hate odd numbers and these two are always gangin' up on me."

"What makes you think Aja is goin' to take your side?" Miri asked.

"She seems more levelheaded than you two pricks." Olivia's tone was snide but playful.

"*Pricks*," Jade sputtered, mocking her friend's word. "Jesus, Liv."

Olivia's pale skin flushed bright red even in the bar's dim lighting.

"*Anyway* . . ." Olivia stressed the word, drawing it out as Jade and Miri laughed. "As I was saying, *Aja*. This group could use a more calming presence, which you clearly are."

"That's true though." Jade pointed a finger at Olivia. "Aja gives me big mom-friend energy."

"That's a compliment by the way," Miri interjected. "Because sometimes I feel like all of us are stuck at seventeen."

"We're not that bad," Olivia whined, then paused. "Are we?"

They all turned to look at Aja, eyes wide, faces expectant. "I mean"—her eyes shifted to each of them—"you all seem pretty responsible to me . . ."

One by one they grinned, the smiles almost innocent but not quite.

"See," Miri said. "She's already lyin' to protect our feelings. She's goin' to fit in just fine."

Aja swallowed, the welcoming words making her feel more emotional than they had a right to. In an effort not to tear up or say something mushy and out of place, she eyed their drinks. Olivia had a beer, but Miri and Jade were both drinking cocktails that she couldn't put a name to.

"I'm going to get us a round of drinks," Aja said, standing up. She'd left her purse in the trunk of her car but had stashed some cash in one of the little pockets on her romper. "What are y'all drinking?"

"I'm drivin' tonight, so I'm good with the one beer." Olivia flashed her a small, grateful smile. "You can get me a bottle of water though."

"I'll take another Long Island." Jade sucked down the rest of her drink, the straw making obnoxious sucking noises once she got to the bottom. "I'm in the mood to get a little sloppy tonight."

"What else is new?" Miri smirked, earning herself a light punch from Jade before reaching into her pocket and pulling out some cash. "You can get me a rum and Coke."

Aja shook her head, denying the cash. "Don't worry about it. I've got it."

"Please," Miri pushed. "I invited you out, I'm not goin' to let you pay for our drinks. In fact"—Miri stood up—"I'll go with you. Come on."

Miri linked their arms and led them towards a clear space at the bar, giving Aja no more room to protest. Both bartenders were busy serving customers, so the women were forced to wait. Aja turned her head to find Miri looking at her, her dark-painted lips curved up softly. She was unsure of what to make of the look, so she returned it.

Miri reached out, twirling a finger around one of the braids Aja had flowing freely, then she tucked it back behind her shoulder. "You feelin' OK?"

"Yeah," Aja nodded, surprised to find that she wasn't lying. "Are you?"

"I'm good. I just want to make sure you're comfortable. Being out somewhere new with people you don't really know can be stressful. I wanted to check in."

Sometimes Aja was positive that she emanated some kind of

scent that amplified how anxious she was. But most people didn't tend to pick up on that scent. And normally, when they did, it was people who struggled as much as she did—like Walker. She wasn't sure if Miri had been able to sniff it out or if she was a little more thoughtful than the average person. Either way, the obvious care in her tone warmed Aja.

"I'm definitely experiencing some anxiety," Aja admitted. "It's been a long time since I've been around so many people, but I promise I'm all right."

"You'll tell me if you aren't?" Miri asked. "We can leave whenever and go back to Jade's or Olivia's. Hell, we can sit outside in the parking lot. Just let me know if you want to leave, and we'll go."

Aja's throat tightened up. She'd been fully prepared to leave if necessary, but she hadn't expected Miri and the girls to come with her. Words were lost on her, and all she could do was give Miri a watery smile and a nod.

"Good." Miri tugged on one of Aja's braids.

"Thank you for inviting me out tonight," Aja said once her throat was finally clear. "It . . . it means a lot to me." So much. It meant so fucking much. More than she would probably ever be able to properly articulate.

Miri shrugged. "Like Olivia said, we had a good time with you. The three of us have been friends since we were little. We could use some new blood in the group."

Aja choked up. She got the sudden urge to hug Miri but held back since she didn't have the wherewithal to ask permission at the moment. One of the bartenders slid up to them seconds later, saving her from making a complete fool of herself. They put in their drink orders quickly—Aja sticking with Sprite. Other than the occasional few glasses of wine, she didn't drink very often. She couldn't trust that a cocktail wouldn't knock her on her ass, or at least get her too tipsy to drive home. And since the rideshare market in Greenbelt was sparse, to say the least, she decided not to risk it.

Jade shot up out of her chair when they got back to the table, bouncing in place as she took a long, deep sip of the drink Miri handed her. "This is my fuckin' song!"

Olivia and Miri shared an amused look but voiced no agreement. It was "Candy" by Cameo, a classic '80s funk song that immediately made Aja's brain flood with happiness. She'd grown up hearing the song at family get-togethers and watching her mother and father dance around the house to it. The groove was infectious, putting an immediate smile on her face. It was also impossible not to move to, which was why her face turned down into a nasty little frown and her head and shoulders immediately moved to the beat.

"See!" Jade squealed. "Aja agrees, come on, come dance!" She took Aja's arm, pulling her towards the little space in the middle of the room that had been cleared as a makeshift dance floor.

"Whoa, whoa." Aja stumbled, struggling to set her Sprite down on the table and pull away at the same time. "Hold up."

"Pleeeease," Jade whined. "Come dance with me."

"I——" She prepared herself to say no but realized she didn't want to. Her eyes strayed to the dance floor. There were already a few people dancing, but no one in the bar was paying any attention. The song *was* really good . . . it made her happy . . . being able to let go and dance to it would make her even happier. She swallowed down every bit of doubt and panic and tried to home in on the only thing she wanted to matter: her own desires. "OK, let's do it."

Heads bobbing, hips swaying, faces grinning, she and Jade made a fucking meal of the song. For nearly six minutes, Aja didn't fear or despair and overthink—she didn't do anything but dance.

Chapter 16

On Monday, Aja felt like she'd been run over by a semi. Her period had come with a vengeance, making her body feel weighed down by pain. Her head hurt, her back ached, and her stomach cramped all the way to high hell. It was so horrible that she'd used some of her sick days to take off work. Around noon she realized that she needed to tell Walker that she couldn't make it to bingo.

She hated that she wasn't going to be able to see him. She also hated that it had only been a few days since they'd been together and already she was missing him. She'd wanted to text him on Sunday. Ask him what his plans for the day were, how Ms. May was, what he'd had for fucking breakfast. Her curiosity felt like it was eating her alive. She didn't know what else she could do with it but lean in. In a compromise, she told herself that when she called, she wouldn't ask him any personal questions. She'd tell him what she needed to, take a little time to soak in the sound of his voice, and hang up.

Walker answered on the second ring, his slow, deep drawl warming her instantly. "What's goin' on?"

"Nothing, just laying here," she coughed. "Uhm . . . I have to pull out of bingo tonight. I'm not feeling too well."

"What's wrong?" He almost sounded pained as he hurried the words out. "Do you have a fever? Do you need anything?"

"No, no. I'm OK, I just . . ." She was a grown-up. It shouldn't embarrass her to tell another grown-up that she was menstruating, and yet, there she was, stumbling over her words. "I have my period and my cramps are killing me."

Walker breathed a sigh of relief. "You had me terrified there for a minute. You sounded so bad, I thought I was goin' to have to run over there and take you to the ER. Do you need anything? I can stop at the store for you or bring you some food or somethin'."

Aja opened her mouth to deny him but stopped herself. Later she'd blame her decision on her hormones—even if that level of bad decision-making was completely unprecedented for her, fluctuating hormones or not.

"No, I don't need anything, but . . . you could come over if you wanted." She threw her arm over her eyes, completely unable to focus on more than one of her senses as her heart thumped. "You know, just to hang out. Only if you're comfortable with that . . ."

It never failed to shock her how easily she could flip-flop between the different parts of her personality with Walker. One moment, she was unsure and anxious, tripping over her words. The next, she was full of confidence, completely at ease and sure that he desired her, that she was desirable. Both feelings were intense, but she could never really predict which one was going to show when.

"I'm absolutely comfortable with that," Walker rushed out. "I can be there in about twenty minutes. Are you sure you don't need anything? I can stop and get a pizza on my way over."

"No, I already have some turkey wraps prepped for lunch. You can have one too if you're hungry."

She could almost hear his smile. "Sounds good. I'll see you in a bit."

Walker ended up making it in fifteen. His knock was so strong against her door, it startled her out of the show she'd been watching. She fought the urge to fall into his arms the second she opened the door. He had on a pair of black track pants and a faded gray T-shirt that looked so soft she wanted to rub her face against it.

"Hey." He looked down at her with soft eyes.

"Come on in." She opened the door more for him and stepped aside.

She became keenly aware that this was the first time he'd been in her apartment. Actually, this was the first time anyone aside from the maintenance staff and her landlord had been in her apartment. She watched as his eyes took in the space, becoming hypercritical of herself for not doing any extra straightening up.

Greenbelt didn't have a ton of free open real estate. When she'd made the decision to move, she'd snapped up the first thing available. The first thing had turned out to be a studio apartment with a little alcove in a four-story apartment building built in the '60s. Honestly, she had very little to complain about. The pipes were old and noisy and the heat and hot water couldn't run at the same time, but everything was sturdy and functional. Plus, it was nearly the same size as her tiny DC apartment for a third of the cost. She used the alcove as her office space and storage area, creating some work and life separation. She'd turned most of the main space into a living area, complete with a comfortable love seat and television. As for her bed—well, she'd taken the doors off the only closet and shoved the top of her queen-sized bed into the space, letting the rest jut into the room.

She liked her place. But she wasn't in love with it. If she planned on staying in Greenbelt much longer, she'd need to find somewhere with a lot more space. But it worked for the time being.

Walker made a strangled noise in the back of his throat as he eyed her bed. Aja figured it was constrained lust rearing its head. But when he turned to look at her, she saw that it was something else entirely.

"Why do you have that in there?" He pointed to the bed.

"Uhm," her mouth gaped. "In the closet you mean? Or like . . . on that side of the room?"

Was he about to insult her interior decorating skills? Was she about to be the first woman in the world to invite a man over only to have him storm out because he thought her furniture didn't flow well together? Honestly, that would be just her fucking luck.

"Yes, in the closet."

Her relief was audible. The question of why she kept her bed halfway in the closet was easier to answer than why she'd gone with a weird-looking green duvet cover.

"Oh, well, I like sleeping in there." She shrugged. "I know it's weird. With my anxiety you'd think I'd be claustrophobic, but I've always liked small spaces. Closets, bathtubs, the inside seats on planes, stuff like that. Being closed in makes me feel safe. Obviously I couldn't get the entire bed in there, but even just being surrounded on both sides of my head helps me be less anxious at night."

Walker stared at her. That look, the one she still couldn't name, stuck on his face so long she feared he'd never be able to look at her any other way again.

"When I was a kid, whenever I was scared or I felt unsafe or anxious, I'd crawl into the back of my closet until I felt better again. It made me feel secure, defended, like nothin' could hurt me because nothin' could get to me."

"That's . . ." Aja had no idea how to articulate the way their admissions made her feel infinitely closer to him. There she was again, seeing him and being seen by him in ways that were completely new for her. With the loss of her words, something else in her chest moved perfectly into place.

"I know," he breathed. "I know."

"I'm—" She shook her head. "I'm glad I met you, Walker."

"I'm glad I met you too, Aja. So glad I'd kiss you if I could."

God, did she want that. She immediately thought back to the kiss they'd shared against her door Friday night. How it had made her so hot and wet and aching that she'd had her fingers in her panties, rubbing her clit, before she'd even made it to her bed. But she couldn't kiss him. Kissing him would lead to fucking him, and that would mean breaking their pact. The pact that she had thought so hard on and had every intention of sticking to—as long as she could keep her traitorous libido in check.

"How about we get those wraps instead," she suggested, leading him towards her small kitchen. "They're pretty simple, just deli turkey, spinach, and Colby jack in some flour tortillas. But I promise they'll make you less horny."

Walker snorted. "That's a glowing review for a lunch recipe if I ever heard one."

"That's me." She poked her head into the fridge, pulling out two of the individually wrapped sandwiches from the bottom shelf. "I can guarantee most of the meals I make will absolutely not make you horny. Can you get me two glasses from that cabinet over there?"

He did as she asked, and she took a few seconds to appreciate the way his shirt stretched over his back and shoulders before averting her eyes back to the ginger ale she was preparing to pour. It was walking a thin line, but she'd promised herself that she wouldn't screw him, not that she wouldn't look. She needed *something* to hold her over if she was going to get through this.

"What do you mean *most*?" He slid the glasses over to her with a raised eyebrow.

"Well, I do make a four-cheese macaroni that'll make your junk tingle a little."

"Damn," Walker cursed under his breath. "And what do I have to do to get a taste of this macaroni exactly?"

"It's my sister-in-law's recipe, it's very special to her, so I don't make it for just anyone." Aja grabbed a bag of chips from the top of the fridge, pouring some in a plastic bowl.

"'Special' . . ." His thumb tapped his chin thoughtfully. "I feel like at this point I've earned the right to a little bit of special mac and cheese. I mean"—he gestured up and down his form—"I let you have my body, after all. Isn't that special?"

"If I made that macaroni for any man who let me have his body, it would definitely cease to be special."

Aja had no kitchen table. She simply didn't have room for one, nor did she have regular company, making it a necessity. Normally she ate her meals on the couch, in front of the television like a recently divorced dad in an '80s family sitcom. She made a concentrated effort not to be embarrassed as she and Walker took their food and drinks and sat down.

"The one time I think my dick is actually going to earn me somethin', and it turns out to be just as useless as the rest of me," he said, laughing.

"I wouldn't say useless. . . ." she mumbled around her sandwich.

Walker had taken a bite too, so he just turned and smirked at her. His cheeks were full, making him look more goofy than suave, but still unbelievably charming. Sometimes looking at Walker was like looking at the sun. If she stared too much, her eyes started to sting and ache, and she had to turn her head before she hurt herself. Even if she hated to look away.

"Before I leave town, I'm goin' to figure out what I have to do to get some of that mac," he insisted. "Because now that you've talked it up all big, tellin' me that it's goin' to make me all tingly and such, I *need* it."

"You know, before I met you, I thought *I* was the most dramatic person in the world," she told him. "But now I realize that I keep my dramatics to myself and you . . . definitely don't."

"I've always had pretty intense emotions." He took his cap off, running a hand through his hair, then setting it on the arm of the couch. "I guess most people do, but for a long time I had trouble namin' them and keepin' them in line, mostly the non-happy ones. When I was sad, it was the saddest thing in the world. When I was scared, no one had ever been more afraid. Shit like that. When I first started counselin', I figured my meds and my therapist would help me not feel those things anymore, to get it under control. But instead he told me that I could feel those things as intensely as I needed to because it's not a bad thing. I just had to learn not to let them overtake my life. So that's what I did. At least . . . that's what I'm tryin' to do."

In an instant, Aja felt like a supreme piece of crap. She understood—at least in some part—what Walker went through every day. And what she didn't understand, she empathized with heavily. Didn't that mean she was supposed to be more sensitive? Wasn't she supposed to recognize that his emotions weren't silly "dramatics" and came from somewhere deeper?

"I'm . . . sorry, Walker." It was simple, but it was what she felt. "I'm sorry I called you dramatic. I've said it before, and I'm sorry about that too."

"It's all right." He shook his head. "I don't view it as a bad thing."

"And I didn't mean it as a bad thing, but with context it still feels . . . gross. Dismissive. I wouldn't like someone calling me hysterical or something and then pretending it didn't have shitty historical context. You don't have to forgive me, but I'm sorry. I promise I won't say it again. Not ever."

He looked at her for a few moments, silent, his eyes dark and contemplative. "OK. Thank you, Aja. You're so damned thoughtful. I . . . I don't even know how to take it in sometimes."

"You don't have to say anything," she smiled. "Just eat your wrap."

He took another bite immediately. "It's good."

"Thank you."

"Definitely better than the pizza I was goin' to pick up."

"Now you're straight-up lying," she snorted.

"I'm not! I can tell there's love all up through this turkey spinach wrap."

"I'm seriously regretting inviting you over. I can see now that I've made a huge mistake."

His answering laugh exposed his neck, long and imperfect with the big red birthmark on one side. She wanted to lick and suck and bite. Was she going to have even a single moment's reprieve from being coiled tight with arousal around this man?

"If you didn't invite me over, who were you going to force to rub your feet after lunch?"

Her head snapped to him, eyes narrowing instantly. "What do you mean?"

"You said you were crampin', right? I'm not so presumptuous as to suggest a belly rub, but Gram always says that a good foot rub can make your whole body feel relaxed."

Could she handle that? His hands on her? She knew some people did, but she'd never thought of her feet as a place she derived tons of pleasure from. But with Walker, she was sure she could get wet with so little as the stroke of his pinkie on her calf. Her mind conjured images of her feet in his hands, his thumbs digging, fingers massaging. She saw herself, moaning on the other side of the couch, completely shameless in her pleasure. The real her, the one sitting next to Walker with a belly full of potato chips and a contracting uterus, shuddered at the thought.

But she wasn't strong enough to turn him down. She just hoped she had enough self-control not to moan like she was having an orgasm while he touched her innocently.

"I suppose a foot rub can be your payment for the free lunch and the pleasure of my company." Her voice came out shaky and uncertain. "As long as we can watch my show while you do it."

"What show?" he asked dubiously.

"*The Bachelor.*"

Walker's audible distress made her cackle.

Ten minutes later they'd cleared away the dishes, pulled up the latest episode of *The Bachelor* on the DVR, and were sitting on the couch with Aja's feet in Walker's lap.

She remained a little tense, worried that if she moved her toes or ankles, she'd accidentally brush against his crotch. And that would definitely be more than she could handle.

"Cute little toes," Walker cooed, lightly flicking the back of her big toe. "I like the white polish. It's sexy."

She raised an eyebrow at him but stayed silent.

"What?" he defended himself. "I can't help it. I find most parts of you sexy. The toes come with the territory."

She'd already known being around Walker was going to be a lesson in restraint. But how in the hell could she exercise that restraint when he made it so hard . . . and wet . . . and aching?

His thumbs rounded the heel of her left foot the second she pressed play on the TV. The touch was light, soft, helping her relax as he continued the treatment around the edges. He didn't apply much pressure until he got to the arch, pressing his thumbs in enough to make her hiss quietly.

"You know, I never understood this show," he said, eyes going back and forth between the screen and her feet in his lap. "All the dudes seem boring as hell. They have, like, no charisma."

"They're not that bad. I mean, they're definitely not the types of guys I'd go for, but I think that's the point. This show is like the supreme escapist fantasy for some people. A bunch of conventionally attractive white-bread women vying for the attention of a conventionally attractive white-bread man. Whoever the guy chooses, whether you were rooting for her or not, she always fits the mold. She's always exactly who you expected."

His mouth turned down as he thought about it. "You don't strike me as the kind of person who's interested in that particular kind of escapist fantasy."

"I'm not, usually."

"So why do you watch it?"

"As ridiculous and slightly offensive as I find it most of the time, it's still addictive. You watch one episode, and you can't stop. You *need* to see it through to the end."

"Eh, I feel like I'll be all right," he frowned, sending his fingers between her toes. "Reality TV has never really been my thing."

She predicted that it would only take him a few minutes to get sucked in and she was right. The season was only a few episodes in and featured a bachelor named Carson, a dentist with dark-red hair and a penchant for sarcasm. Walker's mouth remained slightly open as he watched, still managing to maintain steady massage strokes.

"He's goin' to send her home," he said definitively as the show cut away to a commercial. The bachelor had been on a dinner date with Bianca, a brunette candidate with a bright smile and a generous amount of cleavage.

"How could you possibly know that?"

Aja already had her own idea of who the current bachelor was going to end up with. She always did. More often than not she was wrong, but she never failed to feel a little crushed when her pick was sent home. She also refused to learn her lesson.

"She thinks he's annoyin'," Walker said plainly. "And he can tell."

She looked at the TV as the commercial break ended. The duo was on-screen, the music signaling that their one-on-one date was coming to a close.

"How can you tell?" She searched their faces, trying to get a read on their micro expressions the way Walker apparently had. She found nothing.

"Before the commercial, when he was tellin' that story about breakin' his arm on vacation, she turned her head away from the camera for a second and looked like she was completely over it. It was subtle, but I saw it. I'm pretty sure he did too. Plus, he's spent the entire date tryin' to impress her with no success. *And* all of her laughs have been fake as hell."

Walker moved on to her right foot, immediately going to the arch, digging in hard enough to make her moan involuntarily. His eyes were sharp when they cut to her.

"Uhm, sorry. . . ." Her face heated.

"Don't worry about it." The roughness in his tone did nothing to abate her pleasure. "It's supposed to feel good."

Aja feared opening her mouth, saying something that would easily give away how much she wanted him—how bad of a job she was doing at dampening her desire. So, she smiled, though it was more of a grimace. More teeth than cheek.

Neither of them said anything else. She could feel him next to her though, so keenly that they might as well have been attached. Nearly an hour later, when the episode was over and Bianca was sent home, Walker still had his thumbs pressing into her soles.

Chapter 17

The bingo hall smelled strongly of disinfectant. Normally the strongest scent inside was an odd mix of frying grease and paper. Walker had heard whispers that the staff shut down early on Tuesday night to scrub the place down after someone had gotten so excited about winning that they'd vomited everywhere. Gram didn't buy it. When they'd sat down, she'd told him and Aja that they'd probably just cleaned extra hard in preparation for the health inspection coming up. Last time, they'd narrowly scraped by with a B-minus.

He didn't particularly care why they'd done it, just that the strong mixed scents of Pine-Sol and bleach were incredibly irritating. For the very first time, he found himself sitting next to Aja but eager to leave.

She didn't look very enthused either. She was all smiles and kind words, but he could tell she was tired. It clung around her sloped shoulders and eyes. She sat with her body hunched over the table more than usual, half laying on it. Walker didn't know if her period was the cause of her lethargy or something else, but he didn't like seeing it on her. He found himself wanting to take care of her. To pick her up, take her back to her place, and massage her feet until she was blissed out and rested. But he'd already gotten the chance to do some version of that, and he didn't want to push his luck. So, he found himself willing the game to finish a little early so she could get herself home and into bed.

Gram was barely paying attention as he played her sheets. She had her back to him completely, carrying on a conversation with the woman on her left. He wasn't making much headway. Quite a few numbers on his sheets had been called, but he was nowhere close to getting a bingo. Looking over at Aja's sheets, he saw she wasn't either.

He had to take his disappointment and push it off to the side. Their pact was very much intact, and the time they'd spent together at Aja's apartment had only made his desire to win a bingo and have her again more pressing. The more time he spent with her, the more he got to know her, the deeper his desire became. There had been a shift in his feelings. It wasn't just lust anymore. It wasn't only that he found her physically attractive and as alluring as an enigma. Every day he felt closer to her.

There was other shit now. There was a comfort with her that he hadn't experienced with anyone else, not even his best friends. He could be raw and honest with her about the parts of him that he normally kept hidden away. There was also the fact that he *saw* her. Really saw her. Funny her, anxious her, the her filled with as much hopeless longing as he was.

Those things terrified him, but they also drew him in. They made his want for her even stronger. And they made him want to retreat into his shell.

Walker had never been this eaten up over a woman before. He'd been in love exactly twice. All things considered, the rides had been pretty smooth. When those relationships had started, he'd been giddy and enthusiastic, and when they'd ended, he'd been heartbroken. He hadn't, at any time, felt this conflicted. He didn't really know what that meant.

This thing with Aja didn't feel as easy as the others had been. It felt more intense. Like the stakes were higher somehow. It was thrilling. It was terrifying.

"You doin' OK?" he asked when he heard her release a shaky breath.

"I think my reproductive system is trying to kill me," she joked, but he could see little beads of sweat dotting her forehead.

"You want to leave early? I can walk you to your car."

Aja raised an eyebrow. "Ms. May would kill you if you left her sheets unattended."

He spared a glance at his grandmother. She was still fully engrossed in her conversation, paying him no mind.

"She'll live."

She bit down on her bottom lip, and he could see that she was considering the idea. He'd hate to see her go but he hated to see her in pain even more.

"No." She shook her head. "I want to finish this game. I can still win."

His heart thudded. She hadn't been nearly this concerned with winning before they'd made their pact. It did something to him that she seemed just as eager to win as he did. Against his better judgment, he acknowledged it.

"Sadly, I don't get the feelin' that it's goin' to happen for me tonight."

She looked at him, her dark eyes roaming his face. "I thought you'd have a little more faith than that. Unless . . ." She coughed. "Unless you don't *want* to win."

His hand moved at lightning speed to rest on top of hers. "Trust me, Aja, there ain't a damned thing I want more right now than for one of us to win this game." That was a lie; there was probably one thing. But he refused to allow himself to think on that too much. "I just don't know if it's in the cards tonight. I'm not feelin' very lucky."

"Well, I am," she smiled. "It might be my horny period brain talking, but I feel like it's going to happen tonight."

Her fervor was infectious, and he couldn't help but believe in her odds a little more just because she did.

"All right, play on then."

Unfortunately, it was his prediction that proved true. Aja got close, only two squares away from a horizontal bingo, but ended the game a loser just like him.

As they gathered their things to leave, he took note of the tiny pout on her face.

"Next time." He knocked his shoulder against hers. Gram's attention was no longer dedicated to someone else, so he had to be vague.

Aja rolled her eyes playfully and held up her crossed fingers. "I really thought it was going to happen."

Walker tried not to let his disappointment show. She was already down; he didn't need to kick her with a needless "I told you so."

"You know . . . you can have my body anytime you want, Aja. All you have to do is ask."

She shook her head. "Nope. We have to stick to the pact. That's why we made it, remember?"

"Pact?" Gram butted in, shocking them both. "What pact?"

Aja sputtered, her mouth opening and closing a few times. Walker's face heated as he tried to rack his brain for an acceptable answer. There was no way in hell he was about to tell her the truth.

"Uhm . . . Aja and I made a pact that neither of us would ever leave before a game was fully over."

"Right." Aja nodded emphatically. "We promised each other that we'd always stick it out."

The look on Gram's face was dubious. "Well, I already know that you'll be stickin' to that pact, Wally. I don't drag you in here every week just for you to leave things unfinished."

"Exactly," he said. "That's why Aja here is goin' to keep me honest."

Gram nodded her head once. "I knew she'd be a good influence on you."

She went ahead of them towards the exit. With her casts naturally lifting her bent arms in the air but the bottom half of her moving in a strong stride, the image was hilarious.

"I have to say—pretty sure she's wrong about you bein' a good influence," he said out of the side of his mouth as they followed. "In fact, I think you're goin' to ruin me."

Aja's teeth tugged at her bottom lip. "That's the plan."

Chapter 18

"You have no idea how hard I'm working to convince myself that you aren't marchin' me to my death right now."

She didn't even look back as she led them down the creaky wooden path. "Maybe you're leading yourself to your own death by doubting your instincts."

The sound of his shoes against the ground stopped, and she finally turned to see him standing behind her, legs steeled. They were both silent, the sound of the summer breeze moving the leaves of the tall trees was the only thing to remind her that something other than just the two of them existed.

"Look at me," Walker commanded. "Look into my eyes."

He could have ordered her to get on her back and put her knees up to her ears and she would have followed without complaint. Somehow this felt more difficult. Her eyes met his and they were dark, unrelenting as they bored into hers. Walker was silent as he stared at her. So many seconds passed that she thought she might have slipped into a trance. When he finally pulled his gaze away, there was a smirk on his lips so devilish she was surprised he hadn't sprouted horns.

"You're not goin' to kill me. I can see it."

"And how is that?" She crossed her arms over her chest. "I made you drive all the way out to the edge of town with me, there's nothing around for miles, and you pretty much followed me without question. If I were planning to kill you, I would definitely be succeeding right now."

Walker shook his head, his hair falling into his eyes. He ran a hand through it, pushing it back. "Nah, I'm pretty positive."

"You can't be positive. You've barely known me a month. I could totally be turning on you right now."

"I looked in your eyes," he said simply.

Aja snorted. "I cannot stress enough how little that means, Walker."

"Well, if that's not enough to convince you of my confidence, there's also the fact that I've been inside you."

The words sent her spinning. Whatever words had been planning to come out of her mouth were released sputtering and incoherent. "Walker! Are you serious?!"

"I'm just sayin'—you learn a lot about a person when you've literally felt them at their most vulnerable. And when are we more vulnerable than mid orgasm?"

"I might not have been planning to kill you before, but I'm seriously thinking about it now. . . ."

"This is a good thing, Aja. I know you. You know me. And all because we gave each other the sacred gift of our bodies."

"That is patently false, you are an unserious person, and now

I'm regretting ever feeling anything even remotely close to lust for your goofy ass."

Walker's lips turned up. "We both know that's a bold-faced-ass lie."

"Shut up!" she grumbled, knowing he was right. "I'm going back to the car, you don't deserve to see the beauty of my extra special, super-secret spot."

His arms went around her waist before she could stomp away. He pulled her closer, until her back was flush with his chest. It was hot out, one of those days when it wasn't uncommon to hear "it's too hot out for all that touching" in Black households. They both wore shorts; him, a pair of dark khaki ones that fell just above his knee, and her, a pair of black ones that barely contained her thighs. They'd only been touching for mere moments, but the skin on their arms stuck together as she put hers over his around her middle.

"Wait, wait, wait . . ." The words were said into the shell of her ear. "Maybe I was too quick to judge. Maybe you are here to drag me to my death."

"And . . . ?"

Walker sighed deeply. "And maybe I don't know the true nature of your being just because we've had sex."

She flicked the back of his hand, and his arms tightened around her. "But just so we're being clear," she said with a smile, "you're admitting to me that I could absolutely kill you if I wanted to. And that you don't know me well enough to be absolutely, completely sure that I wouldn't. And for that reason you should always be a little bit scared of me."

"Oh, well, I can tell you right now that I'm completely fuckin' terrified of you. Just not necessarily for that reason."

She tilted her head back against his shoulder and lifted her face up towards him so she could look him in the eyes. "I would like to clarify that you should only be afraid of me because I could, in theory, murder you. Not for any other reason."

"You could do a lot worse than kill me."

She shook her head and pulled away completely. His arms around her were too overwhelming, the feeling of him sweeping her up in something they were actively trying not to get swept up in.

Aja told herself that Walker was referring to her ability to maim him or rob him blind. She was willing to consider any possibility as long as it was far from what her gut told her he was referring to—that she had the power to break his heart. She couldn't go down that road, not right now, not ever. If she let herself think about how she had that power, she'd have no choice but to admit that he might have the same over her.

Unacceptable.

Absolutely un-fucking-acceptable.

She cleared her throat. "We should keep going," she said. "I know you have to take Ms. May to her doctor's appointment later, and I don't want to make you late because we were fucking around before we even got to the spot."

"Right." He looked away from her and into the trees. There was a look on his face, and she couldn't tell if it was anger or hurt. She figured it was probably both.

They continued the trek in silence, the only thing reminding her that she wasn't alone was the heavy sound of his footsteps behind her. When they reached the end of the wooden path, they got an unobstructed view of their destination.

In an effort to convince him to join her, she'd spent days hyping up her super-secret, super-special spot. She'd teased him about how she was relatively new to Greenbelt but still had the inside scoop on a place he knew nothing about. Once he'd finally agreed, she'd realized that she had built a lot of expectations for a spot that, in reality, wasn't very exciting.

It was beautiful, to be sure. A large clearing with lush, well-maintained grass. A small creek ran through the center. The water was barely ankle deep, but it ran swiftly, rushing down its path until it disappeared into the woods behind the clearing. Rocks of varying sizes rested on either side of the creek; some were stones small enough to skip along the water, while others were boulders big enough for multiple people to sit on.

There was no one else in the space, only the bubbling sound of rushing water, the wind rustling the tree leaves, and the two of them, somehow more silent than the nature around them.

"How in the hell did you find this?" Walker asked.

"Some of my friends brought me here last week. Apparently this is where all the kids used to come and get freaky. They call it 'Cunny Creek'."

His face twisted like he'd smelled something nasty. "I've never been here. . . ."

"I figured."

He turned his eyes on her and she realized her words may have come off wrong. "I mean . . . not like that . . . you told me that you weren't very . . . outgoing when you were in high school . . . so I just figured . . ."

"I know, Aja, don't worry," he snorted. "I sure as hell wasn't spendin' any time at Cunny Creek when I lived here. It's nice though. . . ."

"Isn't it?" She walked in a slow circle, slowly breathing in her surroundings. "I found it really peaceful. I thought you might like it."

He smiled softly at her, the awkwardness from before seemingly forgotten. "You're right. I do like it. Thank you for bringing me here."

"I can't give you the full Cunny Creek experience, but I can show you the most comfortable rock in existence."

She took his hand in hers, working hard to ignore how good and natural and *right* it felt to touch him so casually as she led him to the largest rock in the clearing. It wasn't high off the ground, so neither of them had to strain to get on top. It was rounded on the sides but flatter on top, providing a stable base to sit on. The rock had been big enough for her, Miri, Jade, and Olivia together. She and Walker didn't, technically, have to sit so close, but they did anyway. It seemed like whenever there was even the slightest opportunity for them to be close, they took it. Even when it would have made more sense and been wiser to keep their distance.

Walker let his legs hang over the side of the boulder, sitting closer to the edge. Aja crossed her legs underneath her, providing a bit of cushion and hoping that her thighs, shins, and ass wouldn't protest too much later because of her time on uncomfortable makeshift furniture.

"You said your friends brought you out here?" She was surprised when he broke their comfortable silence.

"Yeah." It was still odd to have the girls referred to as friends, but she supposed it was true. "They've decided that me not really knowing anything about what they call 'the real Greenbelt' is unacceptable, so they've started taking me to all their favorite haunts."

"That's really cool of them."

"They're . . . amazing. I've never known anyone like them."

"Hmm." Walker's fingers tapped against his knee. "You didn't have any close friends in DC?"

"No, not really." She couldn't look at him as she spoke, turning to peer into the woods beyond instead. "I mean, I had people, ones who had kind of been my friends in the past, but it was always . . . I don't know. It never felt like this. I always had to pretend like I was OK with them, or it *felt* like I had to. It was like . . . if I didn't play my anxiety off like it wasn't a big deal, none of them would want to be bothered with me. With these girls, it's different. They accept me, they care how I'm doing, they check in when a situation might be high stress and don't make me feel like I'm a burden. It's . . . it's really amazing."

When she found the courage to look at him, he had a faraway look in his eyes. "It is," he agreed. "I came from this place where everybody either ignored me or treated me like shit. When I got out of here, I thought everybody was always goin' to treat me like that. I didn't know if I'd ever have real friendships. I didn't know if I was capable of it. But when I met my best friend, Corey, in college, shit just clicked into place. Now we have the rest of the group, and it ain't the biggest or most exciting bunch of people but they . . ."

"They saved your life," she finished softly.

"Yeah, they saved my life."

It made sense, why he was so adamant to get the hell out of Greenbelt. He hated this place. His memories may have been deeply unpleasant, but that wasn't the only thing driving his desire to leave. He had something to go back to. Maybe not another woman or romantic partner, but the pull of real, genuine friendship could be as strong as the pull of any lover.

It was a feeling she hadn't known before but understood now. What drove him back to the comfort of his support group was the same thing that made her want to keep her feet planted in Greenbelt.

Neither she nor Walker lived simple lives. It didn't matter how undemanding their jobs were or how much drama they tried to avoid, the nature of their mental illnesses meant it was next to impossible to enjoy lives free of complications. Their existences felt precarious, like they were always hanging off a ledge by a thread. At any moment, something could break and send them plummeting to the ground—breaking into pieces.

She was beginning to learn that while those falls were inevitable, they were easier to bear when you had people to catch you. Good friends could be the difference between being left splattered on the pavement or landing hard but steady on your feet.

And there it was, yet another reason why she and Walker couldn't work out. It wasn't just that she lived in one place and he in another. It was that they each lived where they did for a reason.

She'd chosen Greenbelt because it was small and quiet and didn't add to the loud mess that already existed inside her. Walker lived in Charleston because it was as far away from this town as he could reasonably get. She was growing in Greenbelt, changing because of the people in it. She had friends, people who actually had her back. People she felt confident she could call on a dime with a chest full of panic and maybe find a bit of real comfort. Walker had the same thing in the place he called home.

She'd never felt more aware that love couldn't solve everything.

. . . not that she was in love with him.

That would be ridiculous.

Absolutely ridiculous.

The stark reality just meant that she couldn't even consider the possibility of falling in love with him. Not if they each wanted to keep their shit together.

"I'm glad you found them." She meant her words, but they were hard to say.

Walker put a hand on her knee, his thumb stroking along the tensed ball. "Me too. I'm happy you've found some people here who are good to you and genuinely care. It makes me happy to see that not everyone in this fuckin' town is an asshole."

"Same," she laughed. "Or else I have no idea what the hell I'd be doing right now."

"Probably not be at Cunny Creek with a guy you can't make whoopie with."

Aja reared back like she'd been slapped across the face. *"Make whoopie?"*

"What?"

"Walker . . . *make whoopie?*"

"What?" His question came out even more forcefully. "What's wrong with that? Would you rather I said somethin' like *get fresh?*"

"You know, it's never more obvious that you were raised by your grandmother than when we're talking about sex and you all of a sudden start talking like you walked straight out of 1973."

He blushed and it was simply delicious, the tips of his ears turning as beet red as his cheeks. "I never claimed to be cool," he mumbled.

"Trust me, I know. You would have been lying right to my face if you had."

He growled, propelling his upper body towards her until she was flat on her back, nearly underneath him. She looked up at him, and his lips pulled back from his teeth as he playfully snapped them at her.

Her eyes fluttered closed briefly. Having him on top of her, even fully clothed and in a completely innocent way, sent shock waves through her body. She'd been on top when they'd had sex. She hadn't gotten to experience his weight on her, gently pressing her down. Her entire body flushed, heated and singing. She ached to part her thighs, to have him settle between her legs just before he moved inside her again the way she was so quietly desperate for.

His body shifted and the evidence of his same desperation became apparent. He was hard beneath the material of his shorts, and when he accidentally pushed against her crotch, they both sucked in a swift breath.

It was a gut punch when he pulled away, straightening himself up by tugging on the button of his shorts before resuming his earlier position.

"Sorry, I didn't mean—"

"No, it's fine." She cut him off too fast for her words to be honest. "This place is like a beacon of horny energy. We . . . got swept up in it."

He laid back against the rock, moving his legs over the edge more and staring up at her. The sun was high and bright in the sky, so he had to squint. "I don't think I've ever met anyone who could find a logical explanation for being too horny to function quite like you, Aja."

She didn't know what to say to that, so she kept silent.

Chapter 19

The Piggly Wiggly was packed out the ass with people. The store was so old it didn't have any self-checkout lanes, and the three cashier lanes they did have open had lines so long Walker briefly considered herding Gram out of the store and one town over to Beaufort, where they had one of those Walmart supercenters.

One glance at his grandmother and he knew that she'd never go for it. She'd been coming to this store for decades and outright refused to shop anywhere else out of pure loyalty. It wasn't normally like this. Usually he could come in with whatever list she provided, pick up the items, and be loading the groceries in his truck in thirty minutes flat.

Right now, everyone was doing their Fourth of July shopping and it was extra hectic. Walking down the bread aisle, he felt a special kind of tingle in the back of his brain. One that told him he might have to wrestle somebody's hapless husband for the last package of hot dog buns.

Like most small Southern towns, Greenbelt took the Fourth

of July very seriously. In recent years, the celebration had less to do with patriotism than with giving everyone a good excuse to gather and be merry. Each year, there was a town-wide festival that took place at the Mayor's mansion. The town events-planning committee put it together, making sure the start time was agreed upon and supplies were secured. There was always a smoke station for the meats and a huge cake provided by Castillo's Bakery, but everything else was done potluck style. Gram always, always made baked beans and macaroni salad. But, in addition, she made sure to bring extra buns and utensils, just in case.

Walker had only been once. The year after he went to live with Gram, she'd pressured him into going. She'd bought him a new outfit and everything, waking him up, making him wash behind his ears, and dressing him in the cargo shorts and T-shirt she'd picked up. He'd spent the entire first hour following behind her like a lost puppy, hiding in her skirts. There had been no choice but to separate from her once she'd sat down to play a round of cards with her friends though. This was not a scene where children older than five could be "deep in grown folk's business." So he'd wandered off, trying to find some business of his own like he'd been ordered to. It only took him a few minutes to find a peaceful, shaded spot under a big tree, and an even shorter time for some of the other kids to find him.

Like in school, he'd been quiet. Reluctantly taking them up on their offer to play, running after them as they'd enjoyed the picnic, happy to hang out on the margins, relatively unnoticed. Then, like the snap of two fingers, things became much less agreeable. One moment, he'd been fine, only to look up and find himself surrounded by his new "friends" and tons of adults as they prepared to light the sparkling candles on the big cake. The other bodies were packed so close to him that he could barely see the sky. The sounds were loud and unfamiliar, the scent of meat smoke was making his eyes water. It was too much—so overwhelming that he started to panic.

His breaths came hard and fast, and his vision got blurry. He'd gotten so worked up that he'd vomited his lunch all over his new shirt. Looking back, it was one of the first panic attacks he'd ever had. A year removed from his father's care, and his brain was finally reeling from the effects. Walker had been so embarrassed when someone had been forced to carry him over to Gram, and even more so when she'd cut her celebration short to take him home.

His panic attack also made the rumors resurface. By the time he got to school on Monday, the entire building had been buzzing with talk of what had gone down. The new "friends" he'd made regaled their classmates with fake tales about him kicking and biting the man who'd carried him off. Someone said that he'd only started panicking in the first place because someone tried to stop him from biting the head off a live rabbit. It was almost hilarious how he'd gone from baby meth addict to animal torturer over the course of one afternoon.

The only upside to the rumors becoming more unhinged was that they made others keep away from him. If he had to hear the rumors, he'd rather hear them from a distance.

He'd spent every other Fourth of July since at home on the couch, waiting until Gram came home with a foil-covered Styrofoam plate filled with delicious food. He planned to do the same this year.

"Do you think Aja's comin' to this year's picnic?" Gram asked lightly, poking at bags of dark brown sugar to find the one she wanted.

"I don't know, I haven't asked her."

What he didn't say was that he seriously doubted it. He wasn't about to tell Gram all of Aja's business. It was her choice alone to tell people about her anxiety disorder, not his. And if she'd decided that she didn't want Gram to know, he wasn't going to go against that.

"Well, you should." She pointed to the two bags of brown sugar she wanted, silently telling him to put them in the cart. "It might be nice for her to meet some more people in town. I'm sure there are plenty of handsome young men who would like to meet her."

He gritted his teeth as he grabbed the bags. He'd be good goddamned. He had no right to feel the possessiveness that was welling up in his throat, making him ill at the very idea of her with another man. But he felt it anyway.

"Well, maybe you should tell her about it." It took a ton of effort to tone down his smart-assed remark.

"Or maybe *you* could." She pushed her glasses down the end of her nose as she browsed her paper list. "All that time you spend with her, you'd think it'd have already come up."

Walker's brain shorted out and his tongue followed, leaving his jaws flapping but soundless. He hadn't told Gram that he'd been hanging out with Aja alone, outside of Monday-night bingo. He hadn't been forthcoming about them getting dinner sometimes, going to the drive-in together, and certainly not about going over to her house. Frankly, he'd kept it from her because he didn't want to hear her running her mouth.

Nor did he want her to keep entertaining the fantasy that he was going to fall in love with Aja and come running back to Green-belt, pretending history was nothing in the face of newfound love. Plus, just the thought of the type of questions Gram wouldn't be shy about asking sent a shock of fear up his spine.

He tried to recover as quickly as possible before she took her eyes off the jarred relish that he had held up to her face. He'd fold immediately under her gaze, and he didn't want that yet—even if it was still inevitable.

"I don't think I'm the right person to invite her when I'm not even goin'."

"You're still on that?" Gram huffed. "You don't think you'd like to try comin' again this year? Even for a little bit?"

He shot her a bland look, and she pursed her lips.

"Well, I know for a fact Minnie's is supplying peach cobbler this year."

"What?"

Normally answering her that way would have earned him a cuff on the ear. This time she just smirked, her eyes still on the jar.

"Yep, we're still doing the pie competition, but this year, in-stead of that big cake, Mayor Harris is treatin' everyone to cobbler. I figure he had to put in orders for at least thirty of them."

"Do you think you could bring me home a piece?"

She looked at him, finally. "You know how much people love that cobbler, Wally. I have no doubt somebody would knock my old behind over if they saw me trying to sneak an extra piece. The only way for you to get some will be to come."

He thought about it. Over a hundred people attended the Fourth of July picnic every year. Maybe it wouldn't be so hard to sneak in, grab a plate, and sneak out before anyone noticed him.

It wasn't like he was unique in appearance. He wasn't nearly the only blond-haired white boy in town. If he wore a cap low enough on his face, no one would ever know. It wasn't exactly a master disguise, but it was more than enough for Greenbelt.

"All right, I'll come," he groaned. "But I'm not goin' to stay long. Thirty minutes at most. I'll come back and get you once it's over, but please don't expect me to stay the whole time. I'm gettin' in there, gettin' my cobbler, and gettin' out."

"As long as you stop by." Her words were accepting, but the way she said them made it clear she expected him to stay longer. She was in for a rude awakening.

"And as long as you invite Aja," she added.

"Gram . . ." His whine was shameless.

The look she sent him was withering, forcing him to physically draw his body back. "Yes, ma'am. I'll invite Aja."

●●●

July Fourth was the hottest day they'd had all summer. The sky was completely cloudless as they pulled up to the dirt-patch-turned-parking lot near the mansion. Neither he nor Gram had been able to give Aja usable directions, and according to Aja, it was impossible to locate on Google Maps. They'd picked her up instead. Gram had even gotten out when they pulled up to Aja's place, letting her sit in the middle of the cab, right next to him.

The picnic was in full swing when they got there, but Walker knew there were still plenty more people left to arrive. They all piled out of the car, and Walker went around to the truck bed to grab the picnic chairs they'd stored back there.

Gram had very little interest in hanging out with them. After he got her situated at a table under one of the giant netted tents with some other older ladies, she essentially dismissed them. He and Aja were forced to find a spot of their own. It was ninety-two degrees, and the sun was beating down, making the only halfway appealing spot next to the huge wraparound porch. They were under a giant tree that definitely hadn't been this big the last time he'd stepped foot on the property, and they had a clear sightline to the food tables.

It was loud. Music blaring, kids running amok, grown-ups singing and talking and dancing. The entire place was alive, and this should have lifted his spirits, but all Walker felt was agitation. When he looked at Aja, the little frown on her lips told him that she probably felt similar. He didn't bother asking if she was OK; he figured he already knew.

"I told Gram we probably wouldn't stay very long," he told her. "We can leave anytime you want."

"Only after you get your cobbler though, right?" Her tone was playful, and he wished the sunglasses she wore weren't hiding her eyes.

"Exactly." He licked his lips, his eyes narrowing in on the desserts table. "As soon as they put the cobblers out, we're gone."

"At least it's nice out today." She settled back in her chair, stretching out a little bit, allowing him to see more of her.

She was wearing shorts again—little white ones that hugged her wide hips and full ass perfectly. He couldn't see what kind of panties she wore under them, but he'd sure as hell tried. In his imagination, she didn't have anything on. It was a much better image to focus on than his memories.

She also had on a crop top that showed the flesh of her upper abdomen. Aja was, in a word, wondrous.

"What do you mean it's a nice day?" He forced his gaze back to the desserts table, suddenly finding them much less appetizing when faced with something he knew was far sweeter. "It's hot as hell out."

"You could probably use a little sun." She tilted her head back over the chair, face upwards, neck exposed. "I can practically see your hair getting lighter by the minute."

He'd decided to forgo the cap. It was good for the sun—and a disguise—but it also made his head sweat. Once he'd known Aja was coming, the last thing he wanted was for her to watch him sweat like a pig in the South Carolina heat.

A brief moment of self-consciousness made him touch his hair, raking it back away from his face. "Hush, girl."

"I'm serious! By the time we leave, your head is going to be all white."

"I'll have you know my hair has always been this same exact color."

"Mmmhmm."

"For real." His head jerked up. "You know what, I can prove it to you."

"How?"

He had multiple baby pictures in his phone he could pull out if he wanted. If he got really desperate, he could even look up Gram's Facebook page. He didn't have one and had requested that she not post pictures of him there, but he highly doubted she complied. Neither option felt sufficient though. They wouldn't give him time alone with Aja, nor would they allow him a few precious minutes of air conditioner.

"There's a picture of me as a baby inside the mansion."

"Excuse me?" When she took her sunglasses off, her eyes were wide.

"Yep, if you go in that house right now, you'll find a picture of baby Wally Abbott in all of his non-white-haired glory."

Her eyes bugged out in a classically comical way. She nearly tripped getting up out of her chair.

"Let's go."

"Oh, you want to see it?" He stayed seated.

"You know I do," Aja huffed. "Because I definitely think you're lying."

He stood up, grabbed one of her hands, and led her towards the front steps. They weren't supposed to enter the mansion during the picnic. It had been built in the early 1900s. The mayor at the time had found himself dissatisfied with the small two-story home on Main Street that all the previous mayors had called home, so he'd built the sprawling mansion. Six bedrooms, two bathrooms, more sitting rooms than there were asses to sit. Walker had always thought it was ridiculous. No one family needed all that room. And what did it say about them that the person elected to "serve" the community lived on a hill overlooking them all from his plush house while the rest of them struggled to make ends meet half the time? It was ridiculous.

The bathrooms on the ground floor were open, but only to the elderly and parents who needed to change their kids' diapers. Everyone else had to use one of the three Porta Potties they had lined up in the back.

"Shh." He put his finger up to his lips as the heavy front door creaked upon their entry.

He took them through the opulent main hallway, bypassing the living and dining rooms until he reached three closed doors. He'd only been in this house four times: Twice during elementary school field trips, once for a child's Halloween party Gram had forced him to go to, and last as a teenager during a group project with the mayor's daughter, Lydia. So he didn't know exactly which room the photo was in. He remembered that the door on the left was a bathroom. As for the other two, well, he made a guess, choosing the one straight ahead, cheering silently when he turned out to be right.

They had to enter the room to see it, but it was unmissable. Right there, across from the mayor's desk, was an entire wall covered floor to ceiling with pictures of babies.

Some of the photos were black-and-white, some were vibrant and colorful, others were tinged in browned sepia. There were thousands, stacked in rows and columns as neat as their varying sizes would allow.

"What is this?" Aja traced her fingers over the photos.

"This is a photo of every baby born in Greenbelt from 1940 to the present day," he said. "The mayor's wife that year started the project, and every mayor since has kept it up."

"This is so cool." Her eyes were wide and shining. "Show me you."

"You think you can find me?"

She looked over the thousands of images, no doubt laying eyes on all the chubby, towheaded babies she could find, turning her gaze to him when she realized there were too many to guess accurately.

"This one." He threw her a bone, pointing to the photo of him. He was held up by his father, whose face had been cut off just above the nose. You could see the gnarly '80s mustache, the sleeveless Guns N' Roses shirt, and baby Walker in a onesie, toothless and grinning.

"You were right." Her voice was almost a whisper. "Your hair definitely wasn't white."

On his head was a thick tuft of dirty-blond hair, standing straight up.

He'd always loved this picture. It should have made him sad. The ghost of his father's smile was so much like his, yet something he hadn't seen in so long. It made him remember himself as a child. He probably should have hated laying eyes on it entirely, but he didn't. It made him happy, helped him see that there had been a time when he'd been able to smile and laugh with his whole heart—and believe that there could be again.

"You were adorable," Aja told him. "Look at those fat little cheeks."

"If you think that's cute, wait until you see Gram." He located the picture quickly, pressing his finger into it.

She moved her head closer to see, immediately laughing at the black-and-white image of his Gram as a baby with cake smeared all over her face.

"And that's my dad." He pointed to a dark-haired baby. "And that's my mother." Another one.

"Your whole family is here."

"I know," he breathed. "It's weird to see generations of us in the same place." Especially when the real versions had been separated for so long.

He could feel her eyes on him. He wasn't looking, but he knew that they had to be full of questions. He didn't mean for it to, but every time he spoke out loud about his family, his voice took on a very specific cadence—sadness mingled with the frustration that mixed beautifully with the longing. It was the perfect combination of things to invite instant pity, and that was what most people gave him. But when he finally met Aja's gaze, that wasn't what he saw. He couldn't put his finger on what it was exactly, but it didn't make him feel like shit, and he could hardly get over that fact.

"I know your dad drives a truck," she said, turning to look at the photos for a few seconds. "But do you still have your mom? I've never heard Ms. May talk about her."

He took a deep breath and shook his head.

"I'm sorry," Aja stuttered before a slight grimace stretched across her lips. "You don't have to tell me anything if you're not comfortable. I probably shouldn't be asking anyway. It's not my business."

"It's not that . . . it's just . . . it's not that easy for me to be open about it, to be honest." He ran a hand over his face. "It's not pretty, you know? And my feelin's are always flip-floppin', and I never really talk about any of this shit outside of therapy."

Aja touched his arm, her warm hand brushing softly against his bare skin underneath his T-shirt. The room they were in was warm, but gooseflesh raised on his skin anyway. "I get it, trust me. Don't push yourself on my behalf."

He laid his hand on top of hers, squeezing. The look in her eyes was so open, so kind, he found his lips moving of their own accord.

"My mama's name was Colleen," he swallowed thickly. The imaginary pebble in his throat barely moved. "I was named after her grandfather, actually. She and my daddy . . . they had a lot of issues. When I was a kid, they were both strugglin' with drug addiction, and they hated each other and . . . it just wasn't a good situation." He pulled away from Aja completely, a hand running through his hair as sweat beaded at his temples. He started to pace, his jaw clenched tight enough to make his teeth ache. If he was going to tell her about his family's sordid history, he wasn't going to watch the pity play across her face when he did it.

"When I was four, she got tired of it all, I guess. One day she was here, the next day she split, and none of us have heard from her since. It's part of why I don't like being in Greenbelt. All this stuff you just learned about me? The folks who live here had a front-row seat. The drugs, my mama, my PTSD, every single thing. And they never let me forget it. Not for a minute."

"Jesus, Walker." Aja's fingers curled around the back of his arm before he took a step back. "I'm so sorry. I don't even know what to say except that I'm sorry. I'm sorry you had to go through that."

Not that her words weren't comforting, but Walker hadn't been seeking them. He wasn't entirely sure why he'd shared this with her. Maybe seeing the baby photos had gotten his emotions high and acknowledging the why of it had lessened the pressure in his head. Maybe he just . . . *wanted* to be open with her. Wanted her to know parts of him that weren't always easy for him to access himself. It had probably been a bit of both. He didn't tell her everything. Couldn't really. There was only so much of himself he could cut open and flay at a time while still managing to have enough left behind to stand upright.

Even if some tiny part of him wanted to keep going, he stopped himself. It was supposed to be a good afternoon. Warm and sunny and celebratory. And as dark as his mood had gotten, he didn't want to darken more. His time with Aja had become precious to him and he wanted it to be filled with good, happy things.

"It's . . . it's not a big deal." He rasped through his lie.

"Of course it is." She rubbed her thumb across the warm skin of his upper arm, and his eyelids drooped.

Walker shook his head, trying desperately to gain some control of the moment. "It's in the past," he insisted. "I'm . . . I'm a grown man. I'm over it. I should be over it."

"Walker, it's not——"

He shook his head, pulling away again, still seeking control. "Aja, please. I promise it's fine. I've had enough days in my life ruined by the Abbott family mess, I'm not tryin' to add this one to the list."

Her smile was kind but still full of too much sadness for his liking. "You haven't ruined anything."

She was lying, but he was so eager for the moment to be over that he plastered a smile on his face. "Anything else you want to do in here before we join the masses? I could reveal the incredibly humiliating story of how I lost my virginity, maybe? Since I'm dead set on embarrassing myself in front of you."

"Walker, this just makes us even." She finally took her eyes off him, and he let out a breath. "I'd like to do a little more snooping, actually. I'm still not over how wild this room is."

Walker barked out a laugh that was much too loud and shakier than he'd intended. "Snoop away, Peaches."

She let her feet carry her down the length of the wall, looking at all the photos. Once she reached the end she kept going, her fingers dancing over the large built-in bookshelves that took up the wall to the right of the mayor's desk.

"It's really cool in here." She pulled a book out of its place, looking at the cover and turning it face up before sliding it back in.

Walker watched her, his eyes hungry to take in every move she made. The way her thighs flexed when she stood on her toes to fiddle with a trinket, the way her eyes danced like she was discovering something new. He was unabashed in his staring. If he was going to be without her soon, he was going to get his fill.

"If you think this is cool, you should see the shelves they have in the sitting room next door,"

Her eyes lit up. "Can we go in there?"

"You're tryin' to get me in trouble. . . ."

"If we get caught, we can say we were looking for the bathroom. Plus, we can be quick, in and out, I promise. I just want to see."

He had no intention of denying her but left her hanging in anticipation for a few seconds. He loved the hopeful look on her face too much to let it slip by.

"All right." He held his hand out and she took it easily, linking their fingers. "Come on."

Chapter 20

The mayor's sitting room had a type of old-school opulence that bordered on downright gaudy. Completely separated from the other living areas, it was the type of place where the men retreated after dinner parties to "talk business" and gossip. There was a large wood-burning fireplace topped with a giant portrait of Greenbelt's founding mayor. The couches were largely ornamental, all dark wood and red patterned upholstering. There was even a chandelier, glittering gold, hanging in the center of the room. Aja didn't appear to care about the sparkly trinkets or excess; the only thing she seemed interested in was the floor-to-ceiling bookshelves covering nearly every inch of wall space in the room.

"You must really love books." Saying it felt ridiculous, but it was the only thing that came to mind as he watched her survey their surroundings.

"No," she stammered. "I mean . . . kind of. I definitely don't read often enough to call myself a regular reader but . . . I kind of have this thing about bookshelves. I like seeing how people decorate them, what they put there, how they're organized. I can't really explain it. It's just really cool knowing that all these books were somewhere else once. That they were picked out specifically to be read and kept according to someone's particular tastes."

He looked around at the hundreds of books that filled the room. She was right—it was cool as hell to think about.

Instead of rushing her out of the house and back to their spot under the tree, he decided to give her a few minutes. Everyone was distracted anyway, so it wasn't like anybody would be looking for them. As long as they stayed quiet in the sitting room, no one would suspect a thing. He sat down on the largest couch, surprised when it was more comfortable than he'd expected. He spread his thighs some, his arms splaying out over the back.

"Part of me wants to steal one." She giggled. "I won't, because the last thing I need is to get labeled a thief before I've even been here a year, but I really, really want to. A boring one, you know. One nobody would miss."

"That's incredibly evil of you, Miss Owens," he joked.

"It would just be cool to take something home with me that has a little history, is all. Some of these books are so old it looks like they've been here since the house was built." She flipped through the pages of a faded hardcover. "Also, I definitely get a kick out of how the original owners of this house—hell, even the current ones—would throw a fit at the thought of some little Black girl coming in here and taking something."

"Even more reason for you to actually do it then."

Aja looked back and forth between him and the bookshelves, seriously considering it. He didn't want to sway her too much with his opinion for fear she'd end up doing something she didn't want to. But he firmly believed that she should. He highly doubted any of the books in the room had been read in decades. The most action they probably saw was when the cleaning staff came by to do their weekly dusting.

"I don't know. . . ." She slid the book she was holding back in its place. "What if I accidentally end up running off with someone's favorite book? I don't think I can."

She left the shelves, coming over to sink into the couch right along with him.

"If it makes you feel better, the way Mayor Harris governs this place, I doubt he's ever read a book in his entire life."

Aja's laugh reverberated through the room. The apologetic look she gave him when she remembered they were supposed to be keeping a low profile made him chuckle.

"I'm serious," he said. "Choosing to have peach cobbler as the dessert this year is the best decision he's made since he was elected."

"Well, whichever mayor decided to get this couch did a great fucking job." She sank in deeper, throwing one of her legs over his. His hand went to her skin immediately, thumb circling the ball of her knee. "In here is definitely much better than out there."

"I agree. Comfortable couch, air conditionin', the quiet." He nodded. "That's all you need."

"Don't forget about me." She bit down on her lip. "I'm sure my company makes it even better."

He leaned in enough to brush his knuckles against her cheek and bump her nose with his. "You have no idea."

Those brown eyes flicked down to his lips. They were close enough that he could practically taste her breath.

"You should back up." Her lust-roughened voice made him grind his teeth.

"Yeah, I should."

"We have a pact, remember?" Even as she said this, she pressed her face in, rubbing their cheeks together.

"Right—we're only allowed to do this when one of us wins a bingo."

"Yes. Only then."

His dick grew thick against his thigh, dripping like it knew what was about to happen before his brain did. "So why are we doing it now?"

Aja's eyes closed briefly. "Because we're awful, awful people who find it nearly impossible not to be drawn to each other?"

"I don't know about you, but I can't even help myself. Anytime I see you, my body just reacts. The way you smell, the way you move, the way you talk. I don't think there's anything about you that doesn't make me feel like I need to fuck you until we've both had our fill."

"We already tried to get our fill, remember?"

"Oh, I remember all right." His memories were crystal clear, even with his eyes open. "I remember that shit every night, just about."

Aja sucked in a harsh breath, and he could almost smell her arousal in the air. Her leg was still over his, the other on the floor. With her spread open, he had an unobstructed view of her cloth-covered center. Her shorts had ridden even farther up; the skin on the insides of her thighs was a little darker than the rest of her.

"I remember that too," she admitted. "And as soon as I came, I knew that . . ."

"You'd never actually get your fill. That one time would never be enough."

"Yes. Which is why the pact is necessary; it keeps us from chasing that high again and again until we screw ourselves over. Keeps us from almost having sex on the couch in the mayor's sitting room."

"Does it count if we don't actually have sex?" He moved to rub his face against her soft jaw. "Not in the most traditional sense, at least."

"What do you mean?" She tilted her head to the side, giving him more access.

"I mean, what if we just played a little? Did some of the things we didn't get to do last time? Things I've been dyin' to do for longer than I care to admit."

"I thought we did a pretty thorough job of it," she whispered.

"Not nearly. Even after havin' the best orgasm of my life, I was left wantin'. Mostly for a proper taste of you."

Aja's whine was high and hoarse, her legs moved a little as she tried to spread herself wider. "It's been so long since . . ."

"Since what, Aja?"

"Since I've had anybody do that."

"Damned shame," Walker murmured. "If I had my way, I'd live between your thighs." He nipped at the soft flesh behind her ear.

"Those are strong words, Walker. You haven't even gotten more than a taste yet, and you're already ready to devote your entire life to it?"

"One taste was all I needed." He nipped her harder this time, soothing the hurt with his tongue when she hissed. "I told you it was better than cobbler, didn't I?"

"I figured you were exaggerating."

His hands came around to the sides of her breasts; he could feel her hard nipples poking into his chest through her shirt. His mouth ached with the need to suck and bite. "Uh-uh, I was dead serious."

When he felt her hot breath against the shell of his ear, he almost jumped. "Maybe you're right then," she whispered. "Maybe it's not technically breaking the pact if we play a little . . . just this once."

Aja pulled back, just enough that he could rub his thumbs over her nipples. He still hadn't gotten the chance to see them. She'd kept her dress on last time, and she'd been facing away while they fucked. It was risky, but he needed to see them. The need made his skin burn. They had both gotten the results of their STI tests back days ago. The relief they had felt that they both tested negative had been palpable.

"Will you show me yourself, Peaches?" He tugged on the hem of her top.

As much as he wanted it, this wasn't the time or place for her to get completely naked. He'd have to fantasize in real time about what her nipples would feel like under his fingertips. He was being forced to choose which thing he valued more, and the thought of his tongue on her pussy overrode everything else.

Pupils wide, lips spread, chest rising and falling, she was breathtaking. She pulled up her shirt a little, right under her breasts so she could get to the button on her shirt. He took his time, taking in the stretch marks on her plush belly and the way her thick waist looked in contrast to her hips.

Then, right there, in the place where her white shorts met her sex, he saw a wet spot. It was small, just beginning to spread, but it made the material of her shorts appear thin. He pressed his nose to it, groaning at how easily he could smell the evidence of her hunger for him.

He traced a finger along the edge of her shorts and watched her belly quiver. The little silver button popped, then the zipper was down. Aja lifted her bottom off the couch, both of them working the shorts off and past her little barely there sandals.

She kept one foot on the floor but threw the other over the back of the couch, opening herself up to him completely.

"I fuckin' knew you weren't wearin' any panties."

"How?"

His grin was dirty. "I could tell, trust me."

He kissed the dark skin on her inner thighs, rubbing his cheeks against her wet heat as if he could soak it into his skin forever.

She was the only thing he could focus on. Just like he did with the rest of her, he drank her in with his eyes. She was a veritable five-course meal for the senses, and every cell in his body cried out for him to consume her.

He blew warm air against her clit, watching as it pulsed.

"Peaches aren't for staring at, Walker. They're for eating."

It was hard to argue with that, so he didn't. Instead, he ran the flat of his tongue between her lips, letting the tip tickle her clit before taking it into his mouth. Her back arched up off the couch, a loud moan escaping her.

He released her, looking up to see her fingers pinching her

nipples. "Shhh, baby, I need you to be quiet. You don't want to get caught do you?"

Aja didn't answer, nor did she seem able to quiet her gasping and moaning.

"Aja, look at me." He conjured up every bit of sternness he had in him. When he caught her eyes, he made sure to keep them. "Unless you want somebody to come in here and see you spread out like Sunday dinner, you've got to hush."

He opened her up with his fingers, licking at the wetness on the surface of her, spreading her pleasure around.

She gripped the hair at the crown of his head, drawing his face deeper until he felt like he was drowning in her. He made a feast out of her, eating and drinking so heartily he was almost sure he sounded like some type of animal. Behind his zipper, his dick was stiff as a brick. Had his hands not been on Aja's body, he would have reached down to jerk himself off—given himself some type of relief.

He'd always taken a special kind of pleasure in pleasing others, but what he felt while pleasing Aja was different, more intense than anything he'd ever experienced. Whatever it was engulfed him, took him under like a heavy, crashing wave. Everything else disappeared and getting her off became his only purpose in life.

When he felt her start to contract around his fingers and tongue, noticed that the shaking in her thighs was becoming more intense and the movement in her hips sloppier, he knew that his purpose was about to be realized.

"Am I goin' to make you come, Peaches?"

"Yes," she bit out between grit teeth, her digits tightening in his hair. "Fuck yes."

"Can I watch?"

But he was too busy bringing her through it with his mouth to see what her face looked like when she came. He imagined her the way she'd been before, when he'd fingered her against her car. Eyes clenched shut, mouth open in a silent scream, too beautiful to even be real. She kept her grip on his hair the whole time, and when she was done, she pushed his head back, hooded eyes staring at the mess she'd made on his face.

"Come here," she said, her voice rough. "Let me kiss you."

"I don't know if I'm ready to share just yet" He ran a tongue over his lips, making a show of cleaning her off of him.

"Nasty . . ." she remarked, leaning up to chase what she could from his mouth.

"We need to get back out there," he mumbled against her lips.

"You want to go back out there with this thing all cocked and loaded?" She pushed up against his crotch, making him grunt.

"Don't have much of a choice, we're already pushin' it, bein' in here so long."

"Why don't you let me . . ." She reached for him, but he shook his head.

"We really don't have the time," he told her. "I don't need anything in return for pleasing you. I promise I don't have any regrets about how this went down, OK?"

She looked at him through her lashes. "No regrets?"

He snorted. "Not a one."

"Not even knowing that we already broke our pact?"

"Honestly . . . not even that."

"I guess one moment of weakness is to be expected." She

reached down to pull her shorts on. "But this can be enough. It *should* be enough. We can stick to our word after this."

Walker had his doubts about that, but he didn't voice them. He told himself that he'd resist the pull of her as hard as he could. Maybe it would work. Mostly he found himself not wanting it to. Trying to stay away from Aja was more work than he'd thought it would be. It was also a shit-ton more upsetting.

"Of course we can. We're two smart, strong-minded millennials. If there's anything we can do, it's stick to a sex pact." He stood up, checking the couch to make sure they hadn't soiled it. Luckily, it was as plush and red and untainted as it had been when they'd first sat down.

She looked like she wanted to kiss him again, and if she tried, he wouldn't object.

"We should probably go for real now." She swallowed, suddenly looking at the wall behind him instead of meeting his gaze. "We've definitely pushed our luck."

"We should stop by the bathroom to wash up first. If somebody asks us where we've been, we won't have to lie completely."

Aja moved first, and he could do nothing but watch her. The euphoria he'd felt moments before had faded into something else— sadness and longing.

"You coming?" She stopped at the door, eyes half hidden by their own lids but beguiling anyway.

"I'm right behind you."

Chapter 21

When Walker had arrived in Charleston for his first year of college, he'd encountered plenty of classmates who'd called him some version of "country boy." He'd come from farther south in the state, and while most of the people he interacted with had accents, his was certainly thicker. He also figured he had a certain kind of air about him, the type of wide-eyed innocence that could only come from someone who'd spent the majority of their life in a tiny town. His gut told him that their jokes were lighthearted, so he took them in stride, blushing or shaking his head anytime someone brought up how they thought he spent his free time running barefoot through the woods near campus or something.

Truth was, he probably couldn't have been further from That Guy if he tried. He'd spent his childhood tucked firmly under the wing of May Abbott and knew more about the plotlines on *Days of Our Lives* than hunting or mudding. He'd been too to-himself to join Boy Scouts and too anxious to go exploring on his own. Which was exactly why he'd surprised himself one morning when he laced up an old pair of boots that he'd found in the back of his closet and stepped into the wooded area behind Gram's house.

A few days after the picnic, Walker had woken up with something heavy sitting in the middle of his chest. He'd rubbed over the area at first, suspecting indigestion or a pulled muscle. It had taken him five minutes of pain before he finally recognized it as anxiety. He'd spent the last few nights wide awake. Tucked into bed and staring up at the moonlit ceiling for hours, growing more exhausted until his body shut down enough to allow him to crash for a couple of hours. The insomnia wasn't exactly new; he'd experienced it plenty of times before. In recent years, he'd come to think of it as an old friend, a distant memory. But it had decided to visit. Just what he needed—yet another thing to make his life difficult.

Talking to Aja about his family's history had made him feel . . . well, he wasn't entirely sure. There had been some measure of relief; part of him had found opening up to her cathartic. But he hadn't told her everything. A larger part of him still found it necessary to hold back. He didn't have all the words himself, so how could he give them to her? Half the time he didn't understand his own feelings surrounding his family well enough to form coherent thoughts about them, let alone share them with other people.

He also still found comfort in keeping himself locked up tight. The last time he'd been in Greenbelt, he'd had a wall around himself so thick and high that even his own grandmother couldn't scale it. The wall had been chipped away at, block by block, during his time in Charleston. But the second he'd driven into those city limits he'd felt it getting strong again. Not as thick or impenetrable as before, but present nonetheless. It was just another thing to add to the list of reasons why it would be ridiculous to pursue something with Aja. He had too much fucking baggage. And his baggage wasn't the regular kind either. It was monogrammed with about a thousand letters, each one representing something in his life that had served to turn him into a man who, he was afraid, didn't have it in him to allow good things for himself. Not when he'd lived a life so devoid of them.

He'd spent days sitting with those moments they'd shared in the mayor's mansion, the state of his relationship with Gram, and his flip-flopping feelings on Greenbelt. All of them playing second fiddle to the anxious, anticipatory boulder that weighed him down anytime he thought about how he would have to confront his father soon. It felt ominous. Like something straight out of one of those shitty horror movies he liked to watch. Gram had told him the news of Benny's impending arrival weeks ago, and it had followed him around like an oppressive shadow ever since. Made worse by how he didn't actually know *when* the man was coming. It was in the back of his mind at all times. He could distract himself when he was doing errands for Gram or sitting next to Aja at bingo. But anytime he got a few seconds alone, while he was making dinner or in the shower, thoughts of Benny snaked to the front of his mind, instantly making his stomach drop.

Walker hoped like hell that his hike through the woods would tire him out enough to send him into a long, dreamless sleep. Managing his mental health was even harder when he couldn't get something as basic as nightly rest. He knew it was a symptom of the PTSD, not the cause, but he was damned near at the end of his rope.

He focused on the crunching of leaves and grass under his boots, the feeling of his heels sinking into the earth with every step. The trees stood tall above him, but they didn't canopy over top, giving him a perfect view of the clear blue sky and bright South Carolina sun. It was so hot out that sweat made his T-shirt stick to his back within minutes. He'd put a baseball cap on backwards to keep his hair out of his face, but wet droplets dripped down his temples anyway. As uncomfortable as it was, the physical strain kept him present and focused. The stretch in his hamstrings, the contracting muscles in his back, everything distracting from the ache of anxiety and anger in his belly.

He walked in a daze, his feet following the trail that he knew would lead him in a flat circle back to Gram's house. The sun stayed in the same place in the sky, making Walker feel like he'd been walking either for hours or mere minutes.

He cringed when the peaceful silence was interrupted by the shrill ring of his phone. His first instinct was to ignore it, to silence the sound and keep walking as if he hadn't heard it. But it could be Gran calling with an emergency, or possibly even Aja calling for . . . well, he didn't know what, but he didn't want to miss it if it was her.

The number that flashed across his screen didn't belong to either. He didn't have it saved in his phone, nor did he recognize it. It had an area code that he didn't know either. He considered ignoring it, but his thumb hovered over the answer button until it seemed to move of its own accord, pressing down before he could stop himself.

"Hello?" His voice was ragged from lack of use.

"Walker?"

One word. One small, miniscule word that he'd heard a million times. That was all it took for him to know who was on the other end of the line. His father.

He didn't say anything. In fact, he held his breath. His rib cage shook with the force of his pounding heart, but he didn't make a move. He could hang up . . . couldn't he? Yes, he could. All he had to do was pull the phone away from his face and press the button, and it would be over. Hell, he could even block the number. So why in the fuck did his body refuse to do something? He found himself stuck. Feet planted on the ground, hand clenched around his phone so tightly, he thought he might be strong enough to bend metal and glass until it shattered.

"Walker, are you there?"

He tried to speak, but nothing came out aside from an audible puff of air.

"OK, listen . . . listen, Wally." He flinched at the familiarity of the nickname. "You don't have to talk but *please* don't hang up. *Please*."

Goddamn him. Walker, for all his anger, couldn't will his body to move fast enough to do it.

Another breath left him.

Benny released a shaky breath too. "I know Mama told you about my plan to move home. I'm . . . I'm sorry you didn't hear that from me. I was bein' cowardly, lettin' her fight my battles with you for me." He let out a bitter laugh. "What else is new, huh?"

Walker's jaw started hurting from clenching his teeth.

"Anyway, I asked her for your number so I could talk to you about it myself. Now before you go gettin' all mad at her, just know that I had to beg, and she didn't give it up easy. It ain't her fault. She's always had a soft spot for her family, and I pressed on it until she caved. I know this ain't . . . it ain't right of me, but I didn't know what else to do. Even if you don't want to talk to me, even if you ain't even really listenin' right now, I need to say this. I need you to know that I'm not just comin' home for Mama. I'm comin' home for you too."

Walker's knees buckled and he had to throw his arm out against a tree to keep himself from falling into the dirt. What was this? What was happening? He felt outside of himself, completely disassociated from reality.

"It's been years since I've talked to you, and I wouldn't be surprised if you never wanted anything to do with me ever again. I know it's the long shot of a lifetime for me. And . . . if that's what you want . . . I'll have to accept that. I made that bed and it'll be only right that I have to fuckin' lie down in it. But, Walker, listen, if there's even a chance that you don't hate me, that you want to give me a second chance, I want to jump on it. I don't know the exact dates yet, but I'll be rollin' through Greenbelt sometime soon to see Mama and look at a few apartments in town. If you're there . . . maybe we can sit down and talk."

Walker lifted his head and looked at his surroundings. There was nothing but him and nature. So why did it feel like Benny was standing in front of him, eyes imploring and lips speaking words Walker simultaneously did and didn't want to hear? He clenched his eyes shut. He didn't know what the hell he wanted. He didn't have any answers for his father because he didn't have any for himself.

The prospect of rekindling his relationship with Benny was daunting. It was muddled with thoughts and feelings that were neither all bad nor all good. Benny was his father, and he didn't hate him, not at all. But he couldn't deny that the trauma he had suffered because of the man's addiction had altered the course of his life completely. He knew his father had an illness, but everything Walker did and said and thought now were products of it. He'd never been able to escape the repercussions of Benny's actions, but he had been able to escape the man himself. And there was something comforting about that. The type of soothing control that came with denying someone access to you.

It was a multifaceted issue, and Walker didn't know if he had it in him to face it head-on. It was a heavy burden, and he'd never been too proud to cower when things started feeling impossible to handle. He'd thought that if he could ignore his father forever, he'd never have to confront his conflicting feelings about him. It was macabre, sure, but he figured they'd be those people who said nothing then died silently with their hearts filled with regret. But now it was becoming clear that wouldn't be the case.

Benjamin Abbott was here, and he wasn't going anywhere. Even if Walker did decide that he didn't want a relationship, they'd be in the same state permanently. It might not happen immediately, but Benny would start coloring the edges of Walker's life. Especially with him and Gram on better terms.

"Look, I don't want to keep you any longer." Benny spoke quietly after a long pause. He sniffled, and Walker wondered if he was crying. The thought made his heart contract. "Just . . . just know that I love you, boy. More than anything. And I'm sorry. I live with my guilt and my shame every day, but that pales in comparison to the pain and trouble I've caused you. You didn't deserve it. You deserved better than me and your mama both. But I'm . . . I'm doin' well, have been for a while. And I'd like you to see me like this. So, if you'd be willin' to talk when I come into town, it would mean a lot to your old man. I . . . I love you. Hopefully I'll talk to you soon. Bye."

Benny hung up almost as soon as he got the last word out of his mouth. It wasn't until he heard silence on the other end that Walker was able to pull the phone away from his face. He stared at it. Eyes bleary and searching, as if the ridiculous little device he was so attached to had answers to the questions swirling around in his brain.

A bird flew overhead, the flapping of its wings breaking the silence, making Walker jump back into reality. He tucked the phone into his pocket, intending to continue his hike. But he only made it a few steps before he lost interest. It wasn't going to be easy to keep his mind off this anymore. Not when things were becoming more complicated by the second.

He didn't need a distraction. He needed . . . he needed a fucking bright spot. Something happy. Something that made him feel so good that his brain couldn't help but provide him with relief.

Here, in this town, with these people, and his history—that wasn't such an easy thing to come by. But it wasn't impossible. Not when he knew someone whose mere name made him feel light. Not when he knew Aja Owens.

He pulled his phone out, finding her number in seconds and pressing the call button before he could convince himself to stop. Her voice was just as sweet as always when she answered. One word from her and his lips were already quirking up into a smile.

"Hey," he responded, then cleared his throat. "Do you want to hang out today? I miss your face."

He could practically hear Aja rolling her eyes, but he could also hear the smile in her voice when she answered. "I have a couple errands to run in town, if you want to cart me around," she said. "But only because I don't feel like driving. . . . Not because I miss your face or anything. Because that would be weird."

The relief that enveloped him made his head fall back. He didn't care if she wanted him to sit next to her while she watched paint dry—he'd do it happily. He just needed to see her. Anything. He'd do anything to be with her right now. "Give me an hour," he said, already making his way back the way he came. "I'll be there soon."

Chapter 22

Walker had never been to an enjoyable dinner party. All the ones he'd attended had been stuffy. Full of food he didn't care to eat and conversations he didn't care to have. Granted, they'd mostly been work-related, but even the ones thrown by Corey and his girlfriend always ended with him needing a couple of days to recharge afterward.

When Aja had extended an invitation to go to one with her, he'd had half a mind to turn her down. But her question had sounded so desperate, as if she had been holding her breath waiting for his answer, that he hadn't been able to say anything but yes. She'd told him that one of her new friends was throwing a dinner party with her boyfriend. The other two women in the group were bringing along people they were dating, and while they'd said that it would be fine for Aja to come solo, she was mortified at the thought of being a seventh wheel. So on Sunday evening, he found himself dressed in a starched button-down and slacks, sitting at an unfamiliar kitchen island with a fidgety Aja next to him.

"Uhm, I'm sorry we got here so early," Aja told Jade, who was stirring something in a pot on the stove.

"Oh, it's fine, girl. I should have told you that Miri and Liv love being late." She turned to Walker with a sly smile. "Can I make you a drink, Walker? We've got some good whiskey on the bar cart."

"No, thank you. I'm good with this sweet tea for now."

"All right, just let me know. I make a mean old-fashioned. I'll even take my tiny kitchen flamethrower to an orange peel for you, since you're a guest and all."

His laugh was genuine. "I'll keep that in mind."

When they'd arrived, Jade had said that her boyfriend had run out to get some wine and would be back shortly. He hoped that the other guests showed up around the same time as the boyfriend's return. The only thing worse than actively participating in a dinner party was sitting around in stilted silence waiting for said dinner party to start.

On the way over, he'd made sure to think up a few conversation points—general things about his work and popular television shows and movies. He could spend a ton of time making conversation by complimenting the food, even if he didn't end up loving it. He figured he had enough for a couple of hours. Past that, he had no idea what he'd talk about with people he didn't know and would probably never get to know. Which was exactly why he didn't want to waste all his semi-interesting talking points on awkward pre-dinner banter.

Aja looked as tense as he felt on the inside. She fiddled with her fingers on top of the island, dragging her nails across her palms, flicking her wrists, trying to crack her fingers every few moments. He could feel her leg bouncing underneath the table.

She'd told him that her friendship with these people was new, that she still wasn't entirely sure of her place in the group. It was why she didn't feel comfortable being a seventh wheel yet. Walker knew her pain well, understood it in an incredibly personal way. He also knew that nothing he could say would calm her nerves. That would only happen when she started to feel secure, and it wasn't words from him that would help her get there.

From the outside, he could see clearly that Jade liked Aja. When they'd come in, Jade had asked Aja if she could give her a hug. When Aja had agreed, Jade had all but attacked her with her arms, the look on her face distinctly happy.

Walker wasn't sure if Jade felt the need to impress Aja, or if she was always like this, but she'd pulled out all the stops when they'd gotten settled. She'd offered Aja nearly every item in her fridge as a snack. She'd even told her that she would call her boyfriend and get him to bring something back from the store if she needed it.

Aja had refused all but a glass of water and the cheese plate Jade had already set out on the table, and Jade had looked slightly disappointed at the low-maintenance request. When Aja mentioned that the meal Jade was making happened to be one of her favorites, the letdown on the other woman's face immediately gave way to elation.

He sat there, his eyes going between the women like a tennis match, trying to discern their every action and expression. It was obvious to him that they both cared immensely. About what the other thought, about how they themselves were coming off, about the meaning behind accepting only a glass of water when there was perfectly good sweet tea *right there*. It was completely fascinating and clear that there were no bizarre ulterior motives or cattiness going on——just the nervous first blush of a budding friendship.

He wondered if the dance would become more intricate once the others arrived or if their presence would balance things out, make everyone a little calmer. He sure as hell hoped it was the latter. But it might have been hard for Aja to think that far ahead, past the discomfort she was currently feeling towards a different outcome. So he did the only thing he could without possibly embarrassing her in front of someone else. Slowly, he slid his hand up her leg, past her smooth calf and around her shin until he reached her knee. Softer and fleshier than his was, it was pliable under his fingers. When his thumb started to make circles on her skin, her leg stopped bouncing. Her hands continued to fidget, flicking and dragging and stretching, but she smiled over at him——sweet and grateful.

"OK, so——" Jade stopped, shook her head, breathed deep, then spoke again. "Just . . . am I supposed to keep pretendin' like I don't know you or . . . ?"

For a moment, Walker thought she was talking to Aja, but when he looked over at her, he saw her staring right back, eyes wide.

"Oh my God," Aja whispered. "I can't believe I forgot. . . ."

Walker's head began to spin. "Wait, what?"

"You guys went to high school together," Aja whispered. "Olivia and Miri too. They mentioned you when we were hanging out a few weeks ago and I . . . completely forgot. How could I forget?" The last part, she whispered to herself, but he heard it anyway.

His mouth gaped. He was sure that he looked ridiculous, but he couldn't bring himself to stop.

"So I take it you don't remember me?" Jade joked.

He didn't. Not at all. There wasn't a single thing about her that he'd recognized upon meeting her. High school had been a murky time for him. Around eighth grade, he'd realized that leaving Greenbelt for good would be his only real chance at happiness. That if he wanted a good life, one away from the town he hated, he'd probably need to go to college. He also realized that he came from a family with very little money and the only way out would be through grants and scholarships and loans. So, he'd started applying himself. He'd spent the entirety of his four years in high school trying to maintain an A average while making himself as invisible as possible. He didn't try to make friends. In fact, he'd actively rejected the idea. He told himself that it was better if he was alone. There would be less to hold him back and less to lose once he finally left. By the time he got to the College of Charleston, most of his peers at Greenbelt Senior High School were nothing but blurred faces in his mind.

Shame started to creep in, making his ears flame and his chest tight. He thought he'd known awkward dinner parties before, but this one had already taken the cake, and it hadn't even started yet. His brain started flooding with excuses to hightail it out of there. He wondered how shitty it would be, on a scale of one to ten, to fake an emergency with Gram's health.

"I didn't mean to make you feel bad," Jade said, wincing. "It's not like we were friends or anything. I'm not, like, offended that you don't remember me. I just thought it would be weird if I sat across from you all night knowing who you were and not saying anything to acknowledge it."

Walker didn't know what to say. He considered lying, telling her that he did recognize her, just for the relief he might feel once the awkwardness dissipated. But that didn't feel right. He also didn't know how he would keep up the lie if she wanted to take a stroll down memory lane. The only thing about high school that he remembered less than his classmates were the antics they'd gotten into.

"I'm sorry," he said instead. "In high school I was . . . I wasn't very friendly. I was goin' through a lot of shit."

"Yeah, I remember." Jade smiled kindly at him. "And I'm sure all that small-town high school bullshit did nothin' to help. Like I said, I'm not surprised you don't remember me. I was way too concerned with myself in high school to reach out, even to people who obviously needed somebody to reach out to them."

Her words weren't an apology—not necessarily. But they were an acknowledgment, the first he'd gotten in Greenbelt from anyone except for his grandmother. It was a bizarre thing, the way it made him happy and angry at the same time.

"It's not your fault," he told her. "I needed more help than any of you could give me anyway."

Jade shook her head, dissatisfied. "It still wasn't right. Greenbelt should have been better to you, Wally," she coughed. "I mean, Walker. It probably means next to nothin' at this point, but those of us who have grown the hell up have realized that people deserved better from us. You deserved better from us."

His jaw clenched tight, trying hard to hold back an onslaught of tears or words or unrestrained emotions. Yet again, Walker didn't know what to say. Didn't know how to convey what he was feeling because he didn't know what that feeling was. All he knew was that it was more good than bad.

"Thank you," he managed to choke out between his clenched teeth. "Thank you, Jade."

She flashed him an understanding smile, her shoulders un-tightening when she turned back to her stirring.

Walker nearly gasped in relief when he heard the lock on the front door turn. Five people stumbled through the doorway, talking and laughing the way only people who knew each other well could.

Jade seemed a little startled as she put the top back on her pot and went to greet everyone. He and Aja stood, fingers brushing as they watched the exchange of kisses and hugs.

"I really am sorry," Aja said. "I should have remembered we talked about you, that they knew you. Now I've put you in an awkward situation and I . . . I'm just really sorry. We can leave if you're uncomfortable, OK? I'll tell them that I'm not feeling well, and we can go."

He was still trying to wrap his head around his feelings. It was disconcerting to be in a room of people who knew you—or, at least, knew of you—but who you didn't remember. He wasn't angry at Aja though. She wouldn't knowingly put him in an un-comfortable situation.

He hooked his index finger and curled it around hers. "I'm all right, just a little shocked. But you don't need to blame yourself, OK? Somethin' like this was bound to happen at some point. I'm surprised it wasn't sooner."

"But you'll still let me know if you want to leave? I don't want you to suffer just for me. One dinner party isn't more important than your mental health."

"I will let you know if I want to leave," he agreed.

"Promise?"

He lifted their hands and placed a dry kiss on the back of her finger. "Yes, Peaches, I promise."

It was the first time he'd called her that outside of a sexual context, but it felt right. Settled. From the way her expression changed from distressed to pleased, he could tell Aja liked it just as much as he did. He looked at her for a while, glowing under his gaze even in the face of discomfort. Bright and beautiful, outshining every other thing in his head. He felt strengthened by her, and that strength was only bolstered by how she seemed to draw the same thing from him.

"Now, introduce me to your new friends before I start throwin' my emotions up all over the cheese tray or somethin'."

Chapter 23

"My heart is about to get broken."

Dr. Sharp chuckled, unfolding her arms from across her chest to lean forward. Her face was all up in the camera, and Aja found it impossible to stray from her gaze.

"I didn't know you had the power to see the future."

Aja snorted. "I didn't until I met Walker. Now I see the future coming from a mile away, and I'm scared it's going to tear me apart. I thought that if I could prepare myself by knowing it was going to happen it would hurt less, but now I'm not so sure."

"Heartbreak is like any other loss," Dr. Sharp said. "It doesn't matter how much we try to brace ourselves; the blow never comes any softer."

Aja swallowed, tears collecting in the corners of her eyes. It felt like she'd already had her chest cut open, and Walker hadn't even left yet. She was staring down the barrel of absolute devastation and she could do nothing to keep the shot from coming. The pure helplessness of it made her knees buckle.

"How am I supposed to keep it from tearing me apart though?" she asked, tone dripping with desperation. "How am I supposed to be OK after he's gone?"

Dr. Sharp paused, placing her chin between her thumb and index finger. It was such a stereotypically therapist move that it should have been amusing.

"You're very focused on trying to stop the hurt from coming right now. But I don't necessarily believe that's the wisest choice. The hurt is going to come, Aja. You're a person who feels things very keenly, you're only going to harm yourself if you try to push down that part of you."

"So, what am I supposed to do?" Aja sniffed. "Just let myself hurt?"

"Yes," Dr. Sharp said simply.

Aja scoffed. "How is that supposed to help me any?"

"Allowing yourself to experience your emotions fully is only going to make you stronger. You already know what happens when you try to suppress them. They've got to come out sometime, some way, and will likely cause you a lot of harm once it gets to that point."

As hurt as she was, she didn't want to harm herself. She'd come so far with her mental health. She still had a long way to go, would likely always be working hard at being her own version of OK. But seeing the forest for the trees was easier said than done.

"Everyone says it's bad to wallow in heartbreak. I thought that all the crying and ice cream and sad music were bad for you."

"They're wrong." Dr. Sharp's tone was matter-of-fact. "What's bad is trying to force yourself into fake happiness and positivity that you're not ready to feel yet."

"But what do I do?"

"You do whatever you think you need to in order to feel every-thing fully and come out on the other side."

"And if that involves a couple gallons of ice cream and a lot of Adele?"

"Then that's perfectly OK."

• • •

Aja sat through most of Wednesday night bingo with what felt dangerously like a pile of bricks in the pit of her stomach. It was nearing the end of July, and Walker would be leaving Greenbelt in a little over a week. He would be leaving her—leaving them—behind. Not that there was any real, cohesive "them" to leave . . . but hell, wasn't that the overlying issue in and of itself?

They had been very artfully avoiding talking about his im-minent departure in any explicit terms. Instead, whenever either of them brought it up, they'd just say "when Gram/Ms. May gets her casts off." They were absolutely taking the coward's way out, but she didn't really know what to do about it. As much as she wanted to have an in-depth conversation with him about the state of things, she also really, really didn't.

She'd spent so much time over the past few weeks trying to squash her growing feelings for Walker. For a while, she'd felt con-fident that she could keep herself from falling for him. Then, when she hadn't been able to accomplish that, she'd thought she could mit-igate her pain by working him out of her system naturally. Allowing herself to feel all the twirly feelings and act on her sexual cravings so that when it was all over, her fond memories would lessen the sting of his absence. She'd been utterly ridiculous to ever think that could work. The good times they'd had together would only serve as heart-breaking reminders once she finally got left behind.

She needed to talk to him, to tell him that she was almost one hundred percent positive that she was in love with him—a fact that had nearly made her body collapse in on itself once she became cognizant of it. The need to do this wasn't born out of a belief that Walker would change his mind about leaving and stay in Greenbelt forever with her—for her—but because she didn't want to leave anything unsaid. She didn't know how she was supposed to survive knowing that she'd had the chance to tell him something so important but decided against it.

But, fuck, it was hard. Every time she contemplated uttering the words, she froze up. Sweat beaded up on her forehead and her palms, and her mouth refused to make words. Like always, she found herself torn between what she wanted to do and the limitations of what her brain would allow.

Aja was trying to work on it. She hoped that she would manage to get the words out before he left, even if it at the last possible second.

Until then, she did what she'd been doing for months: used bingo to distract herself from her difficult reality. Walker sat to her left and Ms. May to his left, the three of them quieter than they'd ever been during a bingo game.

About halfway through, Aja was closer to getting a bingo than any other time she'd played. One of her blue sheets only had one spot left to fill in the center of the layout. She didn't consider herself lucky by any means. Mostly she considered herself the exact opposite. It seemed almost statistically impossible, but she had never been one square away from winning. She still didn't believe that a random Wednesday in July was going to be the night that it happened for her, yet she couldn't help but get excited.

She knew what it meant if she won. Understood fully that the pact she and Walker had made was still intact. And while either of them could pull out of it at any time if they didn't want to participate, the option was there. The chance to have him again dangled in the balance. That felt exceptionally precarious, since she had so few chances left for it to happen.

Her eyes scanned her sheet with sharper and sharper focus at every ball that was pulled. Each time a number she didn't have was called, she became slightly more demoralized. There were only three balls left spinning in the cage. That meant three very close, very real chances for her to walk out of the hall with a win and an excuse to have Walker inside her again. She shivered. It was so close, but she refused to let herself believe it would actually happen. She would save herself from the disappointment when she had to crawl into her bed alone again. She wasn't going to win. She was not one of the lucky ones. Hadn't she learned that already?

It seemed to happen in slow motion. The caller's thin lips formed words that she couldn't read from across the room, no matter how hard she tried.

"N69—either way up."

Aja gasped, sucking in air so hard that she nearly choked on it. She'd gotten it. She'd won. She'd fucking won.

She looked over at Walker, eyes wide in shock. He looked confused for a second before he looked down at her sheet and saw the horizontal row of dauber prints right in the center. His eyes widened too, realization flooding into his gaze.

"Say somethin'," he said quietly.

"What?" She was too stunned to comprehend much.

"You have to tell them you won, Aja."

She swallowed. Was there anything someone with an anxiety disorder hated more than public speaking? Well, yes, tons of things, but it was still pretty fucking far up the list. She wanted this too much not to claim it though. Wanted to be able to say that she'd won, wanted the prize and recognition that came with it. And more than anything, she wanted the chance to be with the man she loved again.

"Bingo!" A few heads turned to stare, but the caller made no move to show that he'd heard her. It was mortifying. "B-Bingo!" she said again, louder. Raising an arm up, waving it around to draw more attention to herself.

It seemed to take the caller forever to make his way to her. When he got to her side of the table, he had to squeeze past the large pole to her right to get to her. It made her cringe.

She held her breath as the caller looked over her sheet. His slightly shaky index finger tracing the bingo as he made sure it was legitimate.

"B47, I12, N69, G2, O25. Well"—he straightened—"looks like we've got a bingo. Congratulations, young lady."

"Th-thank you."

The confirmation only made her heart beat faster. She took the proof-of-win with trembling hands, turning to look at Walker and Ms. May again. The older woman was grinning, reaching a hand across the table to congratulate her with a warm pat. Walker's gaze was heavier; he'd moved past the initial shock and settled on something else entirely. She knew exactly what because it was mirrored in her own. This win of hers was worth more than the $300 prize. It meant heat and pleasure and closeness and intimacy. It meant everything.

Chapter 24

"You know, I've never actually had sex in this bed before," she said.

Walker's hands seemed to be everywhere, stroking and plucking and caressing her so sweetly that she was breathless without any kind of exertion.

"Wait, what?" He pulled his lips away from where they were sucking at the skin of her collarbones. "Seriously?"

Aja nodded. "I haven't been with anyone since I got to Greenbelt. The only person I've been fucking in this bed is myself."

"Damn." His breath came out in a rush. "That definitely shouldn't be as hot as it is, but fuck if that doesn't make me want to screw you into this mattress even harder to prove I was the first one here."

It was unrealistic to assume she'd never have anyone else in her bed, especially after he left. As hard of a time as she had connecting with people, she still didn't plan on being alone forever. But she might have to toss this mattress for a new one once that happened. This was only the second time Walker had been in her apartment, and his first time in her bed, but already it felt like he belonged there, as if allowing anyone else to encroach on this mattress would be a betrayal to the man who had unwittingly taken ownership of it.

After the bingo game was over, Walker had dropped Ms. May off at home and met Aja back at her apartment in under twenty minutes. Aja had been waiting in her doorway, and the second he'd reached the top of the stairs they had jumped on each other. Chests pressed together, arms tangled, they'd kissed like it was the first and last time. He had walked her backwards, his mouth firmly attached to hers, until the backs of her knees touched the edge of her bed and she descended into softness.

It was the first time she'd felt the luxury of his full weight on top of her. Pressing into her body so exquisitely that she flooded her panties instantly. She spread her thighs, her short button-down denim skirt so stiff that it moved to the top of her legs as Walker slid between them. His length was stiff behind his jeans, and she moved her hips up so she could rub herself against him. The edge of his zipper brushed her clit through her panties, the relief of it so intense that it made her throw her head back.

He'd taken his shoes off at the door, just as she'd requested. Now she watched through hooded eyes as he lifted up to tug his shirt off and push down his jeans and underwear. Instead of getting back on top of her immediately, he stared down at her. She lay there, still clothed but totally disheveled as her eyes raked over him.

It was the first time she'd been able to see him fully naked. To take in the true gloriousness of his broad shoulders and firm chest. His small pink nipples, the dip of his hips, those long, lean legs.

And there, right in the center of it all, his dick. Jutting out of a thatch of dark blond hair, it curved up towards his stomach. Seeing him like this only made her want him more. Her mouth wetted as much as her sex, and she started to sit up, reaching to grab him by the hips and bring him to her mouth.

"I just realized that I didn't get to see you naked either time we did this," he said eyeing her. "You think you could find it in yourself to rectify that?"

There wasn't a single piece of her that wanted to deny his request. Her hands rushed to the hem of her shirt, but he stopped her before she could lift it off.

"Do it slowly. Tease me, Aja. We don't have to rush. Do it like we have all the time in the world together. Like watchin' you bare yourself to me is the only thing I'll ever have to do again."

It was a very tall order, but one she was eager to fulfill. She didn't know how to be sexy in that way. Like the people in movies and TV shows who turned taking off a pair of jeans into a softcore porn production. She figured it would be better if she didn't try to imitate that at all. Instead of biting down on her lip in some fake imitation of sexiness and imagining cheesy music in her head, she focused her attention on Walker. On the way he made her feel every time he looked at her. Like she was alluring enough to make him lose his shit at the drop of a hat.

She let her fingers drag her shirt up slowly, over the fat of her stomach, past her belly button and the stretch marks that she felt no need to hide. Then, farther up, until her bra was revealed. She'd gotten dressed this evening knowing there was a possibility of this happening. She hadn't been sure, but she'd had enough hope to choose one of the matching sets of lingerie she had: a pale pink unlined demi-cup bra covered in delicate lace and a matching thong. She found herself eager to show them to him. Judging by the way his lips curled when she finally pulled her shirt off, she'd made an excellent choice.

"You're perfect, Peaches, the most divine creature ever put on this Earth. I swear."

Her teeth nearly cracked from the force of her shudder. Her mind went blank as rapture rushed through her and made her skin sing. Her mouth opened as she tried to find the words to tell him that she disagreed, because it was he who held that title. But nothing came out. She was too struck. She was no stranger to experiencing brain fog, times when her mind moved sluggishly in reaction to some kind of stimulus. But this was different because it made her feel the opposite of awful.

"Keep goin', baby, we're almost there."

She may not have been able to form words, but she could still follow directions surprisingly well. She popped the top button on her skirt, and Walker wrapped a fist around himself, the skin pulling tight over his knuckles and going slightly white as he squeezed. He stroked his length slowly as she popped each individual button. Normally, she would have only undone a couple before squeezing it down her hips, but he'd told her to make it last, and she felt nothing if not compliant.

He stopped stroking when she got to the last button. She pulled the sides open, revealing the little triangle of her underwear.

"Open your legs more, let me see all of it."

The heat she felt lessened a little as she exposed herself. Walker stared right at her center, eyes burning a hole through the gusset of her panties.

"You're so wet I can damn near see through them," he bit out through a clenched jaw. "Will you turn around on your knees for me?"

She was graceless but efficient, turning herself over and up in seconds. She heard him walk forward, and she settled when he finally put his hand on her ass. His touch burned hot and made her nerves spark. He stroked her, pushing forward some in a silent request for her to lean on her forearms a little more. Then his other hand was there, and both were working to spread her open from behind.

His finger stroked down the seam of her, lightly pressing it between her lips, brushing so subtly against her clit that she whined.

"Can I eat it, Aja? Fuck, Peaches, tell me I can."

"I'll start crying if you don't," she gasped.

Her panties were pushed firmly to the side, resting wetly in the crease between her thigh and her sex. Before she could catch her breath, Walker was licking into her. Hot and wet, she dug her nails into her palms as her legs shook from the sensations.

"So good . . ." She was damned near delirious. "Feels so good, Walker."

He growled into her pussy and the vibrations made her shriek. His fingers were too busy holding her open to fuck her with them. She was so wired up that she didn't need them anyway. He sent slow licks over her clit with the flat of his tongue that made her dip her hips back, fucking his face with abandon.

It was all so much. The position she was in felt good and nasty, she knew that he could see the deepest parts of her. She could hear him too, his light moans as he brought her closer and closer to the edge. And she was there in no time, her hips stopping their rocking to tense as she felt her orgasm build.

She came with her face towards the sky, yelling so loud she was sure her neighbors could hear. Walker drank her down, licking and sucking at her pussy until her orgasm subsided completely.

She waited until he moved back to turn around.

"I want to see your face this time." Her breath was still shallow.

The first time, she'd turned her back to him, hoping that not seeing his face would make things easier. It hadn't, not at all. And since she already knew what the outcome would be, there was no way she was going to deny herself the chance to look upon his face this time.

He was silent as he reached for his jeans, grabbing a condom out of a pocket and coming towards her with intent as he sheathed himself.

He nudged himself against her clit, slicking himself with her before he slid inside. Her nails dug into his back. She hoped that she marked him, created divots or scratches that stuck around even after he was gone. Something physical to remember her by every time his shirt rubbed against his back.

He stared down at her, gaze intense, as he started rocking his hips. She'd never been great at maintaining eye contact, but she found herself unable to look away. She could hear the sounds from outside flowing in through her windows, feel the heat that their thrusting bodies created, even the slick-slide of his dick fucking her was loud and clear.

"Tell me how I'm makin' you feel, Aja."

"You have no idea," she gasped. "No. Fucking. Idea."

"I might have a little bit of one." He pressed a bruising kiss to her lips, his slim hips moving even harder.

Walker buried his face in her neck, gripping her braids just enough to make her gush around him.

Her pussy fluttered, and she felt his dick pulse. Bringing her thighs up, she rested them on his hips, it was a strain, but it allowed him to move in her with more force. It rocked the bed, causing her box spring to creak and moan right along with her.

"Peaches"—he bit her earlobe—"are you goin' to come for me again?"

"Yes . . ."

"Right now?"

"God, yes! Yes!"

She shuddered as his thumb rubbed over her clit.

"Good."

She didn't need time, no more than a few seconds. His words, the dark cadence of his voice, and the way he felt, pressing every single one of her buttons made her second orgasm crash into her like a freight train. It took her breath away, sending her head back into her pillow and her hips harder into his. Stars and confetti and everything good and right exploded behind her eyes. She was so far gone that she barely registered Walker's orgasm until his hands gripped her hips tight enough to make her aware of the outside world again.

"You know what?" Still inside her, his body pressed up close, Walker broke them both out of their trance. "I don't think anything is ever goin' to top that."

Her giggle was damned near girlish. "Missionary is vastly underrated."

"You're tellin' me."

She felt at a loss when he moved off her to settle in at her side. She cuddled closer immediately, her ear to his chest and a leg thrown over his. They were silent as they caught their breath. Each minute that passed had Aja feeling a greater sense of urgency. She needed to tell him how she felt. She didn't care about being cool or waiting for the right time or the right way. She wasn't even sure those things existed. The words bubbled up in her throat, making her gullet feel compressed.

"Walker?"

"Yeah," he sounded half asleep. Maybe that was OK. She could say it, and even if he was too far gone to retain it, she could clear out the need, get it over with.

"I-I think I—"

She was cut off by the shrill ringing of a phone that wasn't hers.

Walker jumped, moving out of bed to grab his jeans off the floor and remove his phone from the back pocket.

"It's Gram," he said, eyebrows furrowed.

Her heart stuck in her throat. She'd been seconds away from saying something that could have changed everything—whether for better or worse, she didn't know. It had taken everything in her to work up the courage to even consider saying the words. She didn't know if she had enough in her to muster up a second attempt.

Walker spoke to Ms. May in hushed tones. Aja turned her attention to her nails, a full set of clear polish with colorful little flowers glued down between two layers. Miri had worked on them for nearly two hours. Placing each flower in its perfect position before she was satisfied. Aja had loved them before. Now they were the only thing she allowed herself to focus on, so she didn't meddle.

She watched in real time, through subtle peeks at his hunched

over body, as his shoulders got tighter. He straightened slowly until his back was a ramrod and a deep line appeared between his
shoulder blades. Something was wrong. She wondered if it was
appropriate for her to comfort him. She wondered if it would be
rude to get dressed.

"All right," she heard him say. "I'll see you in a little bit, bye."

He hung up, and she didn't even have time to admire the sight of
his bare ass before he was sliding his underwear and jeans back on.

"You don't have to go, do you?" Aja hated how vulnerable she
sounded. Damned near pathetic.

He turned to look at her. His face was contorted. Jaw clenched,
eyes drawn, that not-quite-pouty mouth in a dramatic downward
tilt. It was strange to see someone transition from a state of post-
orgasmic bliss to one of what looked like pure terror in a matter of
minutes.

"Are you OK?" She rushed to stand up, not caring about her
naked state. "Did something trigger you? Do you need—"

"No." He shook his head and cursed under his breath, shoving
his shirt awkwardly down his torso. "I mean yes, but I . . .

He stopped again, and she was left floundering.

"I need to go." Even his voice was stressed.

"Home? Is something going on with Gram?"

He took in a heavy, shaky breath that had her moving closer.
"No." Another breath. "Gram is fine. She's fine. I just need to go."

"OK. . . ." Aja tried to wrap her mind around what he was
telling her. "Was it something I did? Did I—"

"No." The word was finite. "It's not you. It's never you. M-my
dad is comin'. He's comin' tomorrow and I need to go. I *can't* be in
the same place with him. I can't."

Her knees went weak, and she had to lock her legs to stay upright. He wasn't talking about leaving her apartment. He was
talking about leaving Greenbelt. Now. As in *right now*. She'd
known this was coming. This had always been the inevitable end
to what they had. So why did it feel so sudden?

"OK, I understand, Walker. But can we talk for a second? I
have . . . I need to say something."

He shook his head, slipping his feet into his shoes. "I can't
think right now. I can't. I can't."

Her eyes watered. "Oh . . ."

He stood up, clothes on, phone and keys in hand. He was ready
to go. Ready to leave her.

Aja opened her mouth to speak, but no words came. What was
there to say? She wasn't about to beg him to stay. Not when he felt
so badly like he needed to go. Who would that benefit?

She grabbed the flat sheet from the bed, wrapping it around
herself, covering her body in an effort to feel less exposed. Her footsteps were small as she followed him to the door.

"I'm sorry," he told her. She couldn't take her eyes off of his
hand as it curled around the knob. "I'm so sorry, Aja. You deserve
better than this. There was no way I could have . . ." He ran a
hand through his hair. "This was always how this was goin' to
end, I think. I was fuckin' foolin' myself."

She could hear his feet thunder on the old wooden steps as they
took him downstairs. She stood at the door until she heard his
truck drive off. Then she waited, convinced that he would come
back. When he didn't, the tears finally fell.

Chapter 25

He was a coward. There was no way around it. Settling into the core of him, right down to his very bones, was a type of cowardice he hadn't even known was possible for him to inhabit.

He'd mulled over his actions a thousand times. Trying to come to some kind of conclusion that didn't leave him believing whole-heartedly that he was an awful person. He never got there though. No justification was enough to quell his self-loathing. How could it? He'd run out on both his Gram and Aja without so much as a real explanation why.

He'd left Aja's in a daze, his head hurting as much as his heart as he pushed his truck hard to get to Gram's faster. When he'd gotten there, she'd been sitting in her spot on the couch, the table lamp on beside her. She hadn't been watching the television or reading the paper; she'd been staring straight ahead. She didn't even look up when he came in. Made no move to stop him when he thundered up the stairs to his room.

He had his bags packed in five minutes. He had laundry waiting to come out of the dryer, but he made no move to retrieve it. He'd just count it as another loss. One in a long line of losses he was experiencing.

He stopped by the couch when he made it back downstairs, bags in hand. His jaw tight. He didn't know what to say. Especially knowing that he was about to hurt her. He tried to lessen the blow by reminding himself that she'd been through this exact scenario once before. Hell, the first time she'd had even longer to prepare. What did it say about him that his own grandmother was so used to him leaving that he doubted this would even be a blip on her radar?

He'd told her that he loved her on the way out. Told her that he was sorry, so, so sorry, but he wasn't ready to see Benny yet. Wasn't ready for whatever life-changing thing was going to roll into Greenbelt along with his father.

She'd said that she understood, but the weariness in her voice was obvious. Shame folded over him, thick like a blanket, but it wasn't enough to make him stay.

He got to Charleston in the wee hours of the morning. The relief he felt upon seeing the city skyline from the highway was nearly enough to make him cry. He made it back to his silent apartment, threw his bags down by the door, and passed out on the couch within minutes.

It wasn't until the next afternoon that the relief of being home found itself confronted with the pain of what he'd left in Greenbelt.

Being back in a place where he could walk down the street and know that the shadow of his past wasn't visible to everyone else felt incredible. So did not being paranoid when he heard people around him laugh or chuckle. Those feelings were invaluable, and he'd missed them.

He was also thankful to be back in his apartment, where the walls were thicker, and in his bed, with a mattress that didn't have his back hurting when he woke up. He also got to be truly alone for the first time in almost two full months. That might have been the best part: the silence, the freedom to walk around his house with his dick out without worrying about anyone else.

He'd missed his friends, the easy camaraderie that he hadn't always realized was so important to him. He'd even missed his office—though he planned on talking to his editor about transitioning to remote work once he got settled in a little more. He had enjoyed the freedom of it and had even been more productive working from Gram's house than at his actual desk.

There was also the tepid relief that came with not having to deal with the state of his relationship with his father. He wasn't completely delusional; it would have to come sometime. It loomed over him, shadowing everything he did.

He had more than one shadow too. One seemed to exist for every good thing he'd walked out on. He missed his Gram in a way he hadn't let himself miss her in years. He missed the smell of her perfume and hearing her whistle as she moved about the house in the morning. Missed the way she threaded her fingers through his hair and made him feel like a coddled child again.

He'd left with the promise that he would reach out to her more, and that when he did, their conversations would be better than they'd been in the past. He'd promised that he'd keep opening up to her and allow her to do the same.

And there was Aja.

Thinking about her made his chest ache. He knew he should try to get his mind off her, but he couldn't bring himself to. She invaded every single one of his thoughts. He didn't have her physical presence with him, couldn't touch her or talk to her—hell, he hadn't even had the forethought to take a picture of her before he fled. When left with nothing but memories, his mind refused to wipe her out.

She was there when he woke up, while he worked, before he went to sleep. He jerked off to the thought of her damned near every day. It was nothing for him to experience something interesting or funny and immediately get punched in the gut with the need to tell her about it. He always forgot that he couldn't. Then when he remembered, he was almost knocked off his feet by the reality of it.

He hadn't planned to end things that way. He hadn't been entirely sure how he and Aja were going to bring about the end of their arrangement, but he knew that they hadn't planned on this. Not him leaving in the middle of the night, right after the best sex of his life, without so much as an earnest good-bye. God, he was an asshole. Every way he turned it, he was at fault, and that made him feel like the most worthless piece of shit in the world.

He had her number in his phone, still sitting right up near the top of his recent calls list. His thumb had hovered over the call button a dozen times since he'd been back in Charleston, but he never pressed it. He didn't know what to say or how to say it. There was no explanation he could give her that would make his actions any less awful. She was probably better off without him. Maybe a clean break was what she needed to forget him completely— though the same could never be said for him.

So he wallowed. Alone in his rumpled bed. He spent the time that he didn't spend working thinking about her. About the count-less different ways that things could have turned out for them.

Maybe the mature thing would have been to try out a friend-ship. Maybe that would have meant they were extra evolved, that their relationship went past the need for a romantic entanglement. But Walker didn't want to be her friend. He'd already tried that, and he'd failed so spectacularly that he had gone and fallen in love with her like a fool.

He resigned himself to spending his days without her, con-stantly wondering, forever longing. He moved through his life as he would have before. Now, though, everything felt sluggish, de-void of vitality. He tried to hide this, tried to make himself look as normal as he possibly could. But he knew people could smell the misery on him. At some point, it became so obvious that he stopped trying to hide it.

Eventually it got so bad that, at another awkward dinner party sometime in mid-August, three weeks after he'd returned, he found himself cornered.

"OK, so, we didn't exactly know how to stage an intervention, but Adya said they were pretty much like dinner parties without the hors d'oeuvres, so we just . . . kept the hors d'oeuvres," Corey said. He was holding hands with his girlfriend on the couch across from Walker, their dark, imploring eyes peering over at him.

Jamie sat next to him, the only other white dude in their small circle, looking just as pale and uncomfortable as Walker felt. An-dre and Nate hadn't been able to make it tonight. But neither were great at emoting verbally, so he wondered if they'd balked at the idea of having to talk to Walker about his feelings.

He'd been looking forward to eating some of the spinach dip Jamie always brought. Now he felt nothing but envy for the two men who got to be anywhere other than Corey and Adya's apartment.

"What in the hell are you talkin' about, Corey? An intervention? I barely like smokin' that awful pot you like bringin' around, I'm not a damned addict."

"This isn't that kind of intervention." Adya ran a hand through her dark hair. "It's an emotional intervention."

"An emotional intervention . . ." He said it like it was the most ridiculous thing he'd ever heard. Hell, maybe it was.

"Yes." Corey nodded. "Ever since you got back you've been walking around like you've got something heavy sitting on your spirit."

He did. A heap of pain the size of an elephant sat on his chest everywhere he went. He knew that there was only one way to get rid of it too, and that would do him more harm than good in the long run.

Walker sighed, trying to think of a way out of this. "I've just been missin' Gram is all. Plus, it's kind of weird bein' back in Charleston with so much around me after spendin' so much time in Greenbelt. The change of pace has me a little shook up."

That wasn't untrue, but it didn't make up the bulk of his shitty disposition, not nearly. Corey and Adya looked at him dubiously, and even Jamie looked unconvinced.

"You can talk to us about anything, man," Jamie said softly. "It's not like we don't know you. Because we do—we know you, Walker. We know when something isn't right."

They didn't know that he'd found himself in love in a matter of weeks. That he'd gotten fully enraptured by a woman who made him feel like he was capable of anything in the world.

They also didn't know that he was struggling like hell to figure out this shit with his dad. Benny had called him two days after he'd arrived in Greenbelt. Walker hadn't answered, but Benny
had left a voice message requesting that he call him back—*please.*
Once again, Walker had found himself at a loss for words, so he'd
put the call off.

How could he tell his father that he didn't know how to be
his son? That underneath all the avoidance and panic was fear.
Stinking, sour, clawing fear that he would open himself up, allow
himself to be close to his father, only to be hurt again. He wasn't a
child, and he didn't need to be taken care of like one. Being grown
meant that he didn't depend on Benny for the same things he had.
It wasn't the material things he was afraid of losing, but the precarious hold he had on his mental health. He didn't know how he'd
survive it if a relationship he cultivated with Benny turned out to
be unhealthy.

He debated whether to tell his friends the truth. What good
would it do? It wasn't like they could fix things for him. Spin the
world around on its axis until he and Aja were able to be together
without causing themselves harm. They also couldn't make his
faith in his father something that he felt like he could hold on to.

But he was tired of keeping it all to himself. He hadn't managed to find a new therapist since he'd returned, and he was feeling
the effects of that more every day. His friends weren't his counselors, but they had never been anything other than accepting. And
the more accepting they became, the harder it got for him to hold
his secrets so close to his chest. Maybe that was why it all hurt so
much—because he hadn't allowed himself to open up about it at
all.

"I met a woman in Greenbelt." Corey's eyes widened, and Walker focused his gaze on an art print behind his friend instead. He'd start with Aja, not because it felt like a simpler issue to tackle, but because, somehow, the baggage of their situation felt less strenuous to carry. "Her name is Aja, and she's unbelievable. Smart and funny and just as fucked up as me but constantly working on it. And . . . I love her."

His words made it sound so easy, but he had no other way to put it. There was no way he was about to recount every little thing that had happened between him and Aja. He was open to sharing with them, but some things were just for him. The little intricacies of their time together didn't need to be shared with everyone for his feelings to be understood.

"Wait," Corey said, leaning forward in his seat, elbows resting on his knees. "You're telling me that you went home to take care of your grandmother and accidentally ended up falling for somebody? And that every single time we talked while you were there, you failed to bring it up?" He paused, but his mouth gaped. "Hold the fuck up, is this that same 'friend' you told me you'd made right when you got there? The one you claimed you weren't going down on?"

Adya flicked Corey on the ear. "He literally said he wasn't going down on her, you damn fool."

"You let her see our texts?" Walker scoffed.

Corey shrugged. "Sometimes she texts for me when I'm driving."

"Jesus Christ." Walker rubbed a hand across his forehead, his exasperation growing stronger by the second. "I was *not* going down on her. I mean . . . not at that point. Later I di——" he cut himself off by clearing his throat. "I didn't bring it up because I knew nothin' could actually come of it."

"Why not?" Adya asked.

"Because I'm here and she's there and neither of those facts are changin' anytime soon."

Adya scowled at him. "It's 2022, Walker—you've never heard of phone calls? Text messages? Skype? There are tons of ways to have a relationship with somebody that you can't see in person all the time. You know that my only other long-term relationship outside of Corey was with someone who lived in London, right?"

He did know. And like the first time he'd heard about her mostly virtual five-year relationship, he found himself unable to see how that could be fulfilling for him personally.

"We made it work for a long time," she continued. "And we were four thousand miles away from each other. You're less than one hundred from your girl as we speak."

"And when that relationship finally ended, was it because y'all didn't love each other anymore, or was it because you realized that the distance between you wasn't as easy to get over as you thought?"

He knew this part of the story too. And maybe it was a low blow, but he found it impossible not to bring up. After nearly half a decade of trying to make it work with each other, Adya and her ex had finally realized they weren't comfortable sacrificing the lives they'd made outside of each other. The fantasy broke, and when it came time to take stock of what they wanted for their actual lives, it became clear that the other person didn't fit anymore.

That was the last thing Walker wanted for him and Aja. He didn't want to spend years simply "making it work" with her, becoming increasingly bitter and disillusioned before everything crumbled. If there were only two types of endings he and Aja were meant to have, he would gladly choose the one that left neither of them broken nor bitter. He would be nostalgic about their time together for the rest of his life. The way she had changed him, turning Greenbelt from a place of complete darkness into a place where he could feel some of the purest, most genuine happiness he had ever known. Not every love story got a happy ending; he just needed more time to try to be content with that.

"Besides"—he gritted his teeth—"I left her without saying good-bye literally minutes after we slept together. I doubt she'd be willing to so much as talk to me now."

All three of their mouths gaped. "What in the hell would cause you to do something like that, Walker?" Adya sounded angry.

"That wasn't my intention." He took his cap off and ran a hand through his hair. "But Gram called to tell me that my dad was comin' to Greenbelt the next day to talk about movin' there permanently and . . . so fuckin' much was goin' on at once. I was dealin' with my feelin's for Aja and terrified as hell of seein' my dad . . . so I ran."

He watched as the shock on their faces turned to sympathy.

"You didn't mention your dad before. . . ." Corey said the words quietly, as if they were the only two in the room.

Walker threw his head against the back of the couch and closed his eyes. The pressure at the base of his skull and his temples was starting to make his head throb.

"I didn't know what to say," he whispered.

"You know that's OK, right?" Jamie asked. "To not know what to say. Like, it's OK to not have all the answers, man."

"Not for me it ain't."

"Sure it is," Jamie pushed. "And your dad probably knows that too. Look, I've never met the man. Don't know a whole lot about him, but it's obvious that as hard as it is, you love him. I know that doesn't always count for a whole hell of a lot, but maybe this time it does. Maybe he's not looking for you to have all the answers or make all the decisions. Maybe he just wants to talk to you, Walker. To see where you're at and how you're feeling about everything."

"It's hard for me to trust people when my emotions are on the line," Walker said. "And that's his fault. So much of what's wrong with me is because of what I went through with him. And tryin' to trust him after all that is . . . it's hard."

"Then don't trust him." Corey said it like it was the easiest thing in the world. "You don't need to trust him yet, not until he earns it. Just . . . talk to him. I wouldn't even tell you to if it wasn't clear that not doing it is eating you up inside. Talk to him, Walker. Suss him out for yourself and go from there. You don't have to decide the entire fate of your relationship with your dad right now."

Hearing that come out of his best friend's mouth made it seem easy. Obvious, even. Just talk to him. . . .

Could he do that? Just have a conversation with his dad without feeling the pressure to have every single thing figured out? Maybe . . . he didn't know for sure. But the thought lessened the constriction that had kept his chest in a state of discomfort for weeks.

Jesus Christ. Was this what friends were for? Getting you out of your own head just enough to make decisions that would unfuck your life?

"You should talk to her too," Adya said after a while. "The woman you love."

He cut his eyes to her, his brain having a hard time keeping up with the switch between two very emotional, very different topics.

"I'm just saying," she continued, like she was scared her words might make his head explode. "You could make it work if you tried. If you really love her, you'd at least try. How are you going to feel in ten years if you let this slip by you without even making a real effort to hold on to it?"

"I don't know. . . ." He blew out a breath. "I feel like that one might be too far gone."

She shook her head. "It might be my love of romance novels talking, but I don't believe that. It's never too far gone to try if you really believe in it. If you actually want it."

"I do." His words were forceful because he meant them.

"Tell her that then, asshole. Tell her all the shit that's been running around in your head since you left her. And make sure you're ready for whatever the outcome may be and let her choose whether she thinks you're too far gone."

As much as he hated to admit it, his friends were right. He couldn't spend the rest of his life like this. Miserable and aching and full of regret. Even if Aja didn't want to forgive him or be with him and his father turned out to be a disappointment, he needed to know. Both scenarios would hurt like hell no matter what. But sitting around doing nothing was even worse. At least this way, he could rid himself of the anxiety that came with the unknown.

He groaned. His tongue thickened at the possibility of count-less words. He had no fucking idea what he was going to say to either of them. The words jumbled up in his head and he had no

clue what order to put them in. He supposed he'd figure it out. . . .
He always did.

He wanted to tell his friends not to hold their breath, but he
held his tongue. "Fine," he conceded. "I'll drag my ass back to
Greenbelt and talk to them. But if this shit turns out bad, I'm puttin' all the blame on y'all." He rubbed a hand over his belly. "Now,
can I get some of that spinach dip I came for or do I have to sit
through another lecture first?"

Chapter 26

More than a month after Walker left, Aja was no closer to getting over him than she had been that night in her apartment. Life went on, and she was forced to go right along with it, but the process of actually moving on was going to be long and wrenching. Especially when her mind refused to stray too far from thoughts of him.

The first week was spent crying in her apartment. She was sure she looked like something straight out of a romantic comedy. The very picture of a heartbroken woman, her hair and face a mess, her clothes dingy, and a tub of chocolate ice cream in her hand. She did as Dr. Sharp had advised and gave herself full permission to wallow and rage, listening to the saddest music in her playlists and watching movies that got her choked up. She let herself cry and scream and despair until her body hurt from the exertion of her pain.

It hadn't lasted forever though. When the week was over, she'd cleaned herself up, opened the windows in her apartment, and made herself leave the house. Even going to the grocery store was a trial, but she'd made it there and back without breaking down completely, so she counted that as a win.

She tried to get her old normal back, rework her schedule to the way it had been before he came into her life. The way it had been before her newfound happiness. Wake up, have breakfast, work, lunch, more work, dinner, then bed. It was boring, sure, but it was also familiar. The work kept her mind from wandering too much, and the process of making her meals kept her busy. Any time she wasn't doing one of those things, she did nothing other than think of him.

She could see him in her mind like he'd never left. If she tried hard enough, she could feel his hands on her. It was like Walker had become a ghost, haunting every corner of her life. Only her grieving process was different because she hadn't lost him to death, but circumstance.

She started to become avoidant again, a trait she'd been actively working on in the months before, but now felt imperative to her emotional survival. Something was clearly wrong, and everyone she knew could sense it. Any time her mother, or Reniece, or Miri and the girls tried to broach the subject of her obvious change in mood, she balked and changed the topic immediately.

The night she'd won bingo had been the last time she'd gone. Every Wednesday, her bones ached with the need for the routine of going, but she couldn't bring herself to. She didn't think she'd be able to sit in the same seat, to play the game the way she always had, without being reminded of him. To her, it didn't seem fair that someone could be in your life for such a short amount of time but still upend it completely.

There was also the issue of Ms. May. She didn't know if her

friend knew the details of what she and Walker had, but if she did, the thought of facing her was terrifying. Would it even be possible for them to have a conversation without the specter of him hanging over them? Would Aja be able to look into her eyes and not see Walker in them? Ms. May was her own person, independent of her family, and it was wrong to associate her with Walker so heavily that Aja couldn't even be around her, but she didn't know what to do about it. So she stayed away and hoped like hell that the woman would understand when . . . *if* . . . Aja had the cour-age to return to the bingo hall.

She recognized that she couldn't be fully alone forever. And as much as she missed Walker, the relationship she'd had with him wasn't the only one she'd built over the summer. She didn't pull away from her new friends completely. But she did hang out a little less, not wanting to bring the vibe down with her crappy mood. When she did get together with them, she found it hard to stay enthusiastic. She hung to the background, speaking less, slower to laugh.

She was still too sore not to stiffen anytime someone dared to try to talk to her about her feelings. She figured she'd wallow on her own, the way she always did. But it took her a while to un-derstand that the reason she'd spent so much time stuck alone in her sadness was because she hadn't had many people outside of her family to wade through it with her.

Her actions surprised even her when she reached out to Miri during the last week in August, finally ready to take her up on her offer to vent her feelings.

They decided to get together, just the two of them, at Aja's apartment. Aja feared getting so sensitive and mushy that she'd cry over a plate of food at a public place. She prepared them a nice dinner at home instead, an Italian pasta dish with enough meat and carbs to make up for opening up to someone she didn't pay to listen to her.

"So, this is about Walker Abbott, I'm assumin'." Miri didn't waste any time getting to the point as she positioned herself on Aja's couch with her plate in her lap.

Aja's eyes widened. She'd been expecting some small talk before getting to the heart of things. But Miri clearly wasn't interested in that.

"Uh . . . yeah." Aja nibbled on a piece of garlic bread. "But I don't want you to think that I only invited you over to talk about some man."

In a way, she had, and she didn't know if that was OK. She cared about Miri, enjoyed spending time with her, and at this point, considered her an actual friend. That meant she was allowed to hog the conversation sometimes, didn't it? So long as she allowed others to reciprocate, that is.

Miri waved a dismissive hand in the air. "Trust me, I have been dyin' to have you open up to me about this since Jade's dinner party. It was so clear that y'all were completely fuckin' in love."

"I guess that's the issue then. He's back home in Charleston now, barely shot me a good-bye on his way out, and I'm here, sad and angry and trying not to be in love with him."

Miri took a bite of her food, taking time to chew and swallow before speaking. "If I had some advice on how to do that, trust me, I would have followed it years ago."

The man Miri had been seeing casually had been dropped shortly after Jade's dinner party. Aja hadn't known her friend was harboring a secret love for someone else. Maybe the conversation didn't have to be all about her after all.

Aja's face must have shown her curiosity because Miri released a sigh that Aja didn't think was nearly as begrudging as she wanted it to seem.

"I was married," Miri said simply, rocking Aja's whole world with three words. "Well, I guess I still am, technically." That made her head spin even more. "We met when we were kids and fell in love somewhere along the way. I had a husband before I was legally allowed to drink. But it fell apart, because everythin' does, and neither of us was strong enough nor wise enough to know how to put it back together. But it's been impossible for me to let him go completely. I don't know how. So here I am, stuck lovin' a man I've loved for most of my life and haven't spoken to in years." She shook her head. "I know that's . . . a lot. But I guess, my point is that I absolutely know what it's like to try not to love somebody. I know how impossible that shit feels, how it takes everythin' out of you."

That didn't make Aja feel any better. She'd hoped that Miri would tell her it got better, that it was actually possible to do.

Aja shut her eyes, appetite gone. "I'm just stuck here, then? Stuck feeling this way forever?"

"I don't know how it's goin' to go for you. It might not even take you that long to get over him. Hell, in a couple months, you might be ready to work your way through all twelve of Greenbelt's eligible bachelors," Miri said with a snort. "But I can tell you from experience that there's no use tryin' to force it. You're only going to hurt yourself tryin' to feel things you're not ready to feel."

They were almost an exact repeat of the words Dr. Sharp had said. But Aja hadn't been fully ready to take them in then. Honestly, she didn't know if she was now either. It was so much better to imagine that there was an easy way out of the pain. That there was some secret door she could unlock that would send her back to a time when she wasn't hurting.

"But it hurts." Aja was ready to cry again. "I can't help thinking that I'm always going to feel this way. It would have been easier if he had been an asshole and broken my heart on purpose. At least then I could feel angry at somebody other than myself."

"Trust me, you definitely don't want that. The on-purpose heartbreak just makes the fact that you still love him even worse."

Aja released a feral sound from the back of her throat, a barely restrained scream. "I honestly can't understand why anybody ever wants to fall in love."

"Because it feels so fuckin' good."

Aja grunted.

"You know it does." Miri's voice went dreamlike. "You're in pain now, but you weren't always. Remember how it felt when he touched you for the first time? How he looked when he was laughing at a joke you made? How everything felt good and perfect and bright?"

"Like a music video," Aja said absently, almost seeing the clips of their love story behind a sunshine-y sheen. It was disturbingly cheesy. She was devastated when the clips turned darker, then ended with her left standing alone, heartbroken.

"A music video with hella sex scenes."

"God . . . the sex . . ."

"Yeah. . . ."

The meal Aja had made went cold in their laps as both women got lost in their heads. She couldn't bring herself to feel bad about it. She already felt bad about more than enough shit.

Miri clicked her tongue. "Girl, you've got me out here remi‐niscin' and shit. Now I feel like I'm about to cry."

"I'm sorry, Miri. I didn't mean to bring you down into my little pool of sadness. I was honestly just trying to vent. I hoped that getting it off my chest would make me feel better."

"Did it?"

"Not really," she said honestly. "Now I can't get Jazmine Sulli‐van to stop playing every time I picture him in my head . . . which is constantly."

"I'm sorry, baby girl. I swear if I had the answers for how to make you feel better, I'd give them to you."

She knew in her gut that Miri had been right when she'd said that the only thing that would help Aja was time. She definitely wasn't focused on moving on from him to someone else—the mere thought revolted her. The more she tried to stop thinking about Walker, the less it worked. It didn't seem like she would ever get to a place where the good memories weren't followed by an ach‐ing heart, but that couldn't possibly last forever. Nothing did. She knew that firsthand.

"It's all right." Aja smiled at her. "Thank you for listening to me whine."

"That's why you fit in with the group so well. We're all just a bunch of whiny little bitches once you get to know us."

A wave of gratitude flooded over Aja. She wasn't sure how she would have fared in this situation if she didn't have Miri, Jade, and Olivia to fall back on. The other two might not be there, but they'd be over in a minute if she called them. Not for the first time, she felt ecstatic that she had real friends. People she could count on and who could count on her. She wasn't at her best right now, but even through her distress, she could see that she'd gotten lucky as hell with them.

"I'm so glad I went into Fresh Coat that day and met you." She found herself unable to keep her gratitude from her new friend.

"Me too." Miri stroked her shoulder. "I'm glad you let us know you, Aja."

Chapter 27

Benjamin "Benny" Abbott was a few inches shorter than Walker. His hair was dark brown and cut much shorter. He hadn't inherited his mother's eyes and hair color the way his son had; they were, instead, the same dark brown as his own father's. His skin was a little sallow, ragged, worn beyond its years. Wrinkles weighed down from a hard life. He was slim—not the type of skinny he'd been while he was using, but of someone who was used to skipping meals.

For all this, Walker had never seen the man look better. Those dark eyes were clear and alert, his entire disposition as calm as it could be given the awkward situation.

It was the first time Walker had seen his father in person in years. Gram had seen her son a few weeks before, but still, she couldn't keep her eyes off him.

They were sitting around Gram's kitchen table, glasses of half-drunk sweet tea sweating on the wood in front of them. The conversation between the three of them had been slow, full of stops and starts. Three days after the dinner party/intervention at Corey and Adya's, Walker had finally given his father a call. He'd apologized for skipping town and ignoring Benny's attempts to reach out. Benny had told Walker that he understood, that he probably would have done the same if he'd been in his son's position. Walker doubted that very much, but he appreciated the sentiment. His voice had been a croak as he'd told his father that he would like to meet up in Greenbelt when he was able. He was ready to talk and listen and try to figure shit out.

They'd agreed to meet at Gram's, to let it serve as common ground for them both.

Gram had been ecstatic, of course. Walker was positive he'd heard her sniffle back a few tears during their phone conversation. He didn't acknowledge it for fear of a scolding, but he'd taken note.

Benny had shown up in a rusted little Toyota ten minutes before he said he'd be there. They'd all exchanged slightly awkward greetings before retreating to the kitchen to catch up.

They conversed about how Gram thought that retirement life was exactly what she'd been waiting for forever, especially with her arms healed. Walker shared that his life was as normal as it could be. He was in the midst of trying to transition to remote work full time while spending most of his other free moments in the company of his friends. He made sure not to mention Aja, who was never far from his mind, so that he didn't clue them in that he was still broken up about having left her the way he had.

Benny was open about what was going on with him too. About how he never thought he'd have a life as good as he did now. About how driving semitrucks across the country allowed him to see things he never thought he'd see and paid him money he never thought he'd make. But also how he could see himself getting older every time he looked in the mirror and was ready to put some roots down. How he couldn't think of any place better than Greenbelt, with his mother close and his only son just a couple of hours away.

Walker had never seen his father so happy. His crooked-toothed smile was big and genuine underneath his mustache, and his voice rang with possibility. Walker didn't have the heart to bring up the heavy stuff yet. Not when he was still trying to figure out what he was going to say. They kept things light, allowed themselves to talk about the kinds of things other families talked about. Like peach cobbler.

"You mean to tell me Minnie is still servin' that cobbler?" Benny looked at them in disbelief.

"Sure is," Gram said. "Makes it fresh every day."

"And it's just as good as it always was." Walker licked his chops at the thought of it.

His father smiled fondly at him. "You always did love that cobbler."

"He used to ask for it in his sleep." Gram laughed.

"Because it's the best thing in the world. Better than fried chicken and biscuits and whatever else is out there." There remained only one thing that tasted better than Minnie's peach cobbler. But he'd likely never taste that again.

"You know what?" Benny rubbed his chin. "I might have to stop by there while I'm in town."

Gram grinned, pushing herself up from the table, her elbows still a little shaky under her weight. "No need. I stopped by and got one earlier today." She opened the cold oven, pulling a white bakery box out and setting it on the table. "I was so happy to have both of my boys with me that I figured we could all use a little treat."

The cobbler was obviously room temperature, but Walker still felt his excitement build once she opened the lid. There it was, almost spilling over the edges of the hefty tin pan. Golden brown and juicy and the second most gorgeous thing he had ever laid eyes on.

He and Benny were so enraptured by the dessert that they didn't notice Gram gathering plates and utensils until they clinked down on the table in front of them.

"I'm goin' to set this here." She smiled at them. "Then I'm goin' to go on up to my room and give y'all some time to talk."

"Gram." He reached for her hand as she tried to turn away, flashing pleading eyes at her, all but begging her to stay.

She smiled softly and petted his head. "You need to do this, Wally. Talk with your daddy. He ain't gonna bite."

He watched as she walked away, the tightness in his chest returning once he was finally alone with Benny. When he looked at his father, Benny's eyes were on him, dark and soft, his brow furrowed. When neither said anything, Benny picked up the serving spoon and dug into the cobbler, cutting out a piece and putting a scoop of ice cream on the plate along with it before handing it to Walker, who didn't touch it until his father took his first bite.

"You know, this was my favorite thing to eat as a kid," Benny said softly around a mouthful.

"Really?"

"Yep. It's why Mama gets such a tickle out of you lovin' it so much.

"I didn't know that." Walker pushed the back of his spoon

into his ice cream, watching it cave under the pressure. Suddenly
he wasn't so hungry for cobbler.

"There's a lot you don't know about me," his father said. "Which
is a damned shame . . . and my fuckin' fault."

Walker shook his head. "Dad . . ."

"No, you don't need to try to tell me otherwise. I know it is. It's
my fault. It sure as hell ain't yours."

Something welled up in Walker, a feeling that he recognized
from deep, deep in his past. The need to comfort his father, to
make him feel better when it was clear that he wasn't doing well.

"You were strugglin', Dad. You were sick. I . . ." He was torn
between his need to follow his emotion and his need to not let his
father off the hook.

"You're right." Benny nodded. "I was. I was sick and strugglin'
and dealin' with all kinds of my own shit, but that didn't make it
right that I drug you along with me through it all. I should have
given you to Mama earlier. Way earlier. Shit, probably shoulda
handed you over the second you were born. Maybe then you
wouldn't hate me so much."

"I don't hate you, Dad." His heart felt heavy at the thought of
his father believing that. "I swear I don't. I . . . I'm scared is all.
All that time I spent with you, and the aftermath of everybody
in Greenbelt knowin' every damned detail . . . it messed me up.
The PTSD changed the way my brain works and the way I feel
and perceive things. It's hard for me to be around you and talk to
you sometimes because I immediately get transported back to bein'
that scared little boy ridin' in the passenger seat of your car way
too young. No seatbelt on, no safety or security, no daddy conscious
enough to make sure I was doin' all right."

Benny hung his head, sniffling, wiping at his eyes with the back of his hand. Walker's eyes welled up, and he begged his lips not to tremble.

"But that doesn't mean I hate you, or that I don't want you around." He kept going, even as his voice shook. "It just means I need you to be patient with me. I need you to understand that you can't just move to Greenbelt and start carryin' on like we're any old family who doesn't have the baggage we do."

Benny's jaw clenched. Walker could see that he was trying to hold himself back from crying. He didn't know what he'd do if his father started sobbing outright.

"I can do that," Benny told him. "Whatever I need to do, I will. I'll take your lead on all of it. I just want to gain your trust. I want to be somebody you turn to. I want to be your father."

"I'd like that too. . . ."

And that was it. Harder than he'd thought by a mile and somehow easier too. No big plans, no sweeping declarations—only the promise that they would both try to be better.

Neither man said anything else. They ate their cobbler in silence. Trying, for the first time, to enjoy each other's company. Now that his taste buds weren't bitter with the acrid taste of anxiety, Walker could finally enjoy his summer peaches and melted ice cream.

Flaky and buttery and sweet. It was the perfect harmony of flavors that never seemed to get old. Walker had been searching for the words to describe what eating this cobbler felt like for over a decade. He'd never managed to nail anything down. Not until he was able to sit in one of Gram's old kitchen chairs across from his sober father at least. Now he realized he knew exactly how eating

that cobbler made him feel. Like he was home. It gave him the feeling he imagined other people had when they were locked up tight
in their cozy houses with their loving families and an unending
sense of contentment.

Before, the cobbler had been the only thing that made him feel
that way. But things were different. Something settled in him
while in the quiet company of his family. Just like something had
settled in him when he'd realized that he loved Aja.

Maybe that was why he'd started calling her Peaches without
a second thought. Not only because the space between her thighs
rivaled even Minnie's best work, but because he unconsciously recognized that she made him feel as at home as the cobbler did.

Wasn't that what he'd been looking for his entire life? A home
to feel safe in? A place where he could be all of himself—from the
scared little boy that hid inside of him to the mostly self-assured
grown man?

He'd spent the past month mulling Adya's words over. She'd
said if he loved Aja, he would try. At the time he hadn't been willing. He thought that if he gave himself enough time, he would get
over her, that his love would fade the longer the distance between
them lasted.

But the longer it went on, the more unbearable it became. When
he'd driven into Greenbelt that morning, he'd had to tighten his
hands on the steering wheel to the point of pain to keep himself
from driving to her apartment. It didn't feel right to be in town
and not see her. It felt like a betrayal. And he fucking hated the
thought of betraying her, especially after he'd broken her heart.

It hit him like a Mack Truck, this newfound openness to the
possibilities of what their relationship could be. He couldn't ignore

the correlation between this and the resolution he'd come to with his father. He'd shown himself that things that were hard were sometimes worth it. He'd proven that he didn't need all the answers *right now*. He could go for what he wanted, what he knew in his gut was right, with both fear and eagerness in his heart, and come through it with something worth having.

Maybe he'd needed this. Needed to set himself on the right path with his father before he was ready to open himself up to Aja. He felt ready to make hard decisions. To risk being hurt. All for the possibility that he might be rewarded with something incredible. A real relationship with Benny. A once-in-a-lifetime love with Aja.

The need to go to her rose up in him so fast that he shot up out of his chair. His father looked up at him with wide eyes.

"Are you OK?"

"Yeah." Walker patted his pockets to make sure he had his phone and keys. "I need to go though. I have somethin' I need to do."

"Oh. . . ." The disappointment on Benny's face was unmissable.

"I'll be back, I swear," Walker assured him. "There's just . . . this woman. I need to tell her I love her. Then I need to beg her to give me another shot because I acted like an asshole the last time I saw her."

"Good luck," Benny called. "Bring her by to see us if she doesn't tell you to get gone."

Chapter 28

There was something incredibly sinister about an unexpected knock on your front door. Every single person she knew, even her landlord, made sure to call before they came over. Most of the time they didn't even knock, instead sending her a quick "I'm here" text once they were outside.

Aja was damned near startled out of her desk chair when a loud, pounding knock sounded against her door on a Thursday afternoon in mid-September. The first thing she did was try to remember if she'd forgotten some plans she had made. She was supposed to go out with the girls on Saturday evening, but that was the only thing set in stone for the week. Nothing was wrong with her apartment, so it shouldn't have been building maintenance. She was anxious as she looked through her peephole. It was too foggy to make out anything other than a faded logo on a T-shirt so she had no choice but to open up to see who it was. One hand on the knob and the other on the mini-Louisville Slugger she kept by the door, she swung it open, dropping her arms to her sides when she saw who it was.

"What the fuck?"

She had convinced herself that seeing Walker Abbott in person again would be a long shot. And if it did happen, it would probably be somewhere awkward, like the Piggly Wiggly. And she'd probably be too angry to say any real words to him. She certainly hadn't thought it would happen only two months after he left and in the doorway of her freaking apartment.

"I'm sorry to just show up like this." His eyes were wide, like he couldn't believe he was there. "I . . . I didn't even think to call."

She didn't feel like she had a right to call him her ex because they'd never gotten that far. But for the sake of the argument she was having with herself in her head, she found it intolerable that her ex still looked so fucking good after time away from her. He was just as tall and lean, his T-shirt still stretched perfectly over his chest, and his jeans fit him snugly in all the right places. There was a ruddiness to his cheeks, and his lips were slightly chapped. The only thing different was the beard. It was blond. Light blond, a few shades paler than the hair on his head. It wasn't thick and rugged like a lumberjack's, but it was full and soft-looking and surprising to see on him. She'd never even thought to imagine him with a beard—what a shame. He had a pink box in his hands, tied with a blue ribbon.

Her mouth gaped, words escaping her. Everything came rushing back at once. The pain when he'd left that night without a good-bye. That he hadn't bothered to send so much as a text to apologize. Sadness and exhaustion and . . . anger.

Aja was angry at him. Mad as hell really. And she refused to be distracted by his absurd bearded face.

She slammed the door, twisting the lock closed like the action would make him disappear back to wherever he'd come from. Her forehead pressed hard against the door. For a few stretched moments, it was so silent she was afraid that her wish had actually come true.

Her hand curled around the doorknob, ready to check for herself, when he spoke.

"I deserve that." His voice was muffled through the door, and she pressed her ear to it to hear him better. "Hell, I deserve worse. But . . . but I . . . I had to try, Aja. I had to come to you and try, to see if you could forgive me for behavin' the way I did and hurtin' you in the process."

"Walker, I . . ." Her head rushed with thoughts, every last one moving too fast for her to convey verbally.

"Just . . . I understand if you don't want to talk to me, but I brought you a cobbler from Minnie's. I guess . . . I guess I wanted to get you a gift or somethin'. Even if you never want to talk to me again, I want you to have the cobbler."

The only issue was that she *did* want to talk to him again. Very much. But she didn't know if her anger and confusion would allow her to. Let alone her pride. He'd hurt her, and she didn't know if she could trust him not to do it again. And if she couldn't, what use would it be to let him in at all?

"Look, I'm goin' to set the cobbler in front of the door, and I'll take three steps back into the hall. I'll give it a minute, and if you don't open the door to get your cobbler, I'll take it with me and leave and . . . and you'll never have to see me again."

"I'm puttin' the box down now," he said when she refused to make a sound. "And I'm stepping back. . . ."

She counted the seconds in her head, trying to use the other parts of her brain to debate if she should open the door or let him walk out of her life entirely. By the time she got to fifty-two, she'd made no real decision. At least not until she twisted the lock on the door and pulled it open to find him still standing there.

The breath he released was palpable in its relief.

"Hi," he said slowly, almost in awe.

Her jaw tightened. Laying eyes on him again brought back the anger, the hurt. But there was something else there too. The very same love that she'd been so close to admitting months before. It hadn't gone away, not even in the face of her suffering. The same lips that had been so callous in their good-bye had kissed hope back into her body. The same body that had run away from her had held her close, gently, like she was something precious, something to be sure and careful with. How in the hell was she supposed to reconcile one with the other?

"Hi," she choked out, bending down to pick up the box of cobbler.

"Aja . . ."

"What?" she snapped.

"I don't want to leave. I . . . I don't want to give up yet."

"What if I want you to give up? What if I already know that I want to be done with you?"

Walker hung his head, broad shoulders slumping along with it. She could practically hear his jaw grinding from across the hall. "I'll have to respect that then . . . no matter how much it—"

"How much it what, Walker? How much it sucks to have to face the consequences of your actions?"

"No." He shook his head, looking like he wanted to come to her. But his feet stayed planted. "How much it sucks to stand here, lookin' in your eyes, seein' how much I hurt you. I'm at your door-step like a goddamn fool, beggin' you for a second chance, knowin' damn well that if you say no, it'll be what I deserve."

"You deserve a lot worse than that. You deserve a swift kick in the nuts."

He smiled, but it wasn't built on humor. It was wry and self-deprecating.

"I'd gladly take one"—he spread his arms—"if it gets me closer to earning your forgiveness."

Her head had started to hurt, and her eyes stung. She wanted to cry. Then she wanted to lie down and pretend like none of this was happening. Like Walker Abbott had never come back to Greenbelt, and she'd never met him, and he'd never made her fall in love with him. His leaving wouldn't have hurt if it hadn't felt so much like abandonment.

"I don't want to hurt you, Walker. . . . Don't . . . I don't know what the hell I want right now."

"What if . . . what if I sat right here until you figured it out?" He pointed to the dirty linoleum floor next to her door. "I don't care how long it takes. Hours, days, whatever. I'll sit right here and wait for you. Just like I made you wait for me. . . ."

Torn between not wanting to let him in and not wanting him to leave, his suggestion seemed like the best option. Torturous, for sure, but maybe he was right. Maybe he did deserve a taste of his own medicine.

"Fine." She nodded. "I'm going in now. . . . I'll . . . we'll see. . . ."

She didn't stick around to watch him settle in, fearful that if she hesitated, she'd change her mind. She locked the door when she got inside, placing the cobbler box on her kitchen counter but making no move to open it.

Knowing that Walker sat right outside her door made it nearly impossible to focus. She tried to sort laundry but ended up abandoning the activity halfway through when the tedium of it became maddening. She sat down at her desk, figuring she could at least answer some work emails, but the walls of her apartment were thin, and she heard Walker shifting around outside, no doubt trying to get comfortable. It didn't matter how loud she turned her music up, she was too aware that she wasn't alone. Not really.

He was out there, so close but still far as hell, waiting on an answer. And she had no fucking idea whether she could give him the answer he so obviously wanted or whether her indecision would last so long, it would drive him to leave.

He did have a life to get to, after all. The thought tasted bitter even though she didn't say the words out loud. Shame filled her, and her vision blurred from the force of it.

What had changed in the time since he'd left? What had made him come back, looking for her forgiveness? Maybe that was all he wanted. To assuage his guilt for hurting her. Maybe she was misreading the entire situation. What if it wasn't love that had brought him to her doorstep but some misplaced sense of responsibility?

Her heart thudded. That was an entirely new thing, wasn't it? Here she was, debating whether or not to reject his love when she didn't even know if he had come to offer it in the first place.

Head pounding, she grabbed her phone and all but ran to the bathroom. She turned the shower on, as hot as she could get it without scalding herself, put one of her playlists on shuffle, and turned the volume all the way up. She needed to use as many of her senses as possible to drown out the turmoil in her head. She scrubbed her body with a cloth that was rough on her skin and soap that was so strong it was almost overwhelming. She stayed under the spray for nearly twenty minutes, then climbed into bed with her towel and shower cap still on.

When she woke up two hours later, it took her a few minutes into her lucidness to remember what had happened.

"Walker?" She called his name and waited to see if he'd answer.

He did almost immediately, his tone eager but muffled, like he was half asleep. "Yeah?"

"Nothing." She threw herself back on the bed, relieved he hadn't left, and stared at the ugly popcorn ceiling.

The second she thought he might have given up and left, her body had tightened up, heart seizing, tears threatening to spring up in her lashes. That said something, didn't it? He'd been out there for four hours, sitting, waiting. No doubt as uncomfortable and unsure as she was.

She couldn't make him sit out there forever. She had to make a decision. Time wasn't going to stand still just because she wanted it to. She pushed up off the bed, slipping on a pair of leggings and a T-shirt and replacing her shower cap with a big satin bonnet. If she was going to get her heart broken, she at least wanted to be comfortable.

She opened the door hesitantly, something inside her breaking when she saw Walker's long, lean legs splayed out on the floor. His back was up against the wall, his eyes were closed, and his lips were parted slightly.

She raised her voice. "Walker."

He jumped awake, springing to his feet, chest heaving. She stepped back inside her apartment, leaving the door open and her hand on the knob. "Come in."

Like the last time he'd been here, he took up a lot of space, not only with his body but with his whole way of being.

"Walker . . . what the hell are you doing here? I want the truth." She found herself unable to hold back on what she was thinking. What would be the use, anyway? She'd agreed to talk to him when she'd finally put him out of his misery and let him inside.

"I spent the entire ride over from Gram's tryin' to think of what I was goin' to say to you when I got here. I spent the last four hours sittin' in front of your door, mullin' the words over and over in my head like I was rehearsin' lines. And now that I'm standin' here in front of you, I can't remember any of them."

Her breaths came hard, lips trembling from building emotion. She tried not to get her hopes up. What kind of woman was she? So excited that the man she loved had come back to her that she was almost willing to jump into his arms with no explanation? Was she pathetic or did she just crave him so much that everything else felt inconsequential? Were those two things even mutually exclusive?

When she didn't say anything, Walker took a deep breath, moving so close to her that she'd barely need to lift a hand to touch him. She clenched her hands into fists to stop herself.

"Aja . . . Aja, I've never had anything in my life as good as you. I spent the entire time we were together tryin' to convince myself that I couldn't have you because our lives didn't match up perfectly. I only thought about the distance between Greenbelt and Charleston and why it could never work because of the baggage

I'm bringin' to the table. I tried to rationalize somethin' that re-quires more faith than anythin'."

He took a shuddering breath. "I've thought about all the ways this could turn out. The good and the bad. And in the end, all I can come up with is that it's like that bingo call—you know: 'either way up.' Either way I turn this situation around, I win, because I get you. Whether just for now or for the rest of my life, I get you."

The emotion in his words made it impossible for her to hold herself back. She pressed a hand to his chest, feeling his heart thundering underneath his shirt. The sheer speed of it told her how nervous he was, but it calmed her.

"I did the same thing," she said quietly. "And maybe we were right to. You don't get to just follow your heart when you spend so much time trying to keep it together like we do."

No matter how much she wanted this—and she did, so much that she felt like she might fall apart without it—she had to make the counterargument. They needed to be clearheaded before they ran headfirst into something that could destroy them both.

Walker's big hand wrapped around her wrist, making her feel small and dainty in a way that made her shiver.

"I don't feel like I've been keepin' it together here lately," he said. "Do you?"

She'd barely been able to get out of bed in the morning. It was all she could do not to sink into her sheets and never come out. But that feeling might be nothing compared to what happened if she lost him a second time.

"No," she admitted. "But you left me, Walker. You left me stand-ing right here in this exact room, naked. You ran out, and you didn't even have the respect for me to tell me why you were doing it. That hurt. It hurt me so much I can't even explain it. And I don't want to be hurt again, Walker. Not by you. There's only so much I can take."

He cupped her cheek, thumb running circles on the apple, catching the slow tears that fell. "Knowin' that I've caused you pain is a stain on my life. I don't think I'll ever be able to forgive myself for it. For makin' you cry, for makin' you think for even a second that you're not the most incredible thing my foolish ass has been lucky enough to encounter. I was just scared, and because of that, I acted like a coward."

"Did I scare you?" she asked him, almost ashamed of how weak her tone was.

"You scared the hell out of me," he admitted. "But it wasn't because you did something to scare me, it was because . . ." He paused, running his fingers over his forehead. "Look, that night, when Gram called me, she told me that my dad was goin' to be rollin' through town the next day. I knew he was goin' to want to hash shit out and talk about our past and our future and I broke the fuck down. I couldn't handle it. I wasn't ready. I've told you a bit about my childhood, but I left a lot out. It was bad, Aja. My dad was so sick that he was just"—he shook his head—"completely out of it a lot of the time. I was doin' everything for myself. Makin' meals out of whatever crap we had in the kitchen, takin' a bath every night . . . I was practically raisin' myself before I could write my own name. Dad would be home, high as a kite, and I'd have to sit there with him, scared to death, watchin' him ride out his high until it was over in case somethin' real bad happened.

"The night I got taken away, he'd had me in the car with him when he went to meet his dealer. And it sure as hell wasn't the first time. I was with my dad constantly. I saw the worst parts of his life. The times he was so high that he pissed himself. When he had to stand on corners in town begging for change so he could feed me and get his fix. I absorbed it all so young, and it fucked me up. He fucked up as a parent and I . . . It took me a long while to figure out if I wanted to let him into my life."

"Jesus, Walker." Her expression was colored with sympathy. She hoped he didn't read it as pity. "I'm so sorry you were put through that. I'm so, so sorry." She understood his reaction a lot better now. It still hadn't been cool to leave like that, but she understood. Walker had been dealing with the culmination of a lifetime's worth of pain and confusion, and he'd thought his only way out had been to run. She could understand that.

"Thank you," he said.

"You're sure that you can handle seeing him now? Even after all that?" She shook her head. "I can't imagine anyone would hold it against you if you weren't ready, now or ever."

"I'm here now," he said simply. "Earlier today, I finished a con-versation with a man I'd been avoiding talkin' to for over a decade. I'd say I'm ready."

She wanted to touch him so badly, but she held back. She didn't know what her brain would start doing if she did. This wasn't something she could afford to just follow her feelings on. She needed to use her head too.

"What do you mean 'you're ready'?" she asked. "Ready for what."

He caught her eyes, staring at her silently. The look on his face was one she'd never seen before. But even before he got the words out, she knew what he was about to say—could feel it somewhere deep inside.

"I'm ready to tell you that I love you." He stepped closer. "I'm ready to be the type of man you deserve. One who's honest and open about how he feels. I want to come to you as whole as possible, Aja. I don't want to put you through the pain of being with a man who can't let you know when he's havin' a hard time."

She looked up at him through teary eyes. "It hurts me to think about letting you go, Walker. It makes me feel like I could lie down and never get up. But if you don't actually mean what you're saying about putting effort into us, I need you to leave. Because I love you too. Of course I love you, how could I not? It seems like every single moment we spent together this summer was perfectly designed to make me fall for you. But I can't put myself in a situation that isn't good for me."

He was forced to wipe away more of her tears, because the longer she looked at him, the faster they came. She was completely overwhelmed. Terrified and excited all at once, vibrating where she stood. So many possibilities stood before her.

Some could lead to a world of pain. Heartache and sorrow the likes of which she'd never known—which was truly saying something when it came to her. The rest could mean a type of happiness she'd never been able to fully envision for herself. A life where she lived with a person who took her as she was, loved every single part of her. Every anxious quirk and panic-induced decision.

She believed Walker when he said he loved her. She could hear in his voice that he meant it. The way he spoke about her was pained and impassioned, a tone she'd never before had anyone speak to her in. She could sense his desperation for her, and that emboldened her. But it didn't make her any less afraid. Because she felt the same, with the same level of intensity that he had for her. And while she couldn't predict the future, she knew that if they did this, she would be all in. What she needed was for him to show her that he would be too.

"I'm not sure what I can give you to prove that I'm serious about this other than time," he said quietly, reverently. "I just need some time to make you see how much I love you, how dedicated I am to makin' you happy. I'm ready for this. Let me show you."

Damn him. How was she supposed to think clearly, to weigh the pros and cons of what action she took next, when his words were so fucking pretty? Not just pretty, but real.

Aja didn't want to deny him. There wasn't a single, solitary part of her that wanted to say no. Parts of her brain clung to that little niggling seed of doubt though, and she needed to push them away. Not just to the back of her head, but completely. If she was going to do this, she couldn't afford to let herself harp on a potential negative outcome. It wouldn't happen overnight, she'd have to work on it, but it was necessary.

It would require faith on her part. The belief that everything would work out because they would make sure it did, together. That their love was enough, not because it could conquer everything, but because the strength of it would make them strong enough to handle all that came with being who they were. And she wanted it.

She took the leap.

"Yes," she breathed. "All right. Yes. Let's do it. You and me."

Walker grinned, making her belly flip.

"I get my girl, and I get to eat a nice, fresh cobbler. My fuckin' Peaches."

Then he kissed her, and she could have sworn the world shook around them.

Epilogue

Beaufort, South Carolina, had a population of just a little over thirteen thousand. It was big enough that it had its own Walmart Supercenter but small enough that you could drive through the main drag on a weekday afternoon and encounter no traffic. It also happened to be roughly thirty minutes from Greenbelt.

Aja and Walker had spent a year and a half making the most out of a long-distance relationship. With Walker working fully re-mote, he was able to travel to Greenbelt during the week, while Aja typically took the hour-and-a-half drive to Charleston on the weekends. They made time to see each other at least two weeks out of every month, and the two weeks they couldn't, they took full advantage of FaceTime and Skype. Most of the time, those calls ended in one or both of them naked and spent, arms straining to keep a phone up to their face.

They were right when they'd predicted that it wouldn't be easy, but it hadn't been nearly as hard as they'd guessed either. Having some time apart was probably a good thing. They got to revel in their relationship without having it take over every aspect of their lives in an unhealthy way. They kept their friendships and their privacy intact while also taking the time to learn about each other. It wasn't perfect, but it worked for them . . . for a time.

When they became dissatisfied with not being able to see each other every day or sleep in the same bed every night, they decided it was time for their relationship to undergo another transformation. Walker still had no interest in settling down in Greenbelt, and Aja believed more firmly than ever that she was not meant to live in a big city. The only option left had been to search for a place that was new to them both.

They hadn't needed to look very far. A trip through Beaufort while on their way to the drive-in during the summer had proved to be enlightening. They'd taken one look at each other and made the decision then and there.

Miri, Jade, Olivia, and Ms. May had been with them when they'd picked up the keys to their rental house days before. The girls had graciously volunteered to help them move while Ms. May had sat on a lawn chair on the porch with a glass of sweet tea in hand and ordered them all around. She was still "healing," of course. Even years after her accident she still claimed she could feel a tingle in her arms any time physical labor was involved. Benny had even been kind enough to bring by a Walmart gift card and order them a pizza for their first night alone in the house. Aja had to stop herself from squealing at the look of happiness on Walker's face when his father had shown up.

Moving had been surprisingly painless, but they had quickly realized that they'd had a suspiciously easy go of things. Completely smooth sailing until it came time to figure out how the furniture was supposed to be situated.

"If we put the couch here, there'll be a glare on the TV." Walker had his hands on his hips like a pregnant person, and she had to work really hard to take him seriously.

"I understand, but the couch is the focal point of the entire living room, and it looks better there. Besides, don't they have those antiglare things you can put on the TV to prevent that?"

He looked at her like she'd committed sacrilege. "And ruin the integrity of the picture with one of those thick-ass plastic things? I don't think so, Peaches."

Aja huffed. "What if we just . . . didn't put the TV in here at all? We could put it in the bedroom instead."

She'd been following a bunch of interior decorators on Instagram in preparation for the new house, and she'd been inundated with all kinds of ideas. Some weren't viable for the way they lived, but she'd gotten so swept up in the excitement that reality had been vacated a while ago. She and Walker were definitely not the kind of people who didn't use their living room to actually live. All the faux-fur throw blankets in the world wouldn't change the fact that they were couch people. And wasn't that just the saddest thing ever?

"Are you actually tryin' to kill me?" He ran a hand through his hair. "Are you bein' difficult because you're still mad I didn't bring you any cobbler home from Minnie's the other night? Baby, I told you, I bought you a piece, but thirty minutes is a long time, and it was sittin' there in the passenger seat just starin' at me, and . . . well, I had no choice but to eat it."

She glared daggers at him, remembering the epic betrayal.

"Yes, I'm definitely still mad about that. But that isn't what this is about. I just want everything to be perfect, Walker. This is our first place together. I want it to be everything we imagined."

He dropped his hands from his hips, coming around the emerald-green couch to take her in his arms. "You're the only thing I imagined when I thought about us livin' together, Aja. Well . . . you and a TV that I don't have to squint to see any time the sun is out."

She pinched his bicep, causing him to laugh and bring her even closer until her face was pressed into his chest. He was a little sweaty from moving furniture all day, but he still smelled incredible.

"I'm serious though," his voice rumbled. "I just imagined you and me together in a space that was ours. Everything else is a bonus. We could be sleepin' on a mattress on the floor, and I'd be as happy as I am now."

She shuddered at the thought. "This is not some shitty first postgrad apartment, Walker. We're not using milk crates as side tables."

"Of course not—we already spent a small fortune on those nightstands from Pottery Barn," he laughed.

"I just want you to be happy here." She breathed her words into the material of his T-shirt. "With me."

"I'm always happy with you, even when you're drivin' me up a wall. How could I not be? You're everything."

He'd never admit it, but Walker always knew what to say. Not that he was some kind of wordsmith with carefully curated monologues that he recited to her anytime she was in distress. He was no Shakespeare, but she didn't need him to be. What he was, was honest. An honest man with honest words that never failed to shake her to her core. And sometimes made her weak in the knees . . . or soaked her panties until she was gasping for satisfaction.

"Fine," she relented. "We can position the couch the other way. I wouldn't want you to strain your eyes too much while you're watching *The Bachelor*."

He made a clucking sound that he had definitely learned from his grandmother. "That's all I ask."

Aja pulled away from him, surveying the state of their living room. There was errant furniture and boxes everywhere, some opened, some taped shut. There was an overwhelming amount of work still to be done. Even small houses were a bitch to organize. They'd decided to do things room by room, starting with the ones that they needed in the most immediate future. Their bedroom and master bath had been completed, the kitchen was mostly done, and the living room . . . well, it was coming along in some form or other.

"We need to hurry up and get through this if we're going to make it to bingo tonight." She picked some stray plastic bubble wrap off the floor, popping the little air-filled circles.

"Yeah." Walker massaged the back of his neck. He looked around the room with an exasperated expression, but when his eyes landed on hers, they softened, and a smile overtook his lips. "Let's get this stuff done. I plan on winnin' big tonight."

"Oh yeah?"

"Yep, I've been on a bit of a lucky streak lately, and I'm tryin' to keep it goin'."

Acknowledgments

We'll start this off with a thousand thank-yous to my agent, Kim Lionetti. Thank you for believing in Aja and Walker and all the ridiculous ideas I will come up with in the future. Thank you for fighting for me and this book. And thank you, maybe most of all, for keeping my time in the querying trenches breathtakingly short.

Thank you to my rock star (but like the cool indie girl, Phoebe Bridgers kind) of an editor, Vicki Lame. In moments of doubt and stress during the process of publishing this book, I've often found myself going back to the words you said after the first time we spoke. I am forever grateful for your guidance and support and superior knowledge of character development. You have been instrumental in changing so much for me and I will adore you always.

To my copy editor, Sophia Dembling. If I've said it once, I've said it a thousand times, but without you this book would be a jumble of typos and constant crossing and uncrossing arms. Albeit, a pretty hot one, but still. I bow to you! Thank you to Kerri Resnik and

Laetitia Charles-Belamour for the gorgeous cover. And to the publicity and production teams at St. Martin's for working so hard to help the world see how special this book is.

Nat, Cici, Demi, Lo, and Soph, you know what you've done and who you've been to me. Meeting you all changed my life. Thank you for the nourishment, the encouragement, and for always keeping me humble. Andy would be proud of all of us assholes. Until the next one.

Mom, Angel, and Ashley, this is the fifth acknowledgment I've been lucky enough to write to you all. I can do nothing but hope that I will have the chance to write countless others. With you behind me, I have all the confidence. I love you more than I can articulate. Always.

To Kaitesi, who was the first to read this book. Your friendship is a beacon of light and your guidance has been . . . whatever a blessing is for this inarticulate agnostic. I can only hope you know how much I adore you.

Authors like Helen Hoang, Talia Hibbert, Love Belvin, Rebekah Weatherspoon, Rosie Danan, Sally Rooney, Alyssa Cole, and countless others whose work has inspired me, moved me, and stolen my heart, I wanna be like y'all when I grow up.

Jade and X.D., who do not know me but whose podcast has provided the most hilarious background to so many of my writing sessions, you two are a wang dang doodle.

And finally, to Rosetta, Gil, and Aunt Laura, you raised me then and continue to now.

Madison Van Zile

JODIE SLAUGHTER is the author of *Bet on It*. She is a twentysomething romance author who spends most of her days hunched over a laptop making fictional characters kiss. While her back is definitely suffering, she wouldn't have it any other way. She loves love, so she writes romance novels full of heart, passion, and heat. When she isn't putting steamy scenes or declarations of devotion on the page, she can normally be found being generally hilarious on Twitter, dreaming about brisket, or consuming way too much television. She lives in Kentucky.